SIX
times
WE

almost
KISSED

(AND ONE TIME WE DID)

Also by Tess Sharpe

The Girls I've Been

Praise for *The Girls I've Been*

'Slick, stylish and full of suspense'
Sophie McKenzie

'A powerful gut-punch of a book that will leave you reeling
long after its final pages. I couldn't put it down!'
Chelsea Pitcher

'Unlike anything I've read before ... immediate, gripping,
incredibly tense, heart-breaking, heart-warming and FUN! '
Holly Jackson

'I could hardly breathe until I finished. The tension!
Absolutely loved it'
Emily Barr

'A captivating, explosive, and satisfyingly queer thriller'
Kirkus

TESS SHARPE

SIX
times
WE
almost
KISSED

(AND ONE TIME WE DID)

Hodder
Children's
Books

HODDER CHILDREN'S BOOKS

First published in Great Britain in 2023 by Hodder & Stoughton
First published in the US in 2023 by Little, Brown Books for Young Readers,
an imprint of Hachette Book Group, Inc.

1 3 5 7 9 10 8 6 4 2

A CIP catalogue record for this book is available from the British Library.

ISBN: 978 1 444 96787 6

Printed and bound by Clays Ltd, Elcograf S.p.A.

The paper and board used in this book are made
from wood from responsible sources.

Hodder Children's Books
An imprint of Hachette Children's Group
Part of Hodder & Stoughton
Carmelite House
50 Victoria Embankment
London EC4Y 0DZ

An Hachette UK Company
www.hachette.co.uk

www.hachettechildrens.co.uk

For everyone who's stayed up too late reading
slow-burn fanfic, waiting for the kiss.

And for the fic writers who fuel us.

PART ONE

Change

(or: the first time, in the hay shed)

Penny

JUNE 21

FAMILY MEETING TONIGHT at 6. Don't be late!

I stare at the text as June scoots past me, tying on her apron.

"You do all your prep work?"

"Yep," I answer. "And I married all the ketchups."

"You okay?" She shoots me a look. I'm holding my phone too tight, staring at Mom's message.

I paste on a smile. "I'm fine. I should go. See you later?"

"Bye, Pen."

I get another text as I leave: Can you pick up Tate at the pool? Anna came home with me, she wasn't feeling well.

So when Mom said *family meeting*, she really meant it. They aren't sisters, Mom and Anna. They like to say they're more than that. Ride-or-die best friends. A bond deeper than blood.

Was Gran there, too? My head's spinning, but I don't know what crisis to land on. . . . Did Mom get all impulsive again? Is there bad news about Anna's health? Those are the two big ones that dominate our lives . . . unless this is some sort of intervention. But I don't need to be intervened on. I haven't done anything, unless you count the color-coding on my wall-sized year-to-date calendar. Tate had told me it was excessive, but she says that about everything I do.

Okay. Maybe that's a little bit of a lie. I have been doing something Mom's banned me from. But if she knew that, she wouldn't have the control to call a family meeting. She would've tracked me down and screamed by now.

So it can't be my thing.

Does *Tate* need an intervention? That can't be right. Tate doesn't do anything but swim laps and roll her eyes when I talk. Tate is like, the perfect daughter. Anna never has to worry about her. My mom likes to say that, all envious. Because I'm so troublesome.

Even though having Tate in my car for more than ten minutes usually spells disaster, I text Mom: Sure.

She doesn't text back. Doesn't give me any more info.

That means someone's dying, right?

No. *God*. Stop freaking out. Don't think about—

Someone already died.

God dammit.

Am I ever going to get through a day without—

Of course not. He was my father.

Of course not.

She wears his ring around her neck. My mom. When she got it, afterward, it was clipped in half because they'd had to cut it off him. She'd thrown one of the halves across the living room, she was so upset. I tried to stop her, but she couldn't be stopped—or maybe I just didn't know how.

Anna had known, though. She held my mother tight and urged me

4

to go outside with Tate. Mom was living with Anna back then, while I was with Gran. Anna found the piece Mom had tossed and she got the ring fixed somehow. Now, two years later, Mom's never without it.

Is it Anna? My stomach twists into knots as I get in my car and pull out of the Blackberry Diner parking lot. It's hard to remember a time when Anna wasn't sick. She had ovarian cancer when Tate and I were little, but she's been cancer free for a few years. But she got sick again. Last year, she was diagnosed with Alpha-1, which is this genetic thing that messes with your liver and lungs. With Anna, it's her liver. My mom's been in fix-it mode ever since the diagnosis.

I turn off South Street, heading away from the diner and toward the other side of town.

The pool's inside a concrete building that's aggressively seventies, down to the weird slanted roof. A remnant of a time when the town was supposed to grow, before the lumber boom went bust. Inside, half the floodlights are already off, making the pool glow.

She's still going hard, the lap clock set where she can see it.

I watch her for a second; I can't help myself. I'd challenge anyone not to be caught up in it, the way Tate moves in water. She's not a mermaid or anything mystical—she's a shark, bulleting through the water like it's where she belongs and she knows where she's headed.

She's alone in the pool. The team doesn't swim together in the summers—or at least, they don't swim with Tate.

Tate's always last to leave practice. I know this, too, just like I know watching her cut through the water will make me have to concentrate hard on my feet for a few steps. She used to be the last to leave because she worked harder than anyone else. She still does, but there's more to it now. She stays in the water until the rest of the girls

5

are gone because she's not friends with any of her teammates. That's my fault, and Tate may seem like she's over it, but I'm not sure how she could be when I'm not.

She hasn't noticed me yet, so I walk over to the stack of kickboards and pull buoys, pick up one of the striped buoys, and throw it into the pool toward her head. It splashes in front of her—I may not be a star athlete, but I can aim—and she jerks up midstroke.

Spinning in a slow circle, she doesn't even take off her goggles when she spots me.

"Seriously?" she asks. Before I can respond, she grabs the pull buoy out of the water and chucks it back at me with the kind of deadly precision I'm barely fast enough to dodge.

The giggle that bursts out of me is entirely involuntary. She knows it, too, because she almost smiles as she swims over to the edge of the pool.

She pulls herself out, and I know well enough to stay far away so she can't shake water on me like a dog. We've been there, done that when we were little. Multiple times, because apparently I can't be smart about *all* things . . . especially when it comes to her.

Tate's got two racing suits layered over each other and drag shorts pulled over them, one leg torn halfway. She wraps herself in her towel as she asks, "My mom send you?"

"No, *my* mom. You should check your phone."

She yanks off her swim cap and goggles as she heads over to her bag and pulls on her parka. I wait, wondering if she got a text or a voicemail. Text, if her frown at the screen is any indication.

Did she get more information than me? Or did she just get the purposefully vague—and clear portent of doom—"family meeting" excuse, too?

I try to read the answers in the sliver of profile I can see. Her nose tilts up at the tip, and her French-braided hair is fuzzy from the cap and the wet and the conditioner she slicks through it before she gets in the water. She needs to shower still to rinse off the chlorine and the swim, but when she looks up from her phone, I know we're heading straight home.

"Let's go," she says, and normally I'd make noise about her getting my car all wet from her swim parka, but now I just nod.

She keeps staring at her phone after we get into the car, and I want to know, I *need* to know more, but I just drive instead. The worry is *there*, looming and tense, and it's like we're both stretching it so tight, any second it'll snap.

"When's your truck gonna be fixed?" I ask, desperate to stave off any snapping or shattering, because it's a ten-minute drive across town and another twenty up the mountain to get to my house.

More silence. I drum my fingers on the steering wheel, waiting, because Tate sometimes savors her words like she's one of those wine-tasting geeks who swish and sniff and swirl to their heart's content.

Sure enough, I'm already turning onto the street out of town when she finally says, "It's not."

I glance over at her. "What do you mean?"

She's resolutely not looking at me when she says, "I sold it."

"What?" She loves that truck. It's a heap, but she's devoted. She puts wax on it and uses those microfiber cloths and everything.

"Don't tell my mom, okay?"

"Tate." I can't stare at her, but I want to. I want to search her face for an answer, because she rarely gives one out loud, but sometimes her face . . .

7

Well, sometimes she can't hide underwater.

She shrugs. "The credit card was almost maxed out. I had to keep the power on. And pay for groceries and meds, and just . . . I handled it, okay?"

My mouth's dry from the realization that it's gotten *this* bad. It's always been bad, money-wise, because how can it not be with all the medical bills? But if it's so bad Tate's selling her truck behind her mom's back . . .

"She's going to notice you don't have a truck!"

"She thinks it's in the shop. Don't worry about it."

"I—" It's like she's asked me to not breathe, if we're being completely honest. Because worrying is kind of what I do. "Fine. But if that's what this meeting's about, don't expect me to argue for your side."

She rolls her eyes. "There aren't any sides, Penny. I'm just trying to keep things going. I thought you of all people would understand. You did the same thing when—"

My tongue clicks against my teeth, a warning sound that echoes with the flash of hurt fury in my chest. "Don't."

Tate's not even shamed by my demand. She just keeps looking at me like it's a dare. "Then don't needle me about figuring out how to pay the bills."

"Maybe you should've asked for help before you sold your truck and made Mom and Anna stage an intervention!"

"That's not what tonight's about. If my mom figured out I sold my truck, she'd talk to me, she wouldn't call a meeting."

I practically leap on her words—"Do *you* know what it's about, then?"—and she lets out her version of a laugh, this huffing thing that never quite reaches her lips or eyes. Her smile does, sometimes. Rarely. You've got to earn it.

"Oh my God," Tate says, all disgusted, and she reads from her phone: " 'Hey sweets, family meeting at Lottie's tonight! Penny will pick you up.' Do you want to pull over and read it yourself to check I'm not lying?" she adds.

Now I'm the silent one. Maybe that was her aim, because we're quiet for the rest of the drive. When I finally pull onto the gravel road that leads to my house, she lets out a relieved breath I pretend not to hear. The kitchen lights are on as I unlock the padlock on the cattle gate I got at the countywide yard sale to replace the one Mom drove through during the bad year. I'm pretty sure the thirty-dollar price tag was because Miss Frisbee felt sorry for me.

I hate that Tate reminded me of that. I hate that Mom's decided to be cryptic instead of clear. I don't like vague. I like ten-point plans with three different exit strategies.

As soon as the car's pulled to a stop, Tate's out of it. I hate it when she does that, too. Impatience, thy name is Tate, I swear.

She's almost to the porch by the time I lock the gate and catch up with her.

"We need a strategy!" I hiss. "What if it *is* an intervention?"

"For what? Have you developed a problem while I wasn't looking? Did you actually fill your closet with Sharpies like you dreamed about when we were seven? If so, then I'm on Lottie and Mom's side. No more office supplies for you. The giant color-coded calendar and the bullet journal of doom are bad enough."

"My calendar is *useful*!"

"It takes up an entire wall of your room. Why do you need a calendar when you have a bullet journal?"

"You'll rip my bullet journal out of my cold, dead hands."

"Mm."

I want to stomp my foot. That's what she does: She inspires *foot-stomping* feelings in me. Like I'm a child about to throw a tantrum because the frustration's just too much.

And then I look up at her, and there it is, in her eyes, because it rarely reaches her lips: her smile.

"Are you just being an ass to distract me?" I demand.

Her eyes crinkle just a little. Oh my God! Why does she do this to me?

Why do I always just trip and fall into it?

"We need to go inside" is all she says back.

"Wait." It's like my hand is two steps ahead of my brain, because I've grabbed her wrist. The inside of her parka is fleece, so her skin's already warm, and there's this long moment when seconds and maybe minutes lose all meaning as she stares down at my fingers around her wrist and then up at me . . . but still, I don't pull away.

It's always so hard to pull away from her.

"If it's not about the truck . . . ," I force out. "What if . . . Tate, what if it's bad?"

She twists in my hold, and time trips back into reality as her fingers hook around mine in a gentle squeeze before pulling away.

"Then it's bad," she says simply.

She goes for the door, but this time, I don't stop her.

I just follow.

Penny

JUNE 21

"WHY ARE YOU in your parka?" is the first thing Anna says when Tate and I walk into the living room. "Girls, you didn't need to rush over."

"Seriously?" Tate asks. She slumps down on the couch next to Anna. The throw pillows—Mom loves throw pillows—almost envelop her.

Anna bumps her shoulder against Tate's. "Go get changed," she says. "You're going to drip all over the carpet."

"Mom?" I call, because she's nowhere to be seen.

"I'm in the kitchen," she yells from the back of the house.

"You let her in the kitchen alone?" I ask, horrified.

"She's in charge of the salad, nothing important," Gran mutters, popping up behind me. I have to bite my tongue to keep from shrieking. Gran is soft-footed and values the element of surprise, and because of that, I've been on edge my entire life. She'll appear out of nowhere like the grim reaper—but one who gives you cookies and teaches you how to hot-wire a car instead of dragging you off to the great beyond.

"I'm just gonna..." I trail off, heading toward the kitchen. Thankfully, Gran's right—Mom's chopping lettuce at the island.

"Almost done here," Mom says, flinging more romaine into the bowl. "We're going to talk after dinner, okay? Go keep Tate company."

"Talk about what?"

"You'll see."

She still won't meet my eyes. She wouldn't be making salad if they were breaking bad health news to us, right?

"I'll set the table," I say. I get the silverware from the basket and the napkins from the drawer in the dining room. When Mom sold our house in town, she still was at Anna's apartment. Mom was beyond the comatose-with-grief stage, but still in the sleeping-all-the-time part. I barely saw her that first year. I lived with Gran until Mom got herself together, and then Mom moved in here and Gran moved into the Airstream she parked across the meadow. It never felt right, driving Gran out of her house. But there's no way Gran and Mom can exist in the same house for months or years.

It wasn't always like that, but it is now.

I'm about to start senior year, and the house is a strange mix of the Conner women: Gran's 1930s buffet with the results of Mom's pottery phase inside, my tools tucked in the drawer, and Mom's biggest, most chaotic stained-glass piece set on top—the one that's all glittery purple shards that should resemble crystals but look like pain instead. Cruder than her other work, it's one of the first pieces she made after Dad died. Her work since then has been different. She used to be obsessed with symmetry and color and precision. Now it's all abstract and jagged storytelling, and it has fancy art people interested in ways they never were before.

12

The silverware is Gran's, too. But the napkins are all Mom again—hand-embroidered with flowers.

I take the time to fold them so the borders match up, because the alternative is to stew some more. I'm setting out the plates when Tate wanders in. She's changed out of her suit and parka into her clothes: sweats and a shirt from last year's 5K to Fight Ovarian Cancer that she cut the sleeves and neck out of because she's allergic to crewnecks or something. She does that with all her shirts. They're always dipping off her shoulder.

It's distracting.

"Penny, you look like you're about to have a panic attack," she mutters as she grabs the plates from me.

"They're acting *weird*."

"I agree."

"Then freak out with me!"

She raises an eyebrow. "Calm down with me," she counters.

"That's . . . ," I sputter, and her eyes crinkle but her mouth doesn't move. "Mean," I finish.

"I'd rather get through dinner without you hyperventilating."

"That was one time, and you know it!"

"It's been a lot more than once, including that time you passed out . . . and *you* know it."

My eyes narrow. She wasn't there the time I blacked out. How does she know about it? And I don't even have to ask, because she sees it on my face and answers and I'm grateful. I'm not someone who can sink into the deep waters of the unknowable like Tate. She never needs to surface . . . and I always end up having to.

"Who do you think Meghan texted all frantic because she knew if she called your mom you'd be pissed?"

13

"Meghan wouldn't."

"Of course she did. She's your best friend and you passed out on her. You're welcome, by the way."

"For *what*?" I want to whip my phone out of my pocket and text Meghan right now, but I don't, because Tate is right. *Again*.

"For not telling anyone."

"There isn't anything to tell," but it's bullshit coming out of my mouth. And because her eyes are still gleaming at me, I add, "I'm fine, Tate."

"Mmm." She doesn't even bother with trying to believe me, but I can't do anything about it because Mom chooses that moment to come out of the kitchen with the salad.

Tate and I finish setting the table, the rest of the food gets brought out, and then we're all sitting there.

I get through four bites of salad before I can't stand it anymore. "So what's going on?"

"I told you," Anna says to Mom, pointing her fork at her. "We should've done it before dinner."

"Done what?" Tate asks.

"After dinner," Mom says again, and it's just enough to make me snap, the way she still refuses to meet my eyes. "We have a plan," she stresses to Anna.

"Mom," I say. "What the *fuck*?"

The entire table goes silent except for a dramatic clatter of silverware on Gran's part—which is a joke, because she swears like a sailor.

Anna starts laughing. "This is your fault," she tells Mom. "Penny, honey, it's okay."

"What's happened?" Tate asks, staring at Anna.

Anna puts down her fork and smiles. No, actually she's beaming.

"Since my liver biopsy, my doctors have been talking about a transplant," Anna says.

"It's what we should've been talking about from the start," Mom says.

"Going on the transplant list like they suggested was a perfectly reasonable thing to do," Anna tells her.

"Wait . . . is there a donor? Do we have to go to the hospital now?" Tate looks like she's about to leap from the table and take my car to get to Sacramento.

"There is a donor," Anna says.

"It's me," Mom says. "We just got the word today that I've been approved as Anna's donor. Why wait for who knows how long when I can give her some of mine?"

"What?" It's my voice. It's loud. It echoes in the dining room and makes my mother's eyes dart toward me *finally*. But only for a second. Then her gaze is gone. She's gone.

"The doctors say even though it's a rarer procedure, there's a better survival rate with a living donor," Gran prompts from the other end of the table.

"You're doing a living-donor liver transplant?" Tate's words come out so fast, they're a terrible jumble that takes me a second to sort out because all I'm thinking is *What did Mom just say?* over and over again. "When?"

"We're headed to Sacramento in four days," Anna says.

"Ninety-six hours, baby!" Mom grins and that's when I realize that they've already decided all of this: The three of them have talked it over days—no, *months* ago. They must have undergone all these tests

15

to make sure Mom was a match and had evaluations to make sure this is what she wanted and . . . we were just left out of all of it.

"Mom!" Tate says, and then she's just hugging both of them, practically throwing herself in their laps like a child, and I cannot stand the joy when I'm about to swirl down the drain of panic and fear.

I can't be here right now.

I'm up out of the chair before I think it through, and I know someone is calling my name, but I keep going.

The backyard is less of a yard and more of a field. This land—the four acres, the house and its corrugated tin roof, with Gran's beat-up Airstream on the access road across the field—is where my dad grew up. I've been here ever since he died. It took Mom longer to get here and for Gran to move into the Airstream. There's no way Gran would leave me alone with Mom after everything. Not that I think Mom wanted to be alone with me—she's always looking for an exit when we're together.

What happens if *she* dies this time? What if she leaves me for good?

Selfish thoughts. Selfish questions. I want to be selfish here. Greedy for the only parent I have left.

Foxtails brush against my ankles as I reach the edge of the field, where a group of volcanic slate formations juts skyward. I perch on the edge of the biggest rock, my fingers searching for the spot beneath the lip of the stone.

There. I trace the initials. *GC + CC = PC*

George Conner + Charlotte Conner = Penelope Conner

My mother has always been so very extra in the love department, down to carving things in stone and giving up her whole heart to Dad

16

so that he took it with him when he was gone... and handing over part of her liver to Anna, because that's what you do for your best friend.

She's great on a team, my mom. When she has a partner, she shines. When Dad was alive, she was brightness personified. But when he died, that light snapped off so abruptly, it left me groping in the dark.

Those first six months—that entire first year, really—she was reeling, needing a teammate, while I needed a mother. Everyone thought I was the stronger one, so I had to be. It's better now. Anna was there for Mom through all of it, because that's what best friends do.

I've been hearing that line my whole life. I've been around the two of them and their stories and their secret language and the fact that they are even closer than sisters or lovers would be. They've created something entirely beyond bonds of blood or romance—an I'll-get-rid-of-a-body-for-you sort of friendship. It's the kind of thing that's so strong it ripples through everything they touch. Half of my life has been spent around Tate just because of them. Gran is as good as Tate's grandmother, and she's the only one either of us has got. There is no part of my life that isn't rippled through because Anna caught my mom shoplifting when they were kids and covered for her.

I should've seen this coming. Of course Mom got tested to see if she was a match. Of course she agreed to do this without even talking to me.

Of course.

I lean back on the rock. I'm out there for long enough that dinner's probably over. But I still don't go inside. I don't even move until—

"Seriously?"

17

My mouth tightens when I hear Tate's voice. I stare at the sky, back flat, knees up. I keep my eyes fixed on the stars even when she walks up and sits down next to me.

I'll cry if I meet her eyes and she's all sympathetic and pitying. And I'll yell if she's mad.

"Penny." It's just my name. I've heard it hundreds of times in my life. I've heard it dozens of times from her lips. But this time, she kind of sighs it through her fingers as if she's trying to hold it in. As if it's suddenly become a secret I'm not supposed to hear.

"This is not..." I stop, trying to figure out a way to say it without hopelessly digging myself into a hole. Because how can I say *Your mom's great, I love her, but I'm scared mine will die saving her* without sounding like a massive selfish jerk?

There isn't. There is no way. So I shut up. This is not her fault. This is no one's fault.

This is just life. Both of us learned it wasn't fair a long time ago.

Silence never swallows me in Tate's presence. It's never truly uncomfortable, with a few exceptions. Maybe because she's mostly quiet unless poked.

So I just wait for her to break the hush.

"I always thought we were lucky," she says finally.

That makes me prop up on my elbows to look at her, because *what*?

"Mom and me," she continues, reading the look perfectly. "We have a lot more people than some. We have Lottie and Marion. I know she's your grandmother, but sometimes she feels like..." She doesn't say *mine*, but it's there.

"She is," I say, because that's true. Gran loves Tate.

"And we have you," Tate adds.

18

"You don't have—" I cut off my automatic denial before I finish it—*You don't have me*—because I don't know why I would even say it. Just to be contrary and cruel when she's trying to wave some sort of surrender flag?

"Yet you picked me up from practice today." And *wow*, Tate, way to fuck over my entire half-denial in one neat declaration.

"It was on the way."

"Did the diner move to the north side of town when I wasn't looking?"

"There's barely enough town to *have* a north side. Everything is on the way to everything else. It wasn't like I went on an extended detour."

"You went out of your way when you drove me all the way to Chico for the bed part last year . . . and spent all that time helping me install it."

"Chauffeur services and fiddling with an adjustable bed frame are not the same as giving up part of your liver, Tate!"

She lets out a breath, long and slow. I'm pissing her off, and I don't *want* to. For once, I really, *really* don't want to needle her or fight. I'm failing at this—whatever this is, this moment when she came out here after me, thinking . . . what? That she could talk me into being okay with it?

Did my mom send her out here? The thought makes me angry. Mom can't avoid me forever . . . or maybe she can. For years, she's been doing a good job of it.

"You're not lucky," I tell Tate, because I can't stand this. "Are you kidding me? Neither of us is. Your dad ditched you. Mine died. My mom lost her mind for a year, and your mom beat cancer only to get

19

sick with something just as bad. The only way you're getting into a four-year college is practically killing yourself to get a swimming scholarship, and the only way I can do anything I want is by bussing tables and tutoring the doctors' and lawyers' kids when school's in session. We're not lucky, Tate. We're perpetually fucked. We're always bleeding money for emergencies. What did you think when you saw that text on your phone about a family meeting? Didn't your mind go immediately to *Something bad's happened*? Because mine did."

"Of course it did," she says. "But then, for once, something bad *didn't* happen. Something good did. She's going to survive."

Then it happens: She smiles. It blooms over her face, so slow I don't realize what's going on until it's halfway over.

I'm dizzy from it. Spinning topsy-turvy in a way that I absolutely cannot be. Tate is motion, a blur of a girl, chlorine-scented and sim-mering. I am not a blur of a girl. . . . I'm not a blur of anything. I am careful, purposeful steps and scanning ahead and behind me for trouble. I try to fix things. And when I can't, I bury them.

But I can't fix this, and I can't bury what's gonna be reality in just ninety-six hours. I wince at the thought. My lungs go too tight, and I can't fight how quick my breath gets, even though I know I should.

Because this *is* a good thing. Anna has been sick for what feels like my entire life, and when her liver started failing last year, it got scary, fast. I want her to be healthy and better—of course I do.

"Hey, *hey*, Penny, breathe."

Her hand presses between my shoulder blades. Gentle pressure. She's always run hot. Like the speed inside her is always burning to get free.

It gets a little easier to breathe.

20

A little easier to talk.

To be honest.

"I don't want either of them to die."

"You can't think like that," she tells me, and when I open my mouth to argue because how can I not, she continues, "No. I'm the expert on the mother-in-medical-peril thing, so you have to listen to me. We cannot stress them out. We have a ton of stuff to do and barely any time to do it. A lot of studies show that psychological stress has a bad effect on transplant patients, so we're going to be on our best behavior and we're going to be fine with the move . . . *and* we're going to make *them* think that this is the thing that makes *us* get along. . . . Okay?"

"Since when do you read medical studies?" I ask it before I've fully processed everything she's said.

"Just because I don't have a giant calendar with my reading time blocked off in purple doesn't mean I don't read," she says, just as my brain catches up.

"Wait. What *move*?" I demand.

"Right. You weren't in there for that part." Tate's not looking at me now. "They're combining households to save money. That's what they called it."

"What?"

"Do you think either of them can afford to pay for everything with all this time they'll have to take off work? My mom will be recovering for months before she can go back, and your mom will be on bedrest for a few weeks at least, maybe more. And they'll have to stay close to the doctors in Sacramento for almost a month. Plus the meds . . . Mom's giving up our apartment. We're going to have to move

21

everything out ourselves while they're recovering. This house is bigger. We're all going to live here."

"*Together?*"

"Well, I sold my truck, Penny, so I can't exactly go live in it."

It bites, her sarcasm. Like a shark. "I don't want you to live in your truck! I'm just trying to understand what's happening, since apparently the family meeting went on in great detail without me, and now I have two new housemates."

"You're the one who walked out like a drama queen."

"I didn't want to cry in front of the moms, Tate. Give me a break. Didn't I do the thing you just told me to do? Not stress them out?"

"They think you're against the idea."

"So my mom *did* send you out here."

"No. I came out here to tell you that if you fuck this up, Penny . . ."

My face twists. My entire *heart* twists. I jump on her words. "Like *anything* I say has any pull with my mom. She never factors me in, and you know it!"

I'm yelling, and we're both on our feet and I don't know when that happened, but it must have, because we're standing on that slab of rock, ready to explode like we're the volcano that spit it out.

"That's not my fault." And now she's as close to yelling as she gets, which is more growly than anything. "Your mom falling apart was not my fault. None of this is my fault. I'm just trying to keep my mom alive."

"And my mom's the best bet." I don't say it like a challenge or like something to hurl at her or even in defeat. It's just . . . a fact. Just like how we aren't lucky. Mom is Anna's best bet. Mom is a healthy match.

Livers regenerate. And I shouldn't be so freaked out.

22

But I am. Because of dozens of things, some I'm not sure I can even name and some that I had in my grasp but Mom yanked away from me.

"Your Mom *wants* to do it."

"But what if—"

"You have got to stop with the worst-case scenario shit," Tate says, and she's not growling anymore. It's a plea.

How? I want to ask her. I want to yell at her more. But now that I'm not, I've realized how close we're standing—if I take a breath, I might brush up against her, and that thought . . .

Oh, no. It's happening again. It starts like this sometimes, and I can feel it—that buzz in my chest.

She just . . . she makes me so *frustrated*. And sometimes I want to reach out and . . .

Not shake her, of course. Never, ever something like that.

Sometimes, I want to reach out and stop her infuriating words and motion and that buzz in my heart and my head, and it's happened often enough now for me to be pretty sure the only way I could do that is to . . . well . . . kiss her.

Which I can't do. Buzz or not.

It's just something that crosses my mind. Sometimes. Like right now. Or when I'm in bed and I'm listing Ways to Shut Tate Up like some girls count sheep.

And it's just something that happens sometimes. That pause. Where everything gets heavy and my lips get dry and there aren't any words, but there is a lot of gazing and . . .

Yep. It's *definitely* happening again.

So I do the only thing I can do: I run. Again.

23

3

JUNE 21

Did you just bolt across the freaking meadow like a deer from me? T

What the hell, Penny? T

You still suck at running, by the way. I could've caught up. T

I thought after Yreka... T

I thought... T

Fuck. T

10:00 PM:

Are we going to ever talk about this? T

4

THE TIME IN THE HAY SHED

TATE

TWO AND A HALF YEARS AGO

THE FIRST TIME we almost kiss, I'm on the edge of drunk. I know this is not a ringing endorsement—of me, how I spent the first half of freshman year, or of this story of the first (but definitely not the last) time I almost ended up kissing Penelope Conner. But stay with me.

I have never existed in a world without Penny. She's two months older, so she got here first. I can't tell you how many times she reminded me of that when we were little. And since Lottie and Mom are Lottie-and-Mom, I've been stuck in Penny's orbit my whole life.

She has a way of doing that. Drawing people in. She's like a magnet. She's like this damn town—even when you think you're free of it, it has a way of bringing you back. But I've never been able to get free of this town . . . or Penny.

I decided she was annoying when I was seven. Wanted to hate her by nine, but it never really worked. Got into what would've been a fistfight if Marion hadn't gotten between us at eleven. By twelve, we'd decided enough was enough when it came to our mothers trying to make us friends. And by thirteen, we were moving toward high school and our separate lives: I was up at five a.m. every day to swim, and she was off color-coding things and terrorizing the school administration via the student council.

Which brings us to the start of high school and that party and the moment that changed everything for me but definitely not for her. (She's not the only one who likes to keep a record of things. Mine's just more in my brain than on the wall in calendar form.)

It's one of the team senior's party. Her parents are out of town and she knows a guy, so there's a ton of beer, and someone's strung lights along the barn rafters. The scent of hay is stronger than the smell of pot, motor oil, and sweat.

Going from a club team to a school team is an uneven balance, because I still swim for the club on weekends, and everyone knows Coach tolerates it only because I'm already faster than all the freshman girls. And the sophomore girls. And the juniors.

I'm not Olympics good or anything. But I might be scholarship good, and it's the only way I'm going to get out of this town, so that's where I put my focus. I already know better than to reach for some things. Some girls don't get some things. And I definitely fall into the *some girl* category.

So I'm at the party. And I'm tipsy off, like, two beers, because I didn't eat, and it's that time before anybody understands that getting shit-faced is kinda boring and makes the morning swim hell . . . and I want so, so badly to fit in with the rest of the team. But I don't know then that fitting in will always be out of reach.

The girls are noisy and so is the music on the speakers someone's hooked up. I don't notice Penny at first, especially because my friend Remington keeps bringing me beer and then making me chase it with bottles of water and hissing warnings about hydrating, because that's the way Remi is. He worries almost as much as Penny.

The whole party, I see Penny and Jayden out of the corner of my eye, and I try not to pay attention, swear to God, but when a guy yells *I'm gonna stare at whoever's chest I want* drunkenly at the top of his lungs, it's hard not to notice.

Jayden Thomas is an asshole. One who *always* blatantly stares at everyone's breasts.

Penny's a crying streak of brown hair and pastel chiffon as she dashes away from him, and I hear Remi say my name, but I don't listen.

I have a problem with not listening.

Which is why I follow Penny. Right out of the barn and toward the hay shed where she goes to hide. It's badly lit and smells like every garden I've ever helped Marion plant.

By the time I get there, not only has she arranged the bales of hay into a chair for herself, she's made a little footstool.

"Gonna make a full-on fort next?" I ask.

There's a little trill in my heart when she says, "Leave me alone, Tate," without even turning around to see if it's me.

"I came to check on you."

"I'm fine." She sniffs. "You can go now."

She kicks her feet up on that hay bale and crosses her arms, and I could leave, I should leave. . . . Another, less drunkish version of me would have left. But drunkish me thinks she looks humiliated and sad, so I have no choice but to nudge her feet to the side and sit down on the hay-bale footstool, facing her.

Her mascara isn't smudged, and I'm relieved that she didn't cry hard enough—maybe didn't care enough—to let him smear her. He doesn't deserve her heartbreak.

"Jayden's a jerk."

"I love him," she says, and I cannot help it, I start scoffing before she's even done with the sentence.

"Penny, you do *not*. That is impossible."

She glares at me. "I'm *supposed* to love him."

"Who says?" I ask incredulously. "Did he say that?"

"No," she says, and sniffs again. "It's part of my plan."

"Your *plan*?" I have that feeling of dread I sometimes get with her, because she tends to take things too far. Like the time we were in grade school and she decided she needed to live off the land for a week to *truly* understand some book we were reading in class. I don't remember the book, but I do remember the week that nine-year-old Penny spent wandering around the woods with an ax, living off blackberries and the fish she caught with a net she wove out of vines.

"My high school plan," she says.

Of course she has a plan. It probably entails numerous color-coded parts and a blueprint of the school she dug up at town hall. And apparently, it includes Jayden Thomas. That thought makes something prick inside me, sharp and angry red. It gets the better of me. Which is why I forge ahead without thinking it through.

"Your high school plan involves a guy who doesn't respect you or any other person enough to stop ogling their breasts? Penny, come on. Breasts are great, I like them a lot, too, but I know not to stare at people's!"

"God, he's such an ass," she moans into her hands. "And a terrible kisser. I don't know what I was thinking."

I'm so relieved that she's not heartbroken that I don't realize what I've revealed until her head jerks up and she's staring at me.

"Wait a second. What did you say about breasts?"

"What?" My heart slams in my rib cage.

"You said..." She's staring at me way too hard, and I suddenly understand the value of running.

Because I just tipsily outed myself to Penelope Conner by talking about breasts.

"Are you..." She stops, trying to give me an escape hatch about accidentally coming out. It's sweet enough—generous enough—for me to shrug and finish the sentence.

"Yeah. I'm bi."

Her head tilts. Curiosity sparks in her eyes. "Okay, that explains some questions I had about Mandy Adams and you in seventh grade."

I kick hay at her. "Shut up. Mandy and I never—"

She smirks, her tears completely dry now.

"We *didn't*," I insist.

"You should've before she moved. She was cute. But maybe she was more my type than yours."

And just like that, I'm the one staring.

Just like that, she's flipped everything, because until five seconds ago, I would've said I knew everything there was worth knowing about Penny. I have—had?—a handle on her, personality-wise.

But this... well, *this* is unexpected.

"Penny, how much have you had to drink?"

"How much have *you* had to drink?" she shoots back. That smirk, it deepens, and the barn rafters stretch shadows across her face for a second, making her look wild.

Because that's the thing about Penny: She's prim and class presidential on the surface, but when you dig deeper, she didn't just spend a week in the woods with an ax—she loved every second of it.

"You're not the only person with secrets," she singsongs at me.

"Well, you've already spilled about your big plan."

"Jayden was just part of it." She waves off his memory like it's a fly.

"How many parts are there?"

"Fifteen."

"You made a fifteen-part plan for high school?"

"It's part of my thirty-five-step plan for life."

She's definitely had too much to drink—she's talking this freely with me. And I've definitely had too much to drink, too, that I'm sitting here, hanging on her words like she's a cliff I've slipped from. But I keep hold instead of letting go.

"That's a lot of steps."

"How many steps would you have in *your* plan?"

"My life plan has one step: Get out of this town."

She laughs. I shouldn't be looking at the way the light falls on her lips, but I am.

So many bad ideas are happening in my head in this hay shed. So many new ideas. Or maybe not new, but ones that were foggy before. Now my gaze is a steamy mirror wiped clean, and there she is, clear for the first time: Penny at her sharpest. More curving thorn than girl, ready to snag you and not let go.

Neither of us knows how to.

"You've always wanted to get out of here." She stretches out on her throne of hay, and I'm grateful for the bad lighting, because my face is red even before her shirt rides up. It's just a sliver of skin, barely visible, a little paler than the rest of her, and I don't know why it's so different all of a sudden. I don't know why it matters more than the skin on her arm or her neck, that strip above her jeans that looks so soft.

But she's not soft. I need to remind myself of that. She looks soft, but she is the girl in the woods with the ax. The girl who spends her weekdays doing all her homework so she's free to spend her weekends on the river with her dad.

The girl who eats rapids for breakfast that'd make experienced rafters shit themselves.

If I'm good *in* the water, Penny is a genius *on* it.

She's terrifying—fearless in an adrenaline-junkie way that her dad eggs on. The last time I went out with the two of them, I was sure I was gonna die.

"Don't you want to get out of here?" I ask, too honest and too curious to stop myself.

"It's not a cage for me," she says. Her head tilts up, toward the open sides of the hay shed, where the horizon—all pine and volcanic rock—looms, and I don't even know this feeling in my stomach well enough to name it. "These mountains . . . that river . . . I could spend my life learning them, and there'd still be more to know."

"Leaving has to be one of the thirty-five steps in that plan of yours," I point out.

"Oh? Does it?" She arches her eyebrow at me, and I've done it again—offended her without meaning to, because we've always ground against each other like parts fused together by a bad mechanic.

31

"You're just going to stay here forever?"

"I don't hate it like you do."

"I don't—"

"You do."

Silence. Because she's a little right about the hating part and a lot right about the cage part, just like she's all right about how she could spend her life here, in these woods, with that damn ax of hers, and never stop discovering new things. I can see it clearly, like I can suddenly see her clearly.

I don't know why it bothers me so much, the idea of her just staying here.

(Or maybe it's the idea of leaving her behind. Because as annoying as Penny is, I could never bring myself to hate her. As much as we clash, I know where she's coming from. And the more we tried to separate the threads of our lives that our mothers' bond braided together, the more I realized how hard it would be.)

She snorts. "At least you're not telling me I'm too smart to stay."

"Well, you're being nice," I say, and she shoots me a puzzled look. "You're not insisting there's no way I'm getting out."

Penny frowns. She has strong brows—dark slashes against tanned and freckled skin—and when she frowns at you, it's a whole experience. "I wouldn't ever say that," she says. "It'll be hard, but that's kind of your area, isn't it?"

She leans forward, elbows on her thighs, and now her feet are close to touching mine. The polish on her toenails is green. Or maybe blue. I can't quite see for sure. But I'm consumed with the need to know, to memorize every detail about this moment.

She is close. (Too close? Not close enough? I can't decide.) Her knees brush against my leg, as she looks me straight in the eye like all the air hasn't been sucked out of the room, and says, "If anyone's getting out, it's you."

"Penny." I don't know anything but her name right now. I can't see anything but her.

I should have never walked into this hay shed.

"I believe it, even if you don't," she declares, and maybe if she'd said it grandly or with a flourish, I could've shrugged it off and blamed the alcohol.

But it doesn't come out grand. And there are no flourishes.

There are her hands, grabbing my wrists and squeezing as she says it. And there is her focus, entirely on me, her eyes so sure, and when she doesn't let go, my entire body jump-starts—a shuddering leap of parts that had been unused now grinding alive.

I pull back my wrists, thinking she'll let go.

She doesn't. She lets me pull her forward.

(I don't know what to do / I know what I want to do.)

(I don't know how to get it / if I should try.)

(Is freezing here better?)

But before I can decide, she does it for me, because that's Penny for you.

"Your eyelashes are so long," she says—and I don't know how to even process the way my heart pounds as she continues, "I never noticed before."

"They're just eyelashes." Is that my voice? I don't even know. My heart's beating too fast. My skin's too hot. It's touching hers.

(She's not close enough. I've decided.)

"Mmm. Pretty." And then like she wants to prove her point, she

33

finally lets go of me. But before I can recover, a finger traces down my face, beneath the curve of my brow, to the corner of my eye, a touch that has me forgetting how to blink or move or really do anything at all.

"You're really pretty."

It's like a cold shock to my system. I don't try to tug away from her, but I know I need to, now.

"You've had too much to drink."

Her smirk is back, God help me. Her fingers are on my cheek now; if they dip a little lower, they'll be cupping it.

"I had half a beer two hours ago. Do you really think I have to be drunk to think you're pretty?"

"I—"

"Because you've always been pretty."

She's cupping my face now. I can't even swallow around how much I want to sink into the feeling.

(She is so close. Her hands are not soft, they're calloused from rowing and ropes, and the catch of rough skin against my cheek is... it is...

It's like being cherished for the first time.)

I say her name. Is it to stop her? Or to urge her on? I'm not honest enough with myself to admit which one I want it to be.

(So close.)

Then someone else is calling Penny's name outside the shed, and we jerk away from each other so fast it makes my head spin.

"Penny? Are you in here?"

Meghan, her best friend, comes hurrying inside a second later.

"There you are! I've been looking everywhere for—Oh, hey, Tate. You keeping her company?"

I paste on a smile. "Just waiting for you to find her," I say, getting up.

"Are you okay?" Meghan asks Penny, but Penny's just staring at me like I'm a tricky stretch of water she hasn't figured out how to navigate, and I want to break away, but how can I when she's looking at me like I'm the most fascinating thing in the world? "You're a mess—we need to get you cleaned up before we go home. Come on."

"I'm fine," Penny says, and she lets Meghan drag her off, but she keeps glancing back at me, brows drawn together in a dark slash like she's determined to figure it out, whatever just happened or didn't-happen-but-almost-happened.

I don't know if it was fanciful, thinking that. Or truthful.

All I know is that she never tries to figure it out. Or maybe she just doesn't have the time. Because that Penny? The one who cried over a boy humiliating her and had a thirty-five-step plan for life and who cupped my face in a hay shed?

That version of Penny dies with her father. And the girl who survives the accident is a whole new Penny. One who's all fears instead of fearless.

(Because some girls, they don't get some things, remember?)

35

PART TWO

Truce

(or: the really sad time)

5

TATE

JUNE 22

"ARE YOU SURE she's all right?" Mom asks me again.

Fortunately, I've got great breath control, because I'm tempted to let out a sigh right now.

"Penny is fine," I say to Mom for the third time. "Didn't Lottie say so?" I prompt when she raises her eyebrows, all skeptical.

"I know this is a lot of change for both you girls," Mom says, and then she stops and settles back in her chair, waiting. She keeps doing this: She makes a statement and then has this kind of trailing look that means I'm supposed to either agree or spill my worries.

"Nothing's really changing other than where I sleep and my drive to the pool and school," I say firmly. "Plus, the whole mother-with-a-working-liver thing. There is that. Big bonus. Pretty good trade-off, I think, for an added thirty minutes to my commute."

She smiles. "You're downplaying it, and you're very sweet to do it, but I want you to be able to talk to me about this. Mothering doesn't go out the window just because I'm having surgery. In fact, it should double or triple afterward, since I'll have all this energy!"

"I'm concerned at the zeal in your voice," I say. "I'm grown, remember? If I was a cake, I'd be baked."

"If you were a cake, you'd be baked but undecorated."

"I'm not sure the metaphor carries—" I start to say, but Mom's glommed onto the tangent, and that's better than being worried, so I let her.

"Seventeen is not *grown*," she continues. "And you . . . you've given up a lot, and I just want—"

Her eyes glimmer, and I'm not gonna let this descend into tears.

"Mom," I say gently. "Yesterday was the best day of my life. You've got to know that."

Of course, that does the opposite of stopping the tears.

"You and Lottie are making the move a bigger deal than it is. I know Penny and I didn't get along when we were little—"

Mom snorts.

"Okay, we've never really gotten along," I amend. "But we're not seven and fighting over toys anymore. We've already talked through stuff. You know, carpooling and our schedules. It's all gonna be great. I'm sure she'll have made a chore chart by now." A complete lie. Penny left me in that meadow *and* ignored all my texts. But whatever. I've got to pack up as much as I can and move it to Penny's house before we leave for Sacramento.

"Penny does like her charts," Mom says, but she's a terrible poker player and it's written all over her face, how little my lies are working on her.

The truth is, I will never say one negative word about this move to Mom. No matter how much she pokes. No matter how much dread or fear or worry or fucking *butterflies* I feel. And I've got a lot of all of those, because moving in with the girl you've never been able to escape is a terrible idea. I've had all the het rom-coms forced on me, too.

But none of that matters. I'd do anything to make this happen. Be anyone Mom and Lottie need me to be. I'd live anywhere. I'd do anything.

There is nothing like this feeling, this proof that's so tangible I can almost hold it: that someone loves my mother as much as I do.

I have held so many opinions about Lottie through the years. They're not wiped away, because I've watched Lottie disappear in grief and Penny shrivel herself up for Lottie's sake, and it's hard for me to overlook or let go of things. I like to turn them over in my head, examine them from all angles, consider the why and the how and the what-if.

There are a lot of what-ifs about Lottie. There's a lot of whys when it comes to her. And not many hows, because I lived on their edges and in their aftermath.

I never thought she'd be our saving grace—she's usually the one who needs saving. But now we're here, the moment we've all been awaiting for so long, and our world is new in a way that we hoped it would be, but I never dared fully picture.

She's going to survive. My mom, I mean.

Every time I look at her, that's all I can think: She's going to *survive*. I said those words out loud to Penny, and it was like standing on a high rock above the water, poised and waiting for years before finally jumping.

Because my life has always had two constants: being stuck with Penny, and my mom on the brink. That's not a pretty way of putting it. But it's not a pretty thing, watching her fade. And I moved past the *putting things prettily* point by the time I was five or so.

"We need to move the beds over tomorrow," I tell her. "Just pack what you need for Sacramento. I'm going to pick up boxes today and I'll take care of all the moving while you're gone."

"I'm sorry we're so rushed," Mom says.

"Don't worry about it," I say. "It's summer. Penny and I will take care of it."

"Sweets," Mom says, after I'm already up and halfway to my room. I look over my shoulder, and the smile she gives me, I want to remember forever. I want to remember her like this, the before, because now there's going to be a before, which means there's an *after*, years of it. "I appreciate you. Both you girls."

"I am pretty great," I agree, to lighten the mood. I don't want her to start tearing up again. She needs to rest and be peaceful and stuff.

"*And* humble." She grins. "Meet me after my dinner shift? We'll have staff meal together?"

"Sounds good."

"I'll see you later, sweets."

I close my door, surveying the mess, wondering if Mom would be mad if I just throw all our stuff in garbage bags and drag them over to Penny's. Probably. Our apartment is small, but it's still an entire apartment. And if I mess up packing the kitchen or lose one of Mom's knives, I'm doomed.

I need someone organized.

I pull out my phone and jab at her name a little too hard. We have to get on the same page or this'll be a disaster.

> If you don't text me back, I'm coming out there. T

I stare hard at the phone, willing *Penny is typing…* to show up. This time, the bubble appears, then disappears. Then it pops up again, before she sends a text that makes me throw my phone across the room, toward my bed.

> **P** You sold your truck, remember?

I hurry across my room and retrieve my phone from the pile of pillows on my bed.

> Are you really prepared to be this big an asshole? **T**

And when she doesn't answer:

> If you don't come pick me up so we can figure out how to live together, I'm going to hitch out there. Either way, we talk this out. **T**

> Your choice. **T**

Penny is typing…

> **P** I'll be there in an hour.

43

6

TATE

JUNE 22

MOM KNOCKS ON my door. "I'm heading to work," she says, peering inside. "Swing by after closing?"

"Okay."

I've only managed to clear part of my bedroom floor of clothes. I don't even want to start thinking about my desk. I need boxes . . . so many boxes. And tape and bubble wrap and—

The knock at the door keeps me from starting my mental list. It's got to be her, so I steel myself when I open it. Only to see Meghan standing there, all earth tones and swishy skirts.

"Hi!" she says, breezing past me in a whiff of orange blossom perfume, her hands full of casserole. "I brought my dad's spinach macaroni and cheese for you and your mom to pop in the oven later. My parents say hi, by the way. And my mom says she owes your mom a text."

Penny's hanging around in the doorway, staring at me.

"Did you call in a chaperone?" I ask her, and Meghan whips around from her trip toward the kitchen.

"Why would you two need a chaperone?" she asks, just as Penny mutters, "Drop it, Tate."

"The energy in here is weird," Meghan comments. To my relief, Meghan has the tact that Penny and I both seem to lack, because she promptly says, "We brought bubble wrap and tape and a few boxes, but not a ton," and turns around and disappears into the kitchen.

"You brought a chaperone," I say again.

"I brought Meghan because she was with me when you texted to demand I come over, so she offered. We'll get everything packed faster with an extra set of hands."

"That eager to live with me, huh?"

"I'm here, aren't I?"

"You ignored my texts."

"I've been busy clearing out the rooms you're going to use," Penny says innocently. "We should move the beds over first."

I breathe. I remind myself *she's going to survive*. I try not to think about the scratch of motel blankets and Penny's tears and the specific hell that is indoor-pool chlorine and how it sticks to everything.

"If you think the beds are the best place to start, I'll take your lead."

Penny blinks, like she thought I was going to keep fighting. "You want me to take charge?"

"I was thinking of just shoving stuff in garbage bags," I say, partly just to get her going, and it does.

"Oh my God, clearly you need me." She's finally moving into the apartment, pushing past me busily, heading toward the living room. "Do you even *have* boxes?"

"Remi's saved a bunch of them for us at the store. I need to pick them up."

45

"Moving the beds would be a whole lot easier with your truck," she suggests, and at first I think she's being mean, but her face kind of pinches as soon as she says it. "Sorry." She shakes her head. "We can drive out tomorrow and get a U-Haul at that place past the lake."

"We can borrow Remi's truck tomorrow. And his grandpa's utility trailer."

"Really?" Her face lights up. "That'd be great. Hey, Meghan, we've got a truck and a trailer to move the beds tomorrow."

"Perfect," Meghan calls back from the kitchen. "Boxes?"

"Gotta go pick them up," I say.

"Why don't you two do that?" Meghan suggests. "I've got enough bubble wrap to start on the dishes and stuff in here."

"Sure," I say, because I want to talk to Penny where she can't run from me. The car is a good place for that. She can't barrel roll out of it if she's driving.

"I—" Penny says, and then she stops, because Meghan is looking expectantly at her and I'm pretending I don't know why she doesn't want to get into a car with me. "Fine," she says. "Let's go."

She doesn't say anything as we walk to the car. There are two apartment complexes in town—the expensive one and the cheap one. We live in the cheap one.

Ronnie, the landlord, is a real asshole. But we've just had to deal. When you can barely afford even the cheapest rent you can find, your options are limited. And Mom and I have been here a long time, since I was eleven.

It'll be weird not coming home from practice to this place. My feet know to avoid the crumbles in the concrete stairs and where the

46

cockroaches like to cluster out by the dumpster, and my hands know every splinter of that shitty stair railing.

Penny unlocks the car for me silently, but she starts talking when we get on the road.

"If we can move the beds tomorrow, we can all leave for Sacramento together from our house on Sunday."

"You really got both rooms cleared out in the last fifteen hours?" I ask.

She shrugs. "If I left it up to my mother, your mom would be coming home from her transplant to a guest room full of unsold artwork. Remember her sculpture phase?"

I shudder. "Those things gave me nightmares."

"Graham still uses them in the Haunted Beer Garden."

"Penny, we should talk about this."

"We are. We're talking logistics," she says, and if she wasn't driving, I think she'd bat her eyes innocently at me.

"We need to talk about what happens *after* we move in."

"We wait for them to come home and don't kill Gran's garden while she's gone," Penny says, like she's reciting a mantra from memory.

"Penny. Please."

Her mouth pinches together. She flips her turn signal with a little too much force and pulls over into the feed store's parking lot. I can smell the hay from here even with the windows closed.

"Fine." She switches the ignition off, unbuckles her belt, and turns toward me in her seat, folding her hands in her lap. "What do you want?"

"Excuse me?"

"I've cleared out the rooms. I've made space in the fridge and my bathroom and the boot rack in the hall. I'm along for the ride, Tate. My mom made a decision, and at least this time I understand why she's doing it, but once again, I have to deal with her choices. So, please, just tell me what you want, and I'll do it, okay?"

Her little speech starts out snotty and ends up in this defeated plea, and suddenly her eyes are welling up and I feel like the shittiest person in the world.

"I want us to have . . . a truce, I guess."

"I didn't realize we were at war."

"Come on, Penny."

Her fingers tap the steering wheel. At this angle, I can see the scars on her hands, the way some of the fingers on her right hand don't straighten without effort anymore.

"I don't want to fight with you," she says softly. "I'm just used to bickering with you. It just happens."

"I know." Because I do. I really, really do. "We just—we have to not bicker. Both of us have to. For the moms' sake."

"I know. You're right." She squares her shoulders, staring hard at her hands on the steering wheel.

"Any ideas on how we do that?"

She laughs. "You're the one pushing it. You don't have a list or something?"

"More your thing."

She bends down into my space for a heart-stopping moment—she smells like the forest, deep and sharp and dangerous—and grabs her bullet journal and pen case out of the purse at my feet. She scoots until she's fully facing me, her legs crossed pretzel-style in the seat.

48

I'm not short enough to do that, so I just tilt toward her the best I can. She grabs a brush pen from her case and flips to a fresh page in the journal, writing out:

PENNY AND TATE'S TRUCE AGREEMENT
(Est. June 22)

"First order of business?" she asks, and oh, it's a mistake to give the ex–class president all the power, but I'm already in it, so I've got to go with it.

"No fighting in front of the moms."

"Agreed." She writes it out, her casual handwriting better than mine on my most careful day.

"No snitching."

She cocks an eyebrow at me. "Is this about your truck? She's going to find out."

"Not from you."

"Fine, but it goes both ways."

"You've got some secrets, Pen?"

She smirks. "Maybe I do."

I tap the bullet journal, because if I keep looking at her, we're going to be in trouble, and this is about avoiding that. "Write it down?"

She writes out: *No snitching to the moms.*

"I have one," she announces. "You are not allowed to use up all the hot water in your showers."

I grimace. Fuck. Sharing a bathroom with her is going to suck. I've been in her bathroom. It's . . . well, it's basically a forest of vines and little bottles of bath salts she probably mixes herself.

"Fine. But you have to move some of the plants and candles out."

She bites her lip, but she adds it to the list. "Deal. What about practice?"

"What about it?"

"How are you going to get there?"

I try to ignore the pinch in my stomach, because I don't know. I didn't know when I handed Pete the keys to the truck and walked the five miles back to town before my mom came home from work at the brewery.

"I'll figure it out."

She lets out an impatient noise. "You are so stubborn."

"No, I'm not."

"I can drive you." The offer, when it comes, is smaller and softer than usual.

"You don't have to," I say automatically.

"I know that. I still can. Though you might have to come to the diner and hang out for an hour or two if practice ends before some of my shifts."

"That's fine. That's . . . Thank you."

She nods. "You're still going to get shit when your mom finds out your truck isn't in the shop."

"My business," I remind her.

"Right. Do you want me to add that?"

"Yeah, actually. Your mom, your business. My mom, my business."

We keep going, back and forth, ironing it out. It takes twenty minutes more, but soon enough, there's a little list on the page that doesn't seem too awful. But then—

"One final thing," she says, writing something down. It takes so long, I'm a curious ache by the time she sets the journal back down, facing me this time, and I see what she's added at the bottom of the list.

No talking about Yreka.

(The rattle of the AC unit in the motel room. Mrs. Rawlins going from door to door on the top floor, a final check on all the girls before she went to sleep. *You two okay in here?* And I'd said, *We're fine*, as Penny hid her tearstained face and broken heart under the covers and we both hoped Mrs. Rawlins wouldn't notice Penny wasn't Theresa.)

Sometimes, Penny looks at me like I'm a dare she wants to take, but forgot how. But now, when I push the bullet journal back toward her, there's something different in her face.

Am I wrong to think it's a challenge?

(I want to yell at her *Now? Now you do this?* But I don't. I won't rise to the bait—imaginary or real. I can't.)

"That's fine," I say.

(It's not.)

PENNY AND TATE'S TRUCE AGREEMENT
(Est. June 22)

- No fighting in front of the moms (or Gran).
- No snitching.
- No using all the hot water (Tate).
- Cut the forest in the bathroom down a little (Penny).
- We'll share the commute.
- Your mom, your business. My mom, my business.
- We'll work together to empty the apartment and move.
- We'll split any extra chores/errands so the moms don't have to do them.
- No stress for the moms. As far as they're concerned, our lives are perfect.
- If there's a life-or-death problem, we go to each other, we don't go to the moms.
- Tate will teach Penny how to make Anna's brownies if Penny teaches Tate how to make Marion's lemon cake.
- No talking about Yreka.

8

JUNE 22

M: So what are we doing about Penny and Tate?

R: Who is this?

M: Who else would be asking about P and T?

R: Meghan, how did you get my number?

M: Tate gave it to me. I've been helping with packing. She said you were helping with the beds tomorrow?

R: Yes.

M: Good. We spent the afternoon boxing up the kitchen and taking apart the beds. So. What are we going to do?

R: We should move stuff in the morning before it gets too hot. Tate and I are meeting up for a run at 6, so maybe 7:30?

M: I'm not talking about the beds. I'm talking about Penny and Tate.

R: What about them?

M: You must've noticed. There's an ENERGY.

R: ???

M: Remington! I know you're more observant than this.

R: It's none of my business.

M: Ha! You admit there is business to be noticed, though, right?! ROMANTIC business?

Remington is typing…
Remington is typing…
Remington is typing…

M: Oh my God, just say it!

R: It's none of our business. Drop it.

M: This isn't over!

I am going to kill Tate for giving you my number. Do not start sending me endless pictures of flowers like you do everyone else.

R

[Meghan has sent a picture.]

Very mature.

R

M

What? You said no flowers. Isn't the ring on my middle finger adorable?

Remington is typing…
Remington is typing…
Remington is typing…

Let me know when you need the truck. I'll be there.

R

M

Tomorrow at 8. If you're lucky, I might actually bake cookies.

9

TATE

JUNE 23

"YOU GAVE MEGHAN my number."

I look up from tying my shoes, squinting in the burgeoning light. Remi's usually at the track before me, but I beat him here this morning. We run together three days a week. Remi's a runner, not a swimmer, but we've always found a kind of kinship in being not just in the loner sports but outliers on our teams.

"Good morning to you, too," I tell him.

Remi glares at me. "You gave Meghan my number," he says again, like I've committed a grievous sin.

"You said you'd help us move the beds today."

"I did. Especially because you sold your truck without talking to anyone first."

"Did you have the seven grand I needed stashed somewhere?" I ask sarcastically.

"I could've tried to figure something out."

I wave him off. "It's done. And Meghan is being really nice and helped me all day yesterday. I don't know why you're always so grouchy about her."

"She's going to send me pictures of flowers," he protests.

"The horror. Meghan's a good photographer. Her flower photos are pretty. You could use some pretty in your life. Are you going to stretch with me? We've only got an hour and a half before we're supposed to meet them."

"Look at what she sent me," he says, holding out his phone. Meghan's smiling face, flipping Remi the bird with an *actual* bird ring on her middle finger.

I snort, and he shoots me another look. Remi is very good at communicating via facial expressions. "What? It's funny. And it's not a flower picture."

"Is this what's going to happen?"

"What are you talking about?"

"You're moving out to the boonies. Does your mom know about your truck yet? How are you even gonna get to practice?"

"I'll figure it out."

"This sucks." He sighs. "We're only going to see each other at school."

He frowns, scrunched and upset, and I'd hug him if either of us were the type. But we've always been more nudgers and affectionate punchers. Which is why he's so bad at saying what I think he's saying.

"Are you trying to tell me you're going to miss me?"

"Oh, shut up," he says, but his ears turn red. "I'm really happy for your mom. I get why you're moving out there."

"I'll miss you, too. But I promise, I won't suddenly start color-coding things just because I'm living in the same house as Penny."

"I'm not worried about that," he says, and then he laughs, too sharp and knowing, and shakes his head. "That's the last thing I'm worried about when it comes to Hurricane Penny."

"What are you talking about?"

"I don't need to worry about you *becoming* like Penny. I'm worried you're gonna get your rib cage smashed open so she can finally reach in and squeeze your heart to a bloody pulp."

For a second, it just hangs there, and it's almost like I can see the words he's said and the imagery he's conjured up, because *fuck*. Those are some words and that is some imagery, all right.

"I—"

"Come on, Tate."

"No," I say. "No," I say again, more firmly. "I'm not in danger of anything."

He scoffs, and it makes my fists clench. "I've known you both since kindergarten."

"That doesn't have anything to do with—"

"I was there the day of the accident," he reminds me.

I hate that my eyes widen when he mentions it. I try not to be obvious about a lot of things. But that day . . .

"In every room you're in, you're always looking for her, Tate."

"Well, she kind of needed finding that one time, don't you agree?"

"You know what I mean."

Of course I do.

"You two are going to be alone in that house for, what, two weeks? Three?"

"Four, probably," I say faintly.

"What are you gonna do, living with her?"

I stare at him, hating that question and how familiar it is.

"Suffer, I guess."

It's too much honesty. I can't bear to look at him. So I take off running, not stretched enough, and I don't even care; I just want to leave him behind, fast as I can.

He knows me well enough to give me a full lap before he joins me.

JUNE 23

M: Thanks for the help with the beds.

M: You seemed kinda off. You okay?

R: I think I kind of fucked up with Tate this morning.

R: Kinda your fault.

M: My fault?!

R: You're the one who was talking about how Penny and Tate are soul mates.

M: I said NOTHING about soul mates.

M: You used that word.

M: Not me.

M: Did you say something to Tate?

M: What did you say?

M: Wait, what did SHE say?

M: Have you two ever talked about this? Cause Penny won't talk about it.

M: Also can you put aside some more boxes while they're in Sacramento?

M: Money has got to be tight with all the medical stuff. Maybe we should organize a spaghetti dinner or something?

M: What do you think?

R: I think you just asked me six questions before I could answer the first one.

R: #1: Yes.

R: #2: I said something I shouldn't have..

R: #3: Tate got upset.

R: #4: Fuck no. I'm not gonna stick my hand in that. All you get is 💧.

#5: Yeah, I'll save as many boxes as I can. R

#6: I vote for a tri-tip fundraiser instead of spaghetti. R

#7: I think it's a good idea and you've been really nice to help out so much. R

M Remington. As I live and breathe. Is that a compliment?

[Meghan has sent a picture.]

Please just start sending me the flower photos you send everyone else. Anything but heart hands. R

M I will send heart hands to anyone I want. Especially when they are being very nice.

11

TATE

JUNE 23

"I CAN'T BELIEVE you did all this in less than a day," Mom says, staring at Lottie's guest room. It took a while, but I've got all her furniture and linens set up.

"Remi was able to fit the dresser into the truck, so we thought we'd bring it over," I say.

"Thank you," Mom says, as she crawls right into bed. She picks up the bed remote from the end table I've placed next to the bed and presses the *up* button, so she's more propped up. "Bliss." She sighs.

"I'll let you rest before dinner."

"Oh, I've got to get up in a second. I promised Marion a game of cards," Mom says. "But I'm just gonna shut my eyes for a bit."

"Okay," I say, knowing that she'll probably be asleep by the time I get upstairs.

Her room is downstairs, with Lottie's, but mine is upstairs, across from Penny's.

I've spent all day lugging furniture up the stairs, and Penny's door is already closed, so I don't bother to knock.

There's something about the upstairs of a house. Something private and secret. I've visited this house through the years. I've spent hours here. But I've only been upstairs a few times since Lottie moved back, and I don't know how I didn't notice it before.

There are no pictures of George downstairs. It's like Lottie's erased him from that part of the house, and I'm only noticing the absence now because there *are* pictures upstairs. There's a photo of ten-year-old Penny and George in life jackets in the cluster of paintings and photos around the stovepipe that runs through the house at the end of the hall. There's also a black-and-white photo of George with his father in the same cluster, and a painting, clearly done by Lottie, of a man's hands, a ring shining on his finger.

"What are you doing?"

I look over my shoulder at Penny, jerked out of my sudden realization. "Just looking at the painting," I say as she stares at me from the doorway of her room. "I don't think I've ever seen it before."

"I saved her from burning it," Penny says, like that's not a crazy thing to have to do.

"You..."

"She put all his stuff in storage," Penny continues, gripping the doorjamb like it's keeping her up. "She won't let me go through it. I guess I should be grateful she didn't burn his stuff, too. But every painting she ever did of him, of her and him, of him and me, of our entire life? She built a big bonfire and burned them."

"Penny..." I don't even know what to say.

"She said I shouldn't be upset. They were her paintings, after all."

"They were your memories."

Her eyes flicker toward me, but she looks away. "I should go help Gran with dinner."

I know she wants to get away from me, but there's no way I'm not going to pull my weight here. And if Marion's cooking, I'm helping.

But when we get downstairs, we find an entirely different setup in the kitchen.

Marion and Mom are playing cards at one end of the counter, a pile of Andes mints between them, and Lottie is bent over her sketchpad at the other end. If you took a photo of it with a black-and-white filter, it would make a quaint and homey scene titled *Women at Leisure*.

"Dinner will be ready in about twenty, kids," Marion says. "I've gotta kick Anna's butt in cards first."

I sit down next to Mom and reach out, stealing a mint from her stack.

"Hey," Mom protests. "Don't you want me to win?"

"I don't think that's possible at this point," Marion boasts.

Mom mock-gasps as I unwrap the candy. But she's gotta understand, if I have to wait twenty more minutes for dinner, I need to eat something. I'm a growing girl.

"Have I taught you no manners?" Mom asks.

"Not when it comes to candy." I pop the mint in my mouth.

"Terrible child." Mom grins at me.

"Awful," I agree.

"You two," Lottie says, shaking her head at us but not looking up from her sketchbook.

Penny looks over her shoulder. "What are you working on, Mom?"

Before she can get close enough to see what Lottie's sketching, Lottie turns the page to a blank one. "Only scribbles," she says.

It's like she doesn't see the way Penny's face falls as she pushes her out. I think about Penny watching all those paintings—her father's face, memorialized in watercolors and oils—burning.

Another layer of grief, brought to her by Lottie.

"Are you girls all packed for Sacramento?" Lottie asks.

"We will be by Thursday," Penny says. "Speaking of all that, we should talk."

"There's nothing to talk about," Lottie says, just as my mom asks, "What do you want to talk about, sweetie?"

Lottie laughs. "She's just worrying again."

"Marion's won this hand anyway," Mom says.

Marion laughs a little too maniacally as she rakes the stack of mints toward her. "I'll be packing plenty of these for our time in Sacramento."

"If I spend almost a month playing rummy with you, I'm bound to get better," Mom warns, but Marion just scoffs.

"I've got years on you, honey-bean."

"What did you want to talk about, Penny?" Mom asks again, and it's like she's breathed a little life into Penny, that she didn't let it go.

"I've made a whole plan," Penny says, setting her bullet journal down and flipping it open.

"Oh, no, not another list," Lottie jokes.

"We've already talked about how we're going to have the apartment moved and unpacked by the time you get back home," I say, because Penny's just staring at her bullet journal and not saying anything.

"I talked to Graham about picking up some weekend shifts at the brewery," Penny blurts out.

We all look at her.

Mom frowns. "You went to our boss? Why would you do that?"

"To help with the wages you're gonna lose. He said it would be fine. He's gonna put me on the weekend lunch shift so I don't have to deal with the night crowd."

"You have a job," I say. How is she going to work at the brewery *and* the Blackberry?

"I can do both," Penny insists.

"You shouldn't have done that," Lottie says.

"Lottie, it's thoughtful of her," Mom protests.

"She shouldn't be bugging Graham or thinking about lost wages," Lottie insists. "The pieces I'm finishing will take care of it all once they sell, Penny. You always worry too much."

Penny's chin lifts. "You don't know the art will sell fast."

"It's like you don't have any faith in me," Lottie says. "My new pieces have been stirring up a lot of interest in the Bay Area. Anna and I have made the plans we need to. That's why we combined households. To make this cheaper. Please just let the adults be the adults, okay?"

Mom's normally smooth expression pinches a little.

"I love how much you care, Penny," Mom says. "Both of you girls."

"But we know what we're doing," Lottie finishes, the condescension dripping like acid.

And Penny reacts like she's been burned.

"How much is the property tax, Mom?" she asks Lottie. "And when is it due?"

It's like she's sucked all the air out of the room, the silence goes so deep. Mom and I sit there, exchanging *oh shit* glances before focusing on the counter. Marion just stares at her granddaughter and daughter-in-law like a mama pit bull ready to bite if need be.

"Penelope," Lottie says, the anger radiating off her in waves.

Penny just keeps going.

"How many cords of wood do we need to heat the house?" She leans forward. "How much is the power bill? We're gonna need to replace the well pump next year—"

"That's enough," Lottie interrupts.

Penny's mouth twists. "The property tax is due in September," she says. "It's fourteen hundred dollars. We have only four hundred of that saved. It takes three cords of oak to heat the house—four if it's pine or something fast burning—plus propane for Gran's trailer. That's at least twelve hundred. We have none of that saved. The power bill—"

"I said, that's enough," Lottie says.

"Lottie," Marion says quietly.

"Don't you get on me, too!" she snaps, and then she's up out of her chair, her sketchbook under her arm as she storms away. I can hear her stomp out of the house, probably off to her studio in the garage where no one will bother her.

A beat of silence, and then my mom, my beautiful, unruffled mom, smooths her hair and says: "You were talking about the power bill, Penny?"

Penny lets out a little noise that could only be described as *relief*.

"Penny's got it set up on her computer," Marion says. "She's been really helpful, sorting out the online accounts for me."

"I pay everything every month," Penny tells Mom. "No autopay, because if we're off by too much—"

"Overdraft fees." Mom and I sigh together.

"Yeah. Mom can be bad about checking the bank accounts before she buys supplies sometimes. But I've got a whole calendar for it. And I can give you the log-in for the power company."

"Great," Mom says. "But, Penny, about the job at the brewery—"

"I can do it," I hear myself say.

Mom looks at me. "Really?"

"Penny already has a job. If it's just the lunch shift, then I can swim before and do the rest of my training after. Until Lottie comes back. The money can go to all the bills Penny was talking about."

When she hesitates, I go in for the kill: "I could keep an eye on Drew and figure out how he's messing up the pretzel dough," I suggest, hoping she'll laugh.

And she does. "Now, *that* I would appreciate."

"So would the rest of us who would like to order the pretzel at the brewery again," Gran mutters.

"Sweets, I'm not going to object to you getting a summer job, as long as you think you can handle it and your training schedule," Mom says. "But, Penny, you've gotta talk to your mom about speaking with Graham."

"I was just trying to help," Penny mutters.

"I know," Mom assures her. "And your mom knows that, too. Because she's doing the same exact thing as you are: helping in any way you can. You two are so much alike."

Penny's eyes shimmer with what she says next. "Anna, I don't want to be like her."

Truer words, I don't know if they've ever been spoken.

I can't sleep. That's not new—I'm a light sleeper. This is a bad trait when you regularly get up before the sun. I have a whole routine—earplugs and everything—but the first night in a room much bigger than the one in our old apartment, combined with the fact that we're in the middle of the woods, not town, and it's *different*. The sounds are different—the forest is quiet, but also loud as the wind rushes through the pines and the space between the two ridges. The house is different—it hums and settles, with creaks I'm not used to. The bed is mine, the stuff is mine, but everything outside of these four walls isn't.

(The girl across the hall isn't.)

Speaking of Penny...

That's what woke me. A creak too loud to be just the house settling. I get out of bed and walk up to the window only to see her in the porch light, and I'm heading downstairs before I really think it through.

(I never think when it comes to her.)

Marion's trailer is dark, but the garage light flicks on when Penny passes beneath it.

I grab my bag in the hallway before I walk out onto the porch. She's already in her station wagon, starting it, heading toward the gate.

I crouch behind Marion's truck as Penny gets out of her car and unlocks the gate, driving through and locking it back up before heading off.

And I follow. I grab Marion's Hide-A-Key under her bumper and take her truck.

(Where the hell is Penny going?)

The road through the forest is hairpin turns along the mountain, a zigzag too narrow for two full lanes. I see a glimpse of her headlights on every curve, but by the time she gets to the on-ramp to the 5, she's far enough ahead that I can follow her without worrying.

I follow her twenty miles down the freeway, the curvy part that the big riggers rush through, with bad consequences, trying to get to the easy straight stretch toward Sacramento. And when I see what exit she takes, I breeze past it instead of following behind her, not because I'm being smart, but because I'm shocked.

She took the lake exit. There's no way . . .

I circle around, taking the next exit and getting back on the 5 heading north, and this time I take the exit she did, my fingers and face numb with *there's no way*.

But sure enough, by the time I get to the docks, her car's parked there in the lot, and she's not in it.

I get out of Marion's truck, and for a second I just stand there, because my mind is telling me a million things, and my body is reacting like there's only one possibility, and that possibility is—

(*No.*)

I move. Toward the docks and the lake that shimmers under the high moon. *What the hell is she doing here?*

My feet slap against pavement, then wood. I don't see her anywhere. But there's no way—

She's in the water.

(That can't be.)

The idea is staggering, because Penny does not go in the water. Not anymore.

Yet here she is, making good time from the dock. Her back to me, headlamp on, paddle strokes sure and smooth as she maneuvers the kayak away from the shore.

I stand there like I don't even care if she turns around and sees me. I watch her get farther and farther away, heading past the inlet, toward the sleek sprawl of water that is Shasta. During the day, it's filled with Jet Skis and motorboats, but tonight it is just her, the moon, and the splash of the paddle in the still water. My heart aches as I remember why she stopped rafting... and wonder why (/when/ how) she came back (and why she kept it a secret).

She lifts her arms. The kayak bobs, tilting back and forth.

She goes under. She just—she flips like a rag doll in the kayak, until the bottom is bobbing along the surface of the lake and there's no more Penny in the moonlight because Penny's underwater. This far away, it's almost like someone's yanked her down from the depths, and I have no choice but to react.

I jump.

And the only thought in my head as I hit the water is: *Not again.*

ACT ONE: THE RIVER

Penny

FIFTEEN YEARS OLD

THE WATER'S ROUGH that day. I'm glad for it. We both are. It's perfect weather—sun's shining bright.

Perfect water—calm, until it gloriously isn't.

Perfect rapids—white as snow.

Perfect father. *Put your arm into it, Pen.*

Perfect day. *Just the two of us this time, Dad?*

Then . . . a perfect nightmare.

On your left! Dad!

When it goes wrong, it is everything and it is all at once. We hit the part of the Wishbone where it funnels into a narrow swirl. It's calm, the start of the rapids twenty feet ahead of us, but whatever hooks the bottom of the raft—a tree branch? Debris from the last summer storm? I will never know—sends us spinning backward into the first rough stretch, and there's no steering, barely any rowing, no recovering. Water seeping along the soles of my feet, then lapping my ankles, so much water, so fast. My focus narrows as the world tilts. Fear flutters. I can't give in to it.

Right yourself. Grab your oar. Don't drop it. Focus ahead. Let Dad steer. Get to the bank.

Stroke. Stroke. Pull hard. Get control.

But there's no getting it back. There's no getting to the bank. Just two strokes before we're in the rapids backward. It happens too fast, there's no way to rope ourselves to something or to try to steer into the shelter of any boulders. We're caught in the thick of it, trying to keep from going down, bailing frantically. Shoveling water and supplies out of the raft as the tear in the bottom and the weight of both of us sinks it deeper.

He shouts about my vest. I can't even check—we're dipping down in more rapids with a teeth-clenching jolt.

All I can do is hang on, no direction, no control, at the river's mercy. He's on the other side of the raft, trying to keep it balanced, trying to steer and failing.

We're going to lose the raft. My fingers clench around the wet ropes until they cut my skin. We slam into the rocks, there's a horrible *crack*, and it takes a mind-spinning second to realize that the crunch was his helmet.

I scramble forward in the slosh, oar abandoned, even as we fall farther into the hell of it. There's blood on his cheek. Trickling down from his forehead. He pulls the dented helmet off and shakes his head—shaking it off?—and he's yelling instructions to me again, so he has to be okay, right? Right?

Throw that last pack. Grab that oar. It's okay, Pen. We've got this. The rapids get nasty up here. Brace for the big fall. After, it'll narrow enough to grab onto something. We've got it.

We don't. We both know it. I have never seen him look so scared. I've never seen him look scared at all. The river's in the back of my throat, swirling in the bottom of my lungs, drenching every part of me, and I know with the certainty of a girl who has spent her life on it: It's going to kill us.

When we hit the bad part of the Wishbone, we won't make it through alive.

He sees it before me: the fallen log. Part of the branch hangs out into the water, and ahead of it is just pure whitewater and too much space, deep dips, swollen by the last storm. The river's turned more waterfall than rapid. His eyes snap to the log, then ahead, then back to the branch, and I look to where he's looking, a few seconds behind his thinking . . . just a few seconds . . .

Rope looped around my hand. Hands around my waist. So tight. We're tilting, we're going to tip—*Grab it, Penny!* he's yelling—and I obey, I reach—do it or die. He hoists me high enough, and I collide with the log, stomach and rib cage hitting it at a speed that has me screaming. The rope around my wrist tightens—the only thing keeping the raft from sweeping away. It snaps me forward, and I can't even hear the rush of the water over the sounds I make. The force of the river, it fights me, determined to move, always so determined to force through any obstacle. That's why I love it.

But now I'm the obstacle. Dad is. And the river hates resistance.

It's okay, Pen. I can barely hear him over the roar—am I sobbing? Screaming? Is there a word for this? I can't think around my muscles, the strain that burns and pops my bones free of their sockets as I try

75

to pull in the rope, yank him in. My body is built for so many things, so useful, so capable, so very strong, but it'll break under this. The churn is all around him. The raft's nothing but deflated rubber and rope tangled up his arm.

It's a battle I cannot win. But I keep trying. The rope's in my hands now, instead of around my wrist. Progress. I can do it. Blood tacky on my palms, rope slipping through the mess, *pull, dammit.* I need to loop it around my hand again. I need six more inches. Just six more inches. I can do it.

I slide farther over the log, pulled by the rope and current. It stretches my body to an inhuman degree, and the *grind-pop* of my elbow is even more painful than my shoulder.

He's yelling something. Over and over, as he splashes frantically in the water. I think it's pure fear garbling it, my own and the rush of the water tricking my ears, until what he's doing finally breaks through.

He's not scared.

He's trying to untangle himself.

He's trying to untether *us*.

He's begging.

Not for him.

He's begging me to let go. *Penelope! Drop the rope! I can't get free— drop the rope!*

I'm soaked. Hanging half off the log, pulled by the churn and the rope and the raft and his weight. He's got the rope pushed off his arm, it's down his wrist. He's almost free.

No. No. I have you. I have you. I promise. I can do it. I'm strong enough.

I have to be.

I pull. The rope slips in the wrong direction, but I catch it, almost falling off the log in the process. The *No, Penny, stop!* he lets out is like nails on slate.

I ignore him. Seven more inches. Maybe eight? I can do it. I can pull him in.

I can. I can. I . . .

"Penny! Look at me!"

My eyes snap to his, across the water, blue against blue.

The rope's in his fist.

"Tell your mother I love her."

I scream. Not a word. Not even a true sound. Just pain. Just realization. Just that awful *knowing* in his eyes.

And then:

He.

Lets.

Go.

13

Penny

JUNE 23

THE AIR RARELY gets cold at night in the summer. It's like the trees and dirt remember the heat of the day and keep spreading the warmth. But the lake cools as the sun fades.

I was scared of dark water once. I was scared of a lot of things for a long time after the accident.

I'm still scared. *You've survived a lot of trauma*, Jane, the therapist Gran sent me to, used to gently tell me, like the label would help. I wish it had, but I acquired a bunch of labels that day that had nothing to do with PTSD, and the weight of them was already too much. Adding more wasn't helpful when I started therapy; it was the way to a panic attack.

That changed, though, the more I went to her. I couldn't talk about the accident. So I ended up talking about other things. About my life. About my quirks. About Mom and that gap that was always there but had now widened to a chasm. About how I used to be able to outrun my thoughts, and now I couldn't.

The more I talked and the more Jane listened, the more she learned, and one day, she brought up something I'd never heard of before. *Intrusive thoughts*. And this time, the sudden knowledge didn't feel like a burden. It felt like a cracked door that'd always been locked before when I passed it.

I feel so stupid, now, looking back. I agreed to a session with Mom, thinking that Jane bringing it up would be better. I was so wrong.

It was like as soon as Jane said that intrusive thoughts were often connected to some anxiety disorders and obsessive-compulsive disorder, everything else she'd said faded away. Mom latched onto the OCD part, ignoring the anxiety part. Jane tried to redirect her; she repeated that it was associated with *both* OCD and some anxiety disorders and even PTSD, but Mom just kept insisting that there was no way I had OCD. My room wasn't clean enough for that.

Maybe it would've been fixable if Mom wasn't so dismissive. Maybe it would've worked out if Jane hadn't started talking about medication and reincorporating rafting into my life to help deal with the anxiety and intrusive thoughts. Mom *exploded*. And that was it. I wasn't allowed to go back to therapy.

I still do the deep-breathing exercises Jane taught me. They help. But talking out stuff helped more. And who knows, maybe the medication and actually figuring out where I fit and how to deal with the anxiety would've helped more. I guess I don't get to find out.

Every time I've tried to bring any of it up, Mom snaps at me. *You know the rules*.

Well, fuck Mom's rules.

Jane had laid it out for me in the session before Mom ruined everything. She told me that everyone has a toolbox. And sometimes, when you're undiagnosed, you build your own toolbox without knowing it. Coping mechanisms that don't look like coping mechanisms.

Rafting was one of the biggest tools in my box. My entire life was centered around it. My mind quieted when I was doing it. And when it was taken away from me, no more quiet mind.

Meghan's tied the kayak to the dock like she does every time I've done this. I flip on my headlamp, flashing it in three short bursts while facing the south shore across the water. Three short flashes answer me back—she's in position.

I trail my hand in the water. I don't even try to block out the echo of his voice, telling me to make sure I've got everything I need before I push off. There's no use trying to squash it—he's in my head and on every curve and line of my face and every path I've walked in these forests and the river and this place. I took after him so strongly it ended up condemning me, because now, to my mom, I'm just a reminder, not a daughter.

I clamber inside the kayak and grab the paddle before untying and pushing off the dock.

The smooth glide makes my stomach clench; there's a part of me that now expects the steep drop and rock of rapids whenever I smell freshwater and pine.

Dipping the paddle into the water, I head across the lake—toward the beam of Meghan's headlamp. My guiding light. She's probably editing photos on her phone as she waits for me to get my ass in gear and actually paddle hard.

I'm supposed to just get across. That's the plan. I've done it a dozen times now. I had to relearn a lot and get stronger. Physical therapy helped. But I'll always have limited movement in my pinky and ring finger. My whole hand will hurt after a while. And it'll hurt more if I push too far.

I've never been good at learning my own limits. This has forced me to.

I clip my paddle to the side of the kayak and lift my arms, stretching up toward the moon. My entire body sings with it as I make a split-second decision.

One. Two. *Flip*.

I don't slip under. It's not graceful, hand rolling in a kayak. It's a *slap-crash* of a movement, abs clenching, skin peppering with bumps at the cold shock of water, and then . . .

Silence. Peace. Home.

I revel in it, because I didn't in the past. Now I can. There was no big moment in being able to do this. There were so many little steps. Forward and backward. And I'm not sure I would've made it without Meghan just . . . being there. No matter what. Even when I was crying and when I was raging and when I was having a panic attack on the riverbank at the thought of sweeping away like he did. She always showed up, and yeah, sometimes she told me it was a bad idea, but she always *showed*, and I have a thing about people leaving, you know?

I let out a string of bubbles. Controlled and slow. My chest is starting to get tight—my lung capacity still sucks—and I'm just about to pull myself back to the surface when I feel it—a ripple under the water before something wraps around my waist.

My mind doesn't even filter through possibilities. My mouth's open and screaming all my air out before my brain goes online. Fear floods. Teeth clench. *Don't suck water in.* My body reacts, fighting, knowing that it's always been this, it was always going to be the water that takes me, that's why Mom's so scared—

—and then I'm out of the kayak. I don't even know how—my mind's blank with panic—but my legs are free and my body knows enough to kick up, away, but I forget about not sucking more water in, and when I surface, I'm choking on it.

She bobs up to the surface seconds after me, and it takes dripping, numbing seconds to actually *see* her. To make out the wet blur of Tate.

"What are you doing?" I will never know who yells it—I think maybe we both do, almost at the same time. I think maybe in that moment, we feel exactly the same for opposite reasons.

Her arm hooks under mine, and I'm startled into sagging against her as she tugs me into her wake. We tread water, her legs brushing against mine in restless circles. My headlamp bobs away, carrying the light. In the growing dark, my hands scramble along the slope of her shoulders, and her tank top strap slides down with my fingers, and it's like my mind's come alive with that one detail.

"Get off me!" I push—not really hard, but enough that it propels me away from her and the slip of her skin in the moonlight. Water surges around me, and she swipes a hand over her face, tucking back strands of hair that have come loose from her French braids.

"What the fuck, Penny?" Tate shouts.

"You grabbed me! You could've killed me!"

"You went under! I thought—"

She stops. A thunderous kind of silence as the rest of her words become glaringly clear. She jumped in without even taking off her clothes.

She thought . . .

Anger spikes before I can get ahold of myself or think it through. I'm so mad I shove water at her, splashing her like we're eight and

82

forced into another picnic at the creek. "How could you think I'd do that to my mom? To Gran?"

To you?

"You went under!" she shouts again, like she's on a loop, and her eyes are huge. . . . Her shoulders are shaking.

Thwap, splash. Thwap, splash.

Meghan's headlamp hits us like a spotlight. We jerk away from each other, distance and water between us again, squinting in the brightness.

"You two," Meghan snarls. "Get to the bank."

"I—" Tate starts, because she clearly hasn't realized that when Meghan uses the scary voice, you listen.

"Now!"

I obey, and Tate follows as Meghan secures my kayak to hers and paddles alongside us, her mouth twisted in disapproval.

I push forward, pulling my arms through the water. I'm not like Tate—power and speed in every stroke, a body designed to cut through any churn, broad shoulders, long limbs and wide hands that look like they can cup both of mine. She speeds past me, even though she's not even trying.

Meghan beats us to shore, pulling both of the kayaks onto the dock by the time I'm halfway there.

When my feet finally touch the sandy lake bottom that fades into the concrete of the boat ramp next to the dock, Tate's already out and sitting at the damp edge of the ramp, her bare feet in the water. I wade until it's ankle deep, feeling slow and useless all of a sudden. I want to shake water on her like a dog, I'm still so mad. She *followed* me. How did she even manage that without her truck?

The answer to that's over her shoulder—Gran's truck is parked in the lot.

"Did you follow me here?" I demand. "Did you *steal* Gran's truck? What were you thinking?"

"Marion told me to use the truck when I needed to," she hisses back. "How about what *you* were thinking, paddling out in the middle of the night with just a headlamp? Since when do you get in the water at all?"

"None of your business!" I shout just as Meghan calls over her shoulder, "We worked up to kayaking ages ago."

I glare at her.

"What?" Meghan asks, staring at both of us from her spot on the dock. "She's not going to tell anyone. Tate, you're not going to tell Lottie, are you?"

Tate doesn't respond, and my entire world tilts harder than I did in that kayak. If she tells my mom, it's over before it's begun. And I can't let that happen. Not again. Mom destroyed everything the first time. I have a chance to make it right, and I won't let her ruin it again just because Mom hates the river.

"Truce agreement," I remind Tate. "Rule Two: No Snitching."

"Your mom can't *still* be on the river thing," she protests, and a smidgen of hope rises in me because she sounds baffled.

"Oh, she absolutely is," Meghan says. "There's a pool rule."

"A . . . ?" Tate looks confused.

"I'm not allowed in any body of water but a pool with a lifeguard," I explain.

"Seriously?"

"Thus the subterfuge and late-night kayaking trip," Meghan adds. "We have to practice some way."

"Practice for what?"

I shake my head at Meghan, but it's too late.

Meghan holds out her hands. "I'm going to let you two talk this out," she says. "Pen, Tate's right. We've got to figure something out so we can do this during the day. Especially when—" She presses her lips together. "I'll let you two talk," she says again.

She completely abandons me, but she grabs the kayaks and will end up doing all the work of putting them away, so I can't be too mad. Especially because this is kind of my thing to explain, even if it is *our* thing. As in Meghan and mine's.

But first, it was Dad's.

I sit down next to Tate, and the lake laps over our feet. The boat ramp is ridged, not smooth, and I can feel it through my leggings. I shift, trying to get comfortable, but I just end up closer to her.

"What are you practicing for?" Tate asks. "Are you going to raft again?"

"And if say yes?" I know Tate's not like my mom, but all I can think of is Mom's reaction to Jane. How after the session, she'd sold Dad's business. How she'd exploded when I confronted her about it.

"You loved rafting."

"I did," I say. "I do," I correct myself. It's rusty, but it's real.

"Then great. If it makes you happy. And you can—Your hands are okay, right? With the paddling?"

"I had to build up to this. Adjust. Do my exercises. But it's not bad so far."

"Does it hurt?"

I'm quiet for a second. I'd messed up the tendons and nearly severed two of my fingers on my right hand trying to pull Dad in. A tug-o'-war injury, the doctors called it. . . . I get why they call it that, but it sounds like a kid's game instead of what it is: this physical representation of loss that I can't run from. For the right hand rebuild, I'd lucked out with really good surgeons, and Gran had made sure I did the physical therapy. Some things are hard now, but not impossible. So far, at least.

"My hand's always gonna hurt sometimes, I think."

"That sucks."

I shrug, because that's just life now.

"So you're just building up to rafting again and you don't want Lottie to know."

"Yep. That's it."

There's a moment where she just looks at me. "You're lying."

Gillian Tate, everyone: the witness to all my worst moments and the seer-through of all my lies.

"Why is Meghan so involved in this?"

"Because I needed someone to help me." That is the truth, but it's not the whole truth. She's looking at me like she knows it's bullshit.

"She and I have a plan," I add.

"What plan?"

"My mom, she sold my dad's half of the rafting business to his partner, remember?"

"Yes, I remember."

"She had no right to—"

"Penny, what does this have to do with rafting again?"

86

"Tom was the money-and-numbers guy. He wasn't the outdoorsman that Dad was. He wants out, and he's agreed to sell the equipment and client roster to me and Meghan when we graduate."

She's quiet for a moment. "Where are you gonna get the money?"

"The life insurance. My dad had two policies. One for Mom, one for me. I get it when I turn eighteen. Meghan has an inheritance from her grandparents. We're gonna pool the money and go into business together."

When she doesn't say anything, just looks at me in silence, my skin prickles. "It's what he would've wanted," I say. "Me owning the business. I would've gone to work for him after I graduated."

"I know," she says.

Two words. Why do they mean so much? Why was I so sure that she'd laugh at me? Or yell at me?

"You do?" My voice is shaking, and so are my hands, and maybe I want hers to still them. . . . I cannot ask for it. But I remember the day they buried him.

Did her promise hold?

"Your dad understood you," she says, and my eyes are welling before the words are fully out of her mouth, because yes, yes, he did. And now no one does . . . or am I wrong? Does she?

"He would've loved working with you," she continues. "Your mom . . . she wants you to use the money for college, right?"

"Yep."

"And you're planning on breaking this plan to her when, exactly?"

"I was thinking *after* I turn eighteen and after Meghan and I buy the equipment from Tom so she can't mess it up."

Tate lets out a whistle.

"She'll try to sabotage it," I insist.

"No, I get keeping it from her. She's just gonna be . . ."

"Yeah," I say, when she doesn't finish, because there's just too much Mom's gonna be when she finds out, and Tate understands that better than anyone. Meghan gets it, she's heard it from me, but Tate's *seen* a lot of it.

Sometimes even stuff I didn't see, because Mom ran away from me.

"Maybe make a ten-point plan to break it to her?" Tate suggests.

My cheeks heat, because I think she's teasing me, but when I look at her, she's earnest.

"You're not gonna tell?"

"Not unless you keep pulling this late-night shit."

"You'll have to help cover for me, then," I say, and it maybe comes out like a challenge, because her eyes spark.

"Fine," she says, rising to it. "I will."

"Why?"

"Because your mom is wrong," she says. "And because I told you once, if there were sides, I'd be on yours. It's easy to do that when it's the right side."

"And . . . what if my side is the wrong side?"

Another of her silences as she chews on her words. "I've known you my entire life, Penny. When it comes to the important stuff I haven't seen you be wrong yet. Just . . . a lot of wrong done to you."

Then she gets up and holds out her hand as water drips from her plaid pajama pants and tank top.

I take it like it's a step forward.

It feels like it is.

14

ACT TWO: SEARCH

TATE

FIFTEEN YEARS OLD

THE DAY OF the accident, Marion is supposed to pick me up from swim practice, because Mom's in Sacramento for some medical tests.

When Remi shows up instead, I know something's wrong. He just got his license, but his mom is so paranoid about him driving, she doesn't let him *ever* have the car. But he's standing there with his keys in his hands, waiting for me, and I almost break out into a run to get to him.

And thank God for Remi, because the first thing he says when I'm close enough is "Your mom's fine."

"What—"

"Something happened at the river."

All that relief gets sucked out of me in a second. "Penny?"

"I don't know. Marion called my mom a few hours ago, said that Penny and her dad didn't show at the pickup point."

"George is always extending trips," I protest, even as there's a dull thud in my head. It's my heartbeat, I realize too late. It's beating too fast, trying to catch up with my racing thoughts. (When was the last time I saw Penny? What was the last thing she said to me? What was this reality I'd stepped out of the pool into?)

I can always breathe, but suddenly I can't.

"They found the raft," Remi says.

Thud, thud, thud.

"It was really torn up."

Thud, thud, thud.

"It looks like they had to bail."

Thud, thud, thud.

And then he's cursing, and his hands hook under my arms, because otherwise I'm going down in the parking lot.

"I'm fine," I tell him, and then I move out of his grip and lock my knees.

Thud, thud, thud.

"Where was the raft? Where are they searching?"

"Near Devil's Fork, where they found it."

"They should be looking around the Wishbone," I say. "George was talking about taking Penny up there for her birthday, last time I went out with them. Call your mom. Tell her."

"You know she doesn't get reception out there."

"Okay. Then drive."

He raises an eyebrow. "I'm supposed to take you home."

"Remi."

"Fine," he says. "Come on."

Remington is my best friend. Which is why, on the drive out there, he plays music from my phone instead of his, and he doesn't say a word, just lets me stare out the window and bite my nails bloody.

She'll be fine.

Even if she had to bail, she's a strong swimmer. And she had to have a vest. George wouldn't let anything happen to her.

(The first thing is true, the second thing, I don't know for sure, and the third . . . I think I'm just lying to myself, because some things are beyond even the best men.)

The pines are beautiful any time of year, but they're a blur out the window as the road climbs higher. We twist along the street, snaking curves through the cliffs and trees, the river only a slice of blue and white through the thick pines when you look the right way. I try to focus on them—on anything—but when Remi slows down where the road splits, I can't.

"We can go find my mom—" he starts.

I shake my head. Devil's Fork is a few miles down on the south road. The Wishbone is fifteen miles north. We can't waste any time. If she's hurt—

"Wishbone. Now."

"My mother is going to lose it." He sighs, but he heads north instead of south.

Nothing is easy in the forest. It's the first rule anyone ever taught me about it. The forest is work. It requires effort. And it'll make you earn things.

You have to respect it. What it can give you. What it can take away.

(Has it taken her?)

"There's a pack in the back seat," Remi jerks his head. "Emergency stuff. We should take it with us."

I unbuckle to grab it, a heavy canvas bag zipped up neatly. Remi's mom knows her stuff, of course, so I clutch it like the lifeline it is.

We follow the river down, and then the road turns sharply upward, climbing in zigzags that make my stomach clench. Remi takes a right when there's a fork, and a few miles in, the road roughens to gravel and then to pure dirt that's more potholes than anything. A few miles more, and we have to stop. There's a forestry utility gate.

"Shit," Remi says.

I get out and test it, but it's chained shut, with no way around it. Remi gets out of the car, the emergency bag slung over his shoulder.

"Let's do a check," he says, ever the Boy Scout. But I don't blame him.

We assess our supplies: The bag has a first-aid kit, bottles of water, a blanket, clothes, granola bars, two whistles, a knife, and a flashlight. Remi loops one of the whistles around his neck and gives me the other.

I pull out my phone and set a timer. "We walk for thirty minutes. We should cover two miles at least. We call their names every ten or fifteen steps, so they have time to call back and we can hear them."

"Okay, let's go."

We set out, determined and at a clip.

"Penny!"

"George!"

(I count the steps. One. Two. Three. *Please.* Four. Five. Six. *She can't be.* Seven. Eight. Nine. *If she's okay...* Ten. Eleven. Twelve. *I'll do anything.*)

"Penny!"

"George!"

I'm wearing flip-flops with no tread, and they slip on the thick fall of dried pine needles that carpets the access road. No one's been down here in a long time. Since maybe last fire season.

"Penny!

"George!"

Sweat trickles down my back as we move, steady and sure, down the road.

"Penny!"

"George—"

Remi grabs my arm. "Tate, look." He points, and it takes a second to see what he's spotted: a flash of bright orange through the trees.

Hope—it's a terrible thing. This is what I have learned.

I run. The road steepens and the trees clear as I finally get the right vantage point. From here, I can see down to the river—and I can see *her*, on the sloped embankment. She's sitting up. She's alive. (Oh, God, she's *alive*.)

The orange is her life jacket. She's still in it, her back to me, staring out at the water below.

"Penny!"

She doesn't even glance toward me. Can she hear me? I raise my voice. "Penny?" Still nothing.

I need to get down there.

Where's George? I look around frantically as Remi comes up behind me.

"Remi, go get the car."

"The gate—"

"Find a way. Go get your mom, then."

"I can't leave—" He stops, he looks at her, he looks at me. He swallows. "Okay. I'll figure it out."

"Be fast."

He nods. I hear him scramble away, and all my focus goes to her. I need to get down there. I could go farther, searching for an easier way, but she's *right there* . . . and it's like she can't even hear me.

So I sit down on the edge of the slope, grit my teeth, and push off, feetfirst, and slide down in a skin-scraping rush. My back stings as gravel and branches snag, and one of my flip-flops flies off before I hit the bottom, but I get there.

"Penny." I crawl over to her.

She is . . . destroyed. Her hands. Oh my God. Her *hands.*

"Penny?"

It takes her a second, but now that I'm crouched in front of her, she focuses on me. "Tate." And then she giggles, a high-pitched, hysterical sound that sparks panic in my stomach. "You found me. Of course. Of course."

"Everyone's looking for you." Focus on the facts. "Penny, I think you're really hurt. Your hands—"

"They're fine," she insists, waving one of them—I'm pretty sure I glimpse *bone* through the swelling and wounds, holy shit—and her voice . . . it isn't *hers.*

"Penny," I say slowly, looking around. None of her stuff is here. Not even a water bottle or an oar . . . or anything. The river is at least seven feet down. How did she get up here with her hands like that? "Where's your dad?"

"He's dead," she says, so matter-of-factly it sends a jolt through me.

"No—"

"He's *dead*." She snarls it at me, shifting into feral in the space of a blink. And suddenly, there's Penny again, but it's not the Penny I know. Her eyes have never burned so—I'm ashes in the brunt of it, dirt grinding into my knees.

"Okay," I say. "He's dead."

It's like I've shot her; she jerks, and then, *oh*, then, bit by bit, she sags into my agreement.

"Thank you," she whispers.

Then she sobs it, swallowed up by the grief of it, and then I am destroyed by the horror of it.

I can't think of what to do first. Something like panic bubbles under my skin. I need to be calm. I need to be the rock.

(I need to be her rock—oh, God, she needs one.)

She's a *mess*.

Broken and battered and branch-whipped across her face and legs. Two of the straps on her vest are broken; there's only a buckle left. Her hands are raw, red and purple gore. Some of her fingers are bent in directions they shouldn't be. Does she even have all of them? My mind trips over the horrible thought as I try to count them. She's holding her arm oddly, like she can't straighten it. Is it broken? I need to get her to the hospital.

"He let go. In the water. He let go of the rope. I told him I had him.

I had him. I was strong enough. I *was*. Tate, I was strong enough. I had him. I promise. I had him. I had him. I *had*—"

"I know you did."

Her hair is hiding half of her face, and I start to reach out, but then I realize I shouldn't, because there's blood matted on the side of her head. Did she hit it? Where is her helmet?

"Why did he let go?"

God, her hands are *mangled*.

"He didn't want to."

I look over my shoulder. Can she walk? Should I get her up?

"But he *did*." Her hand brushes against her knee, just barely; it makes her cry out.

How long has she been like this? All day? Longer? Her hair isn't wet anymore. So, long enough for it to air-dry. Long enough for the blood to mat in her hair and congeal along her legs and arms. Long enough for all the bruises to rise under her skin, livid.

Much too long.

My brain is going in a million directions. She needs doctors. Drugs. Antibiotics. Probably surgery. Where's Remi and the car? We need to get her into town, then down the mountain where there's a hospital, not just a clinic.

"Why did he let go?" She just keeps repeating it, like she's on a loop. That extraordinary focus of hers—the thing that makes you feel so seen when she turns it on you—it's suddenly fixed on this awful question, and she's caught in it, unable to tear free.

I reach out, trying to be gentle (wanting so badly to be), and I don't cup her face but hold it. She stiffens but doesn't fight it. Her eyes meet mine. And then it slows, the shaking, until it's just trembling, her body all adrenaline and pain and whatever else it's doing to keep her upright.

"Tate," she says again, sounding puzzled. "You're real."

(It's like she's bestowing that status on me.)

"Yeah," I say. "I came for you." I lick my lips. Simple. I should keep it simple. Keep her talking and focused, away from whatever happened. "We should...we should go home. That sounds good, right? Home?"

"Home," she echoes the word distantly, and then her face *crumbles*, folds in on itself like a handkerchief crushed in a pocket. "Home," she says again. "Oh, God. *Mom*."

"You're okay. She'll be so relieved."

I know it's a mistake the second it's out of my mouth.

Penny laughs. It's not hysterical like before. This is horrible: knowing and grieving all at once.

"She'll hate me," she says, with the same certainty she'd said, *He's dead*, and I can't help but believe her, because George is the metal to Lottie's magnet.

Was, I guess...Fuck.

"Why did he let go?" she asks hopelessly.

"I don't know," I say, even though I'm pretty sure I do.

He let go to save her.

(I would've let go, too.)

97

15

TATE

JUNE 24

IN THE LAKE parking lot light, Penny wrings out her ponytail, the water splashing on the pavement.

I'm soaked, too, my pajama pants and tank top sticking against me in kind of embarrassing ways because I'm not wearing a bra. My wet sleep braid is dripping steadily down my stomach, and I want to take my hair out and twist it dry like she's doing.

"Did you even bring a towel?" I ask. My swim bag isn't in the truck, since it's not my truck.

"I wasn't expecting to take a full dip."

"You flipped in the kayak!"

"That was kind of spontaneous. I was feeling the moment. One you kind of ruined by scaring me."

I glare at her, and she lets out a sigh. "I have blankets in the car. Come on."

She unlocks the station wagon and roots around in the back, coming up with two fleece blankets. She hands me one, and I turn around, my back to her so I can wrap it around my body like a shield.

I shimmy out of my pants and tank top under the blanket and fix it toga-style around me.

Bending down, I pick up my wet clothes, and when I straighten—I don't mean to look, I swear—but I catch a glimpse of her, and then I am looking.

She's not undressed.

I would've looked away if she were. (That isn't what I want, not like that.)

She's got her blanket wrapped around her like me, shoulders bare, but she's twisting her hair up now. Practiced movements that my eyes follow like my hands want to, her head tilting to the side, and it shouldn't gut me, this simple thing, this thing I've seen her do before, even. (But it's somehow different here in the parking lot light, in the wake of fearing, then jumping, and this new knowing.)

"Are you okay?"

(It's not different, Tate, what are you thinking? Some girls don't get some things.)

"Yeah," I say. "I'm fine. Thanks for the blanket."

"We should get going. It's almost two."

"Yeah. I'll just—" I jerk my thumb behind me toward the truck, and then I'm backing away from her.

(I can't look away and I turn only after she does—what a foolish fucking girl.)

I get in my car, but Penny drives off first. Thank God she does, because I hold it together just long enough for her brake lights to fade.

My lungs haven't caught up with my breathing since I jumped into that water, and once Penny is out of sight, I lose it.

There's no graceful or good way of putting it. I just fucking lose it: white-knuckling that steering wheel as tears join the lake water dripping down my front.

(I really thought she—

I didn't even hesitate.

I just jumped.)

My head feels fuzzed. Adrenaline will do that to you. (And Penny really has a way of upping my adrenaline, doesn't she?)

The movement out of the corner of my eye is the only warning I get before she taps on the truck window. I don't startle, even though I hadn't heard her drive back up. But I want to crawl through the floor of Marion's truck and burrow into the earth to get away from her, since there's no hiding my blubbering.

I roll the window down, raising an eyebrow like my eyes aren't as red as my nose.

"You weren't following me. I was worried the truck didn't start."

"It's fine."

She places her hands on the window—does she think I'm gonna roll it back up? That absolutely crossed my mind. Her fingers—painted copper with little black triangles at the tips—curl around the glass.

"I guess I freaked you out as much as you scared me," she says.

The shuddering breath I let out is humiliating, but I'm desperate for air. "I guess."

"I'm sorry."

"Are you?"

She flushes like it's an accusation. I didn't mean it to come out that way.

"I guess it's a little hard, Tate, having you bear witness to all the disasters in my life."

"I—Is that how you think of me?" My voice shakes, because she's shaken me. Is that really who I am to her? Some forever figure in all her worst memories?

Her eyes widen. "No. No. I just—" Her fingers tighten around the edge of the window, swaying toward me instead of away. "Our lives, Tate, they're fucked in different ways, right?"

I nod.

"But you just...you always seem to handle everything. And I can't. Like, at all. I run around trying to fix things, and it explodes in my face more than half of the time, and you're always there. And I just—I want to be—"

"What?"

"I would like it if I didn't keep failing in front of you, okay?"

"Penny, I—" My mouth doesn't know what to say, but my body seems to, because I'm reaching for her, my fingers sliding over hers gripping that window's edge, and the breath she lets out—

—is it electric for her, too? Like that jolt in your stomach when you dive in for the first time—warm body, cold water—the shock you can't run from?

If I look at her, it's over, so I stare at our hands. Hers and mine. My fingers laid over hers, both of us chilled from the lake, but that's not the reason why goosebumps pepper.

At least not for me.

"Just because I seem like I've got a hold on things doesn't mean I do."

But I've got a hold on her, right now, and she's got a hold on me—actually, metaphorically...maybe eternally.

"You're better at all this medical stuff than me," she whispers. I know her enough to know how much it takes for her to admit that.

"I've had more practice than you on the caretaker side," I said. "But you're the only one of us who's actually had surgery and recovered in a hospital."

Her eyebrows twitch, like she wants to scowl. "That's not the same. My hands—it's different."

"Yeah, but you still have more experience when it comes to being a patient. I bet you know which hospital Jell-O is best."

"The green, of course."

"Lime? Ew." Partly I say it so she'll scoff, and she does.

She rolls her eyes. "You're a philistine when it comes to Jell-O."

"I like the red kind."

"It tastes like cough medicine."

"Delicious cough medicine."

"Obviously I will be making my mom *and* your mom's Jell-O choices, if need be."

"Obviously." I nod very seriously. "They must be protected from bad Jell-O decisions."

"I know what you're doing," she says, and her fingers flex beneath mine, not like she wants me to pull away, but more like she wants to just feel my knuckles against hers (or maybe that's just wishful thinking).

"What's that?"

"You're trying to distract me."

"*You're* the one who came back here and distracted *me*. I'd be almost home by now if it weren't for you."

"I thought you were broken down!"

"But I'm not. I'm just trying to recover from you taking ten years off my life."

"Are you seventy? That is the most Gran thing you have ever said," she declares.

"Marion's not even seventy."

"Tate!"

It makes me look at her (big mistake), and her expression makes my stomach clench (bigger mistake), and one of my fingers rests against the scar on her ring finger (biggest mistake).

"It's just a day away," she says softly.

"I know," I say. On Friday, everything changes.

"It's too soon. I mean, I know it's not. I know the sooner, the better. I just—"

"You want what we don't have. More time."

"It's not only—" She stops. I can feel her pulse pick up, the way her blood thrums under my skin. "I did think I had more time," she says.

I wait, because her hands are almost shaking under mine.

"I thought I'd have more time to get her to love me again."

I'm silent, and she finally looks up when it stretches. "Aren't you going to tell me my mom loves me?" she asks, and it's a challenge, it's a dare. I may be the witness to her worst, but she's the challenge of my life (the dare in my damn heart).

"Your mom has been real shit at loving anyone, even herself, for a long time," I say.

"She's giving *your* mom part of her liver."

"She is. And I will drop anything for your mom for the rest of my life because of it. But that doesn't mean—"

"What?"

"That doesn't erase what happened. It's not some get-out-of-shitty-mother-jail card. It shouldn't be."

"She's not a shitty mom—"

"She *was*." I'm not going to dance around it. That's what being on Penny's side means. "Not because she got lost in grief. But because when she got better and pulled it together, she didn't say sorry or make amends. She just pretended like it didn't happen. But it did. I know it did and so do you. That's why she avoids my eyes sometimes—because I was there when Mom was taking care of her. And it's why she avoids way too much with you. She doesn't need to avoid Mom—Mom is her ride-or-die. They are what each other has left."

"*We* are what they have left," Penny bursts out.

"We are. But it's different, the two of them," I say. "We're almost grown. Hopefully, we'll move out. Move on. And they are—"

"Forever," she finishes, almost bitterly.

"Old ladies knitting on the porch," I say, because it's what Mom and Lottie like to laugh about.

It doesn't make her smile, though. Her fingers pull away, and in their sudden absence, mine feel cold.

"We should get back," she says, and I notice how careful she is about not calling it *home*.

But it is now: our home. We have to learn the new shape of it as we learn to share space we've never had to; we're so used to being only children.

"I'll follow" is all I say back, because if I keep talking, too much will spill out.

(Because I was there, in those deep-grief Lottie days, and Penny was not, and I am thankful for that, but it's like there are wary grooves worn deep in my heart from those months, the impulsive shot in the dark that was Lottie and the wake of her pain, with me counting pills and checking pulses and running what-if scenarios.)

I'm close behind the red glow of her taillights all the way back home. I'm quiet as I follow her through the gate and up the driveway and as we creep into the darkened house. But I have to slow down in the hallway because I can't see, and I can't remember if the coatrack is on the right or left and running into that cast-iron monstrosity would really top off this night.

I step forward tentatively. One step. Two. I can see the shadows of the stairs now.

A light in the living room flicks on.

"Hi, girls," says a voice.

I freeze. Penny drops her keys, she's so startled.

And Mom?

She just smiles kind of sarcastically at us from the couch.

16

ACT THREE: THE FUNERAL

Penny

FIFTEEN YEARS OLD

THINGS ARE FUZZY for a long time after they take me to the hospital. Probably because the doctor shoots me up with a ton of drugs and antibiotics as soon as she gets to me. I'll understand why later on, because they have to operate on my hands and put my shoulder back in place, and a few ribs are broken, but they can't do much about that except wrap up my middle and drug me some more. At the time, I try to fight it—and them; everyone except Tate, really—but I fail.

I'm in the big hospital for days. Maybe weeks. I lose track after the third day.

On the third day, the search and rescue people find him. The only moment my gran leaves my side is to identify his body.

I don't see my mother the whole time.

"She's ill, sweetheart," Gran says. "She needs to rest."

I know the truth: She doesn't want to see me.

It's cemented as fact when they bring me home...but I don't go *home*. I go to Gran's.

I sleep in the bedroom my father slept in as a child, and I want to feel him in the walls, in the books and fishing poles he left behind, but I don't feel anything.

I'm not just numb. I'm not here.

Penny has left the building and the state and probably the planet. I float. I am nothing.

I like it more than I should.

Anna comes. She brings Tate, and we do not look at each other the whole time they're there.

She knelt with me, there in the dirt. She cupped my face.

She tethered me.

I haven't even said thank you.

I haven't said anything.

Before they leave, Anna kisses my forehead—she hovers a little at first, like she's unsure where to touch, where it will hurt less.

"It was nice to see Tate, wasn't it?" Gran asks me as the sound of car wheels on gravel fade.

I shrug. I can't turn away from her in bed, because I still can't rest on my side. But it's enough to get her to drop it.

Mom decides to bury him.

When Gran tells me, I just stare at her, and she has to look away. The shame burns red in her cheeks.

107

I'm already failing him again.

"It's your mother's choice, Penny."

This time, I don't care how much it hurts to turn away from her. The pain's the only thing that keeps me from screaming.

The morning of the funeral, I finally see my mother. Gran has to take me to the house to get my black dress, and there she is, in the living room, already dressed and pristine, not even a mascara smear. She's frozen on that couch, staring straight ahead, and when the door shuts behind Gran, her eyes snap to us so fast it's almost jump-scare creepy.

"Marion?" I hear Anna's voice call from the back of the house. "Is that you?"

"Yep, it's us," Gran calls. She has her arm around me. "Lottie," she says gently. "We're here. So we can all drive together. Remember?"

Mom nods just a second too slowly. She's staring at my bandages, and I have to fight the reflex to hide them, because it hurts to move them or think about them or just to stay still.

"Hi, honey," Mom says.

"Penny, do you want to go get dressed?" Gran suggests when I don't answer.

But I've zeroed in on my target now. I shake my head, and I'm moving, out of the foyer and into the living room, until I'm directly in front of her. Until I'm towering over her, my bruises and bandages right in her face.

There is so much I want to say. I hate her and I love her and I need her and I *needed* her and she was here this whole time, and she *knew*, she knows now, and she's still just . . .

Frozen.

I really am nothing. To her.

"Why are you putting him in the ground?"

It's the first thing I've said in days. I spit it at her, because it's something that should be spat. It's ludicrous. It's *wrong*.

It's not what he wanted.

"Penny," she croaks out. "Honey. Please, don't do this to me. Not today."

"Don't put him in a box, then."

"Penny." She shakes her head. "I need my medicine."

"Honey," Gran says behind me. "Come on. You need to get dressed."

But Gran can't grab my hands or my arms or guide me away by the shoulders, so I use it to my advantage and stay put.

"This isn't what he wanted."

My mom just keeps shaking her head. "Anna?" she calls. "I need my pills."

"Honey . . . ," Gran stresses.

But I keep going. It's all I've been thinking about since Gran told me. Dad in a box. Dad locked up tight, forever. Dad, who loved to be outside more than anything, in the deep, stale dark.

"You *know* what he wanted," I continue. "He wanted to be on the water. He wanted to be on the riv—"

"Don't you dare." She comes to life in a second, like a snake startled into striking. She's up off the couch and in front of me, and I'm almost as tall as her, but not quite. "You think I'm going to give that damn river any more of him? You're crazy."

"Lottie!"

109

It's not Gran who says it. It's Anna, hurrying in from the back bedroom, Tate next to her.

"Did you hear her?" Mom asks, and it's almost mocking, when she continues, "The river *kills* him, and she wants me to put him back there. Crazy!" This time, when she calls me crazy, she almost yells it at me.

I want to cower.

But I'm nothing. And I guess there are advantages to that.

"That's enough," Gran growls.

"Lottie, you need to *stop*," Anna says. "Penny, sweetheart, go with Tate, okay?"

"No," I say.

My mother looks down, but I chase her gaze. I move with it. I refuse to let her dismiss me. "You do this, I will never forgive you."

Then she does look at me.

Then she laughs at me.

"I am not the one who needs forgiveness."

And that's how my gran ends up slapping my mother on the day of my dad's funeral.

I don't go. Gran pleads, Mom doesn't bother, Anna tries to make the case, but I just can't.

I stay outside on the back porch as I hear them rustling inside the house. Gran calls my name one more time, but when I don't come, she sighs, and her footsteps fade. When I hear the car drive away, I finally relax—

—only to stiffen up, because the sliding glass door opens behind me. I turn, so slowly—I hate how slowly I move now—and Tate's standing there, in her black dress, her hair French-braided like always.

"Your mom's unhinged," Tate says, walking across the porch and folding herself down next to me. "I get why she is. But don't listen to her."

I don't say anything. I don't know what to say.

Will she forever be the audience to my worst moments? Am I as weak and broken in her eyes as I feel?

Does she know what she did that day?

I need to thank her. But if I do, I'd have to acknowledge it.

I had floated above that river. Maybe I would've drifted away for good. I'd wanted to—maybe still do. But before I could, she was there, when I knew she couldn't be.

And I thought, *Of course.* Of course my brain conjured *her* up. I must be dying, to dream her there.

She couldn't have been real.

But then she touched me, and she was. She was there.

She found me.

And for the first time since he let go of that rope, I wanted to keep breathing. Just a little.

"My mom's right," I tell her, because Tate's already seen my worst. She might as well get my truth.

"Your mom is full of bullshit, grief, and Valium," Tate says bluntly. "She doesn't even know her own middle name right now. But I don't care about the excuses. She should've been at the hospital with you."

It rises in my chest so fast, I can't even prepare for it or try to suppress it. It's like she's punched a hole in the dam inside me, and what bursts forth...

"Oh, fuck, Penny," she says when I start sobbing. "I'm sorry, I didn't mean—I know your mom's dealing with a lot, too. But you almost *died*—"

I can't hug her. I'm too scared I'll bump my hands against something too hard. But I carefully put my right hand—the one that has only one pin in it—on her knee, and then the left joins it even more gingerly, and she falls totally silent. Her breath goes out of her in a *whoosh*. Her hands fidget in her lap, just inches from my bandaged ones.

For a long time, that's how we stay. Touching, but through so many layers, almost not. Her fingertips could brush mine if she just straightened them a little.

"Thank you," I finally tell her.

Her eyebrows rise. "For what?" Her fingers stretch....Is it on purpose?

"For finding me. For staying. For being on my side."

Tate's fingers touch mine. The slight weight of her hand through the wraps makes me want to start crying again.

"I will find you when you need me," she says. "And I will stay if you want me. But, Penny, there shouldn't be sides here."

Tate's fingers skate gently over my hand. She licks her lips. Her eyes are a lifeline. I can't look away.

"There are always sides."

I have to look away, because if I don't . . .

Grief makes you think crazy things. That's what they say, right? My mom is right. I *am* crazy.

I just so badly want someone to hold me.

Tate is the one who looks away.

Tate is the one who bends—

—to press her lips against my bandaged hands.

First the right. Then the left.

And Tate is the one who tethers me back to the ground when she says, "If there are sides in this, I'm on yours."

PART THREE

Surgery

(or: the time in the pool)

TATE

JUNE 24

WE STARE AT Mom lounging on the couch like a triumphant queen. Oh, God, she's so smug. She's never going to let me live this down.

"Did you two have fun sneaking out?" Mom asks.

Penny tugs at the strap on her blanket toga and runs a hand over her head like it's gonna hide her damp hair. It's obvious we've both been in the water. It's not like you can hide that from a swim mom, even one as low-key as mine.

"We were just—" Penny's at a loss for a lie, looking at me desperately.

"Skinny-dipping?" Mom asks, all arched eyebrows and barely hidden amusement. Even in the dim light, I can see how her eyes are practically glittering.

I'm so glad my teenage awkwardness is such a delight to her. Seriously, I am. She needs all the laughter she can get.

"No!" Penny says, sounding so horrified it seems almost fake.

"Penny wanted to show me the deer by the creek," I say quickly, so she won't dig a deeper hole. "They only come out at night. I slipped and fell in. She had to help me out."

"Mm-hmm," Mom says. "Penny, honey, why don't you get some sleep, okay?"

"Are you—"

"We'll talk in the morning," Mom says gently.

Penny looks at me one last time before dashing up the stairs, mouthing *truce* at me like I'm about to forget. I won't rat her out, truce or not. Especially because Lottie's no-river-rafting rule is all about Lottie, not Penny.

I'm not lucky enough to get to follow Penny up to bed, though.

I don't pull shit like this. I am a good daughter. I don't sneak out—I don't have to. Because Mom and I, we have trust. And I know how valuable—and rare—it is, because I see what not having that has done to Penny.

"Come sit," Mom says, patting the top of the mountain of throw pillows on the couch. "You need a towel?"

"I'm fine."

"You have anything to tell me?"

"We really just went down to the creek to see the deer. I didn't mean to freak you out."

There's a moment when she looks disappointed.

Then she grabs her phone off the coffee table, opens an app, and hands it to me. I glance down at the screen: It's her credit card app, and I see the payment I made.

"I got an email saying there was an extra payment made," she says. "I thought it was a mistake at first."

"It isn't."

"I realize that. Tate, sweets, what did you do?"

It's too hard to look at her, that open face that's told me my whole life, *You can always talk to me.* I've believed it and I've cursed it and I've loved it, this promise she's always made me. *Us against the world.*

I betrayed it, bypassing her like this.

"My truck. I sold it and used the money to pay off the card and some other bills."

"Why would you do that?"

"Because the card was almost maxed out and I knew we'd need it in an emergency, because there's always an emergency. And I was right, wasn't I? We've got to pay for a rental in Sacramento and anti-rejection meds—"

"Tate, being able to predict the sporadic downward trajectory of being chronically ill doesn't make you Cassandra personified. It just makes you my daughter. And my daughter shouldn't be seizing control of my bills."

"I didn't—"

"You went behind my back instead of talking to me. We don't do that."

"I just wanted to take it off your plate. You have enough to deal with."

"You built that truck up from a skeleton with Marion. It was important to you."

"I'll get the money together to buy another junker and fix that one up before I graduate," I say. "But this was more important. I—this was important to me."

"Why?"

"Because," I say. "Because—" And then I just shake my head, eyes burning.

Some things, they can't be unsaid. Some things mothers shouldn't hear.

(Because I will always feel the weight of almost losing her in the back of my throat, because I will always worry about her more than I worry about myself, because I am greedy enough to still pursue what I want, but decent enough to understand I'm selfish for it. Because on the outside, some people might look at us and think *she's* the burden, but really, I am.)

"Okay," she says, and she rubs circles on my damp back as I try not to shake under her touch. "It's okay. Let's just . . . let's make a deal. If you want to contribute, you talk to me first. Like we did with the weekend job at the brewery. I can't be on your team if you don't tell me your plans. And we need to be on the same team more than ever now."

"I know. I'm sorry."

"It's *my* job to take care of *you*," she reminds me. "And I know it's been the other way around—"

"—that doesn't matter."

"You've still lost things."

"As long as I don't lose you."

"Oh, sweets."

"One more day, Mom," I say.

She squeezes my hand. "One more day," she repeats, and we bask in it—the knowledge that soon, that maybe, this is the turning point.

I get up early. I need to pack some more stuff at the apartment before we leave for Sacramento tomorrow. And I need to make some sort of cleaning plan so we can get the deposit back. Ronnie, our landlord, is notorious for withholding it for any little reason.

So I wake up at five-thirty, and by the time it's six and light out-side, I've got my suit and sweats on and my bag packed.

I sneak downstairs, having learned about the squeakier of the stairs last night. But my caution is in vain, because Penny's sitting on the bottom steps of the narrow staircase, waiting for me.

"What are you doing up so early?" I ask quietly.

"We need to start packing up the apartment kitchen, right?"

"I can do it—"

"And I can help. My shift starts at noon, so you've got me for five hours; then we can drive back for the dinner the moms are making us have. Oh! And I packed up some cleaning supplies to leave there." She taps the crate with her foot.

"I was going to swim first," I say, and I hate how guilty I feel for saying it.

She just shrugs. "That's fine. I can pack while you train."

"Are you sure?"

"Yeah. But let's go before they wake up, because my mom will want to come to supervise and then wander off to spend two hours getting lunch for everyone, and your mom will try to do all the work . . . and they both should rest before our trip tomorrow."

"Marion's the only sensible one in this whole house," I mutter.

"Damn right," her voice calls from the kitchen, followed by a laugh when Penny and I shut up.

"Bye, Gran!" Penny stage-whispers before grabbing the crate of cleaning stuff. I shoulder my swim bag, and we hurry out of there, Penny looking over her shoulder at me and grinning like we're in on the same joke.

I unlock the gate, and she drives through it so I can lock it behind us. After getting into the station wagon, I buckle up and start rummaging through my bag.

She looks at the purple gallon jug I've pulled out of my bag and starts laughing. "That's *enormous*."

"It's useful."

"No wonder your skin glows, if you're that hydrated."

"My skin does not *glow*."

"Meghan has asked me several times to get a look at your skincare routine—so yes, you glow."

"My skincare routine is sunscreen."

"Oh my God—of course it is. That's so unfair. Meanwhile I'm over here keeping the pimple patch companies in business. Hormonal acne is the *worst*."

"My mom says to drink spearmint tea for that," I offer as we weave along the curved road toward the highway.

"I'll try anything. Like cramps are not enough to deal with each month." She shakes her head and asks, "Was your mom really mad last night?"

"She was. But not about us."

"What was she—"

"She found out about me selling my truck."

"Oh, shit."

"It's okay, though."

She looks over at me, pure skeptic. "Seriously?" She turns onto the highway on-ramp, heading toward town. "She let it go? You were so worried."

"I don't think my mom has the energy to punish me," I say.

"I would say *lucky*, but it's a pretty shitty reason to be lucky." She gets into the fast lane to pass a logging truck full of pine.

I don't know why, but it gets a smile out of me. "It's not lucky. She and I have a deal."

"What kind of deal?"

"We don't sweat the small stuff. We focus on the bigger picture. I thought this was gonna be a big fight. That's why I worried. But now there's a lot bigger stuff to worry about. I didn't know we were going to need to rent a place in Sacramento for like a month of their recovery. Now I do, and so I guess maybe you're right: It is lucky I sold it."

"No. I was wrong. It was you trying," she says. "Like you always do."

I have to look out the window then. Focus on the blurred trees. Otherwise I think I might reach for her, to see if her hand remembers mine from last night—because mine does.

Penny

JUNE 24

IT'S WEIRD BEING in Tate's apartment alone. I dropped her off at the pool and drove right over, hauling my crate o' clean up the seventies cement stairs.

The trash hasn't been emptied, so I grab that first and head back downstairs.

The dumpster's across the parking lot, and as I walk toward it, a door on the bottom floor at the end of the building swings open. A man steps out, leaning in the doorway, watching me with a slow up-and-down look that makes my skin crawl. I think about just hurrying up the stairs; sometimes avoidance is the best. But I shoot him a hard look—sometimes ignoring the creeps is worse, because then they'll do anything to get your attention. Cutting off creepy with *don't fuck with me* sometimes makes them scuttle away. But it doesn't work this time—he just keeps watching me, and the alarm bells in my head are going off. Shit. I chose wrong. I should've just kept my eyes down and scurried.

I dump the trash and go back upstairs, trying and probably failing not to look like I'm hurrying. He doesn't move from his spot.

It's a good thing, Tate and Anna getting out of here. It's safer at our house.

I make sure the door's locked before I start assembling boxes. I turn on my white-noise app and start taping while crickets chirp, trees rustle, and birds caw. When Tate comes back, she'll want to play music. But I can have my soothing forest right now.

As I tape up boxes, my thoughts drift, my mind buoyant, bobbing in the current. Less than twenty-four hours of living together, and Tate's already figured out my big secret.

There's no way Anna believed us. She was going to follow the mom code and tell my mom something was up. That's the way they are.

When Dad died, a part of me was so glad Mom had Anna. And part of me was so mad she had Anna. Because it meant she didn't need me at all. Maybe it was selfish. But I needed my mom, and I got broken promises and denial . . . glassy eyes and rules that made me want to run even as they hauled me closer to someone who could barely look at me for months.

Would it be easier if we stopped pretending? Or would it be as hard as we both think?

Isn't that why we keep pretending?

I've just finished up the front of the cupboards when I hear the door open.

"Tate?" I call. I had locked the door, right?

"Penny, is that you?" Anna's voice asks.

"In the kitchen."

Anna peeks her head in. "What are you doing here?"

"Packing stuff up. Tate gave me the keys. She's at the pool until ten."

"Penny—" She smiles. "I really don't deserve you two."

"Yes, you do. You should go home and rest. We have a long drive tomorrow. There's sweet tea in the fridge and lounge chairs in the shed. They're nice if you put them by Gran's garden with all the butterflies."

"I should help—"

"You should rest. I bet my mom's resting."

She leans against the counter. "How are you doing, Penny?"

I think about the truce. *No stress for the moms.* "I'm great."

"Yeah? I know this is scary. What your mom's doing for me—"

"It's great."

She smiles, too much understanding in her eyes.

Anna has a gentle knowing about her. You can't escape it. It pulls at you. Welcomes you. It makes you want to trust. But I have to resist.

I love Anna. I'm grateful to her, because my mom may be keeping her alive now, but I'm pretty sure she kept my mom alive after my dad died. Anna always knows what to do. I love her for it—she knew what to do with Dad's ring and Mom's heart and mind in the aftermath— and I hate her a little for it because she has all the answers about Mom that my mom can't, or maybe won't, give me.

"It's still scary," she says. "You've lost a lot the last few years."

"I don't want to talk about that."

Tell your mother I love her.

"I know," she says. "But if you ever do . . ."

It flares inside me, irritation that I shouldn't have toward her. "You don't want me to talk about it, Anna," I say, and her eyebrows

126

draw together. She's lost weight the last few months. She looks sick again—like she did during chemo. I shouldn't push her like this.

"I want you to be able to talk about everything that happened."

"You really don't," I tell her. "You love my mom."

"I do," Anna says. "And I love you."

"*Because* you love my mom."

"Oh, Penny," she says, and it's so sad the way she says it. I can't tell if it's because she knows it's the truth or because she knows I'm the kind of girl who can't imagine any other truth.

"I really have it handled here," I say, grabbing another folded box. "And Tate will be done in an hour."

"All right," Anna says slowly. "I'm just going to pack some things. I have to check on Drew at the brewery before I head back home."

"The pretzel dough, I remember."

"He can't get it right to save his life." Anna tsks. "I've got no idea what they're gonna do while I'm gone. So I'll leave you to it if Tate's heading back soon."

"She is."

"I just have one more thing."

"Yeah?"

"About last night?"

My stomach twists and my fingers clench around the spray bottle. "Algae-covered rocks and only one flashlight was not a great idea, I'll admit," I say, trying to keep my voice light instead of begging. Can she just let it go instead of following the mom code?

"Okay. I get that you don't want to talk about this either. I know it's probably awkward, considering. But let me just ask: Are you being safe? Are you and Tate both being safe?"

It scrambles my brain for a moment, because the first question kind of makes sense, but the second question does not, paired with the tone of her voice. The look on her face isn't right; it's more amused and resigned than upset I broke Mom's rules, and I'm so confused until she keeps going:

"When you're together, I mean. I know sex ed isn't great with queer stuff, but just because you two don't have to worry about pregnancy doesn't mean you don't need to be safe. Especially if you were sexually active with other people before you got together."

The PSA sex talk makes it click. She's not talking about rafting. She's talking about . . .

Anna saw us last night together, all rumpled and, well, *not dressed* under our blanket togas, paired with that terrible excuse from Tate. . . .

Oh, shit.

Anna thinks we snuck out to—

I blush so hard, I'm pretty sure it covers my entire body. She thinks we're together. *Together* together. Like, *sleeping together* together.

If my brain was scrambled before, it's even worse now. I'm running through what's better: Anna thinking I'm sleeping with her daughter or Anna realizing she's got it wrong and I'm kayaking on the lake at night. And the entire time I'm trying to decide, that night's playing in my head like a movie as if Anna's assumption has unlocked something I'd hidden away. My fingers running down Tate's shoulder in the water, her tank top strap coming with them, and not stopping this time—what would it be like to touch the freckled parts of her collarbone? Tate's hand wrapped around mine over the car window like she could hold all of me in her palm—what would it be like to let her?

128

To let her in?

"I don't want to snoop," Anna continues. "But I just want to make sure you two are being—"

"Yes!" I say quickly, before she starts, like, asking me if I need dental dams. "Yes. Of course we are."

She smiles, relieved. "Good. I'm glad." She squeezes my shoulder. "Not just about that. I'm glad you two girls finally figured it out."

And then she walks out of there, and I just stand there because, oh my God, what is she talking about, she's glad we *finally* figured *it* out?

I just let Tate's mom think . . .

Which means *my* mom's gonna think . . .

And I just let myself think about . . . her. Like that.

Like that night in the hay shed—her skin had been so soft I sometimes think I *had* been drunk, that I'd imagined it. Like that day on the porch—her lips hadn't even touched my skin, just the bandages, but I still feel like I know them. Like that night in the motel in Yreka—

No. I can't think about that.

I won't.

19

P !!!!!

P Meghan! 911!

M What's wrong? Did your mom find out about last night?

P Anna caught us coming back.

M Did she tell your mom?!

P No.

P Anna thinks...

Penny is typing...

Penny is typing...

P Okay, idk why but Anna thinks Tate and I snuck out to...well, YOU KNOW.

M Wait. What.

M: Are you telling me that Tate's mom thinks you two were having sex in, what, the woods?!

P: By the creek.

P: That's where Tate told her we were.

M: Sounds adventurous.

M: But kind of cold and dirty.

M: One-way ticket to a yeast infection.

P: Meghan!

M: What? This is hilarious.

P: It is not!

P: Why would she think that?!

M: Yes, why would Anna think you and Tate were secretly banging? I wonder.

M: What did she say when you told her she was wrong?

P: I kind of let her keep thinking it.

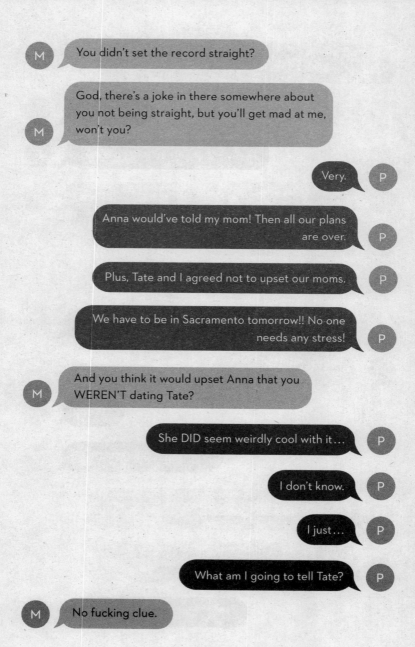

M You didn't set the record straight?

M God, there's a joke in there somewhere about you not being straight, but you'll get mad at me, won't you?

Very. P

Anna would've told my mom! Then all our plans are over. P

Plus, Tate and I agreed not to upset our moms. P

We have to be in Sacramento tomorrow!! No one needs any stress! P

M And you think it would upset Anna that you WEREN'T dating Tate?

She DID seem weirdly cool with it... P

I don't know. P

I just... P

What am I going to tell Tate? P

M No fucking clue.

20

M This is some rom-com shit, Remington.

R What happened now?

M Apparently you and I are not the only ones who have noticed the Penny-and-Tate thing.

R Oh?

M ANNA thinks they're dating.

R But they're not.

M Of course they're not. Then they'd both have to actually acknowledge the FEELINGS.

R Tate is bad at feelings. She pushes them down.

R That's kind of shitty of me to say, I guess. I do it, too.

M We all suck at feelings. I think it's part of being human.

M: I mean.

M: Penny runs from hers.

M: I bury myself in hobbies.

M: It's just easier sometimes.

M: You know?

R: Yeah.

R: I know.

M: Sorry—didn't mean to get all serious. I just...I want Penny to be happy. She deserves it. Her AND Tate.

R: I get it.

M: Okay, let's change the subject. Heavy stuff over. What about the fundraiser?

R: ???

M: The tri-tip fundraiser we were talking about.

I didn't realize you wanted to do that. R

M Well, I've been reading about transplant recovery. It's a LOT. For the transplant recipient and the donor.

M There's no way Anna or Lottie will be able to go back to work soon.

M It's going to be a ton of $$$.

We could crowdfund online? R

M I asked Penny about that. She said their moms weren't into the idea of making their story public.

Okay. R

We'd need more than the store grill, though. R

M The brewery has one.

Do you know how to grill? R

M Can you teach me?

Sure. R

M We can sell chips and soda, too.

M We can also ask the Blackberry Diner to donate some pies.

M I'll make a list and some calls.

I'll ask my manager about the meat and the grills. R

21

JUNE 24

M How are you doing?

P I'm packing for tomorrow.

M You're not packed?

P I'm trying to chase down all of Mom's stuff.

P The woman has never heard of packing cubes, I swear.

M So...did you tell Tate?

M Or did you go with the truth w/ Anna?

P Too busy for that rn.

Meghan is typing...
Meghan is typing...

M Okay.

P I know you want to say something.

M I do!

M But timing, you know?

M You've got a shit-ton of stuff to deal with.

M So...

M I'm just here, okay?

P I love you, you know that?

M You better!

M Ilu2.

22

JUNE 25

Grill is ours! Plus a meat donation. R

M That's amazing!

Do you know what time they're leaving tomorrow? R

M Early, I think.

M I'm going over there in the morning so Marion can show me how to water her garden while they're gone.

M Want to come help? You could see Tate.

Yeah. R

I'd like that. R

Thanks, Meghan. R

23

JUNE 25

M · Don't stress about texting me back. I know you're driving.

M · I'm sending everyone all the good energy.

M · We love you all so much, and if you need ANYTHING, I can be there in six hours. Maybe five, if I really speed.

M · Even if you're just bored or need a break or want to kick someone's ass in Scrabble. I'll be there.

M · Not very fast, obviously.

M · But I'll come.

M · Love you! Text me when you get there!

24

JUNE 25

R Hey.

R You're probably still on the road.

R I know tomorrow's surgery is big.

R My mom told me to tell you she's praying for all of you.

T You know I don't believe in that stuff.

R I told her that.

T What'd she say?

R She just sighed.

R I'm not praying for you. I know you're not into that. But I am thinking about you all, okay?

R It's gonna go great. All of it. I know it.

R: If you need me, I can be in Sacramento in a few hours.

R: I cannot guarantee Meghan won't tag along, though.

T: We're pulling up to the gas station. Gotta go.

T: Thanks, Remi.

25

Penny

JUNE 25

THE TROUBLE STARTS as soon as we get to the front desk. The motel is two stories high on the lot near the highway. And the parking lot is packed.

It's forty minutes from the hospital, which is not recommended, but I'm pretty sure those recommendations were written by surgeons who haven't ever had to worry about paying city hotel rates. Or maybe they have. There have to be some surgeons who came from poor backgrounds.

I'm not really listening at first as I sit down next to Tate and Anna after helping Tate make sure their luggage is out of the way so Anna can stretch her legs out.

"Thanks, girls," she says as Mom greets the clerk.

"Hi, we have three rooms for tonight. Under Tate."

"Of course. We have three queen rooms booked for you," the clerk says.

"How are you feeling?" I ask Anna.

"Just tired," she says.

"We'll get checked in so you can rest," Tate says, looking over to Mom.

"There was supposed to be one queen and two rooms with double beds," Mom says to the clerk. She looks over to us and mouths *Just a sec.*

"Oh no." The clerk begins typing into her computer. "There must've been a mistake with the booking. I'm afraid we don't have any double rooms available for tonight. I'm so sorry."

"Oh, well, that's fine," Mom says. "It won't kill you to share a bed, will it, girls?"

She's directed the question to us, looking over her shoulder with a smile.

Neither of us answer. Because, oh my God, what kind of answer are you supposed to give? I try not to side-eye Anna, because is she gonna object?

But Anna just laughs. "Does that mean I have to bunk with you?" she asks Mom drily.

"What's wrong with that?"

"You hog the blankets! I learned this from countless sleepovers."

"You want *us* to share a bed?" Tate asks, and my cheeks heat, because she sounds horrified.

"Well, I suppose one of you could share with Marion—" Mom starts.

"No way," Gran says. "I am an old woman. I don't share beds."

"I—" Tate looks over at me, and then quickly away, and I'm bright red. I have to be. My face is too hot for it not to be. Anna's looking at the both of us kind of curiously.

Shit. Of course she is. She thinks we're dating—God, she thinks we're sleeping together. In her mind, we should be *delighted* with this. But Tate isn't delighted; why should she be when...

We don't have a good history. Motel rooms and Tate and me. Not after Yreka.

My life is a soap opera. But I'm the only one who knows it.

"It's fine," I say quickly, because what else am I going to say? There's no other option here. I'll just... sleep in one of the chairs or on the floor or something. I'll figure it out.

No stressing the moms out. Especially not now, hours away from everything getting better for Anna and Tate.

"The rooms are fine," Mom says to the clerk, and she hands over the keys. "Here, girls," she says, thrusting the plastic keychains at us. "Let's get all unpacked and settled, okay? Anna and I are just down the way in number 201, and your gran's in 208." I take the key, looking down at 215 stamped on it.

"I'm gonna go unpack" is all Tate says, and I'm about to follow her out of the lobby when Gran hooks an arm around me. "Come help me with my bags, will you?"

I follow her to Anna's car and grab Gran's big Samsonite suitcase that's from the time when they didn't put wheels on suitcases. It's heavy, so I have to use two hands to lug it up the stairs and into her room for her.

"Perfect," Gran declares, sitting down on the bed and propping her hands behind her head. "Come sit." She taps her foot against the end of the bed, and I obey.

"How was the drive?"

"Fine," I say.

"You and Tate fight over the radio the whole way?"

"We split the hours," I say. "And we played stuff from our phones. You really should let me download some music on yours—"

"I have my records," Gran says. "I don't like having all those goo-gahs on my phone."

"They're called apps. And the records get scratched."

"Scratches give character. Nothing in life comes out unscathed."

"That's . . . okay, kind of true."

"How are you doing?"

I smile brightly at her. "Great."

She shifts in the bed, her head tilting toward me. "Yeah?"

"Of course."

"You bullshit just like your daddy" is all she says, and then she waits. She thinks she can wait me out. She's wrong. "You haven't been back to the hospital since—"

"—it's not that. I'm not a baby."

"It's not about being a baby," Gran says. "It's about acknowledging that you went through a lot in that hospital. So did I."

"Mom didn't."

Silence. It's pointed, because it always is with Gran.

There'd been times in those months after Dad died when I'd wondered if my mom was ever going to come back for me . . . and I'm sure Gran wondered the same. Gran was with me for every step and tiny accomplishment in the healing process. I tried to thank her once, in the beginning, when everything was painful, not just in my body, but in my heart. And she'd scoffed at me and kissed my head and whispered, so low and tight, *I will never leave you, honey-bean.*

Because she knew I'd been left, not just by Dad, but by Mom, too.

"Your father would have been very proud of Lottie for doing this," Gran says.

It startles me. I've spent too much time trying to step around the thought of him—like Mom's trained me into it through her silence—that it never crossed my mind to wonder how he'd have felt about this.

Sometimes I'm scared that Mom's erasing him, the way she did from her art, that it will ripple into the rest of our lives. That it's already happened: That not talking about him will lead to forgetting him faster.

Is losing someone just a perpetually growing ball of grief? Like snow rolling down a hill, growing larger until it swamps you? It's supposed to get better, not worse. Is that what Mom's trying to save me from?

Is Gran right? Would he be proud? I search myself for the answer, picturing his smiling face.

Yes.

He would've been proud. He would've called her *my wife, the hero.* He would've been down here with Mom and Anna, instead of Gran. Gran would be with us up in Salt Creek, taking care of us while Dad took care of their recovery. He would've thrown fundraisers and moved mountains and made everything happen.

It takes my breath away, allowing myself to picture this alternate life for a second. He's been written out of our stories, a terrible conclusion wrapping up his so abruptly, and picturing him here . . .

It's a novelty. It's a wound. Something I didn't think to do because—oh.

He would've made things easier.

God, it would've been so much easier.

"Penny," Gran says, and I sniff, shaking my head and hoping the tears don't spill.

"I'm fine," I say. "It was just a long drive."

It's been a long week. Month. Year.

It's been a long life, and I'm just seventeen.

"Your mother . . . she's doing something very brave," Gran says.

"I know."

"But there have been times when she wasn't brave," Gran says. She squeezes my shoulders, looking at me closely. "I want you to know I understand that. I see it."

I nod. "Thanks," I force out.

"Why don't you shower and rest for a little bit, and then I'll take you and Tate out to dinner? There's no eating before the surgery, so they're going to stay in. I believe a movie marathon was mentioned."

"Oh, God, they're going to watch rom-coms all night and quote all the lines," I say. "Yes, please, take us out of here."

Gran laughs. "Your wish is my command, honey-bean. Go unpack and tell Tate the plan; I'll come by in an hour, and we'll pick a restaurant."

I get up and lean over, pressing a kiss on her forehead. "I love you," I tell her.

"You'd better," she says, brushing a hand over my hair. "I love you, too, honey. It's going to be fine."

I go down to my car and get my suitcase. Then I walk up the stairs and down the open-air hall toward my—no, my and Tate's—room, trying not to drag my feet. But the closer I get to room 215, the harder it is to move. The harder it is not to remember—hammering on the door of the motel room in Yreka. Room 143. Knowing Tate was on the other side. Knowing it—she—was the only safe place after Laurel . . .

I push it out of my mind. There's no place for it here. Not now. Preferably not ever.

Taking a deep breath, I shove the key into the lock and push the door open, then wheel my suitcase inside with me. She's already got her swim bag on the luggage rack. It's unzipped, a spill of clothes draped over one side, and my eyes fix on the blue lace straps that have to belong to a bra, and I just—

I don't think I can handle this.

The door swings shut. She looks up from her bag.

And then we're totally alone in the motel room.

26

TATE

JUNE 25

THE ONE WAY to guarantee you're even slightly distracted from
your mother's impending liver transplant? End up in a motel room
with only one bed and the one girl you cannot share a bed with.

I spend the first five minutes trying not to freak out. The next ten
trying to unpack but really mostly freaking out. And then she shows
up after helping Marion with her stuff. I should've offered to help. It
was selfish of me to just walk out of there.

We stand there, me on one side of the queen bed and her on the
other . . . and who knew a bed could seem so big and so small at the
same time? The silence stretches, and I am certainly not going to be
the first one to break it.

It's déjà vu, and I'm trying not to feel it or think it.

Because we made a rule. It's on the truce list.

No talking about Yreka.

That means not thinking about it either—because if I do, I'll lose
myself in the swirl of it, and I can't. No distraction is worth that.

I can feel her eyes on me, but I just focus on unpacking. She walks over to the bed and starts doing the same with her purple suitcase, shuffling between the bathroom and the bedroom, then turning her attention to hanging up her clothes.

I didn't bring any clothes I need to hang, so I finish before her and don't know what to do. I head to the bathroom with the last thing in my bag: my gallon Ziploc of shampoo and sunscreen and stuff.

"My gran wanted to take us to dinner," Penny calls.

"Okay," I say, before shutting the door. I lean against it for a moment, trying to breathe while I eye the bathtub, wondering if I'd fit okay in there with some towels as a makeshift bed.

Maybe there's a way to convince Marion at dinner to let me share a bed with her . . . but even as I think it, I know it's not going to happen.

I am in hell. Oh my God. This is hell. Penny's on the other side of this door, and it's even worse than being across the hall from her like at home, but not as bad as sharing a *real* bathroom with her, where her bubble bath collection is and her candles scent the air, and this is why she always smells a little like everything, like flowers and vanilla and a little spice, instead of a specific perfume. She uses a rosewater toner and keeps her cotton rounds in a green Depression-era glass container, and these are details I cannot forget.

She's already placed her makeup kit in here. It's a fuzzy lavender bag in the shape of a cloud, and the contrast between us suddenly strikes me in this one little thing.

(I am the Ziploc bag with a toothpaste smear on the bottom because the cap came loose, and Penny is a fuzzy cloud designed to be touched and loved.)

I'll just sneak out once she falls asleep and sleep in the car and slip back inside before she wakes up. She'll just avoid it, like she did before.

(Fuzzy morning Yreka light and warmth heavy across my stomach—her arm wrapped around me, but since I was half asleep, I didn't quite know that. . . . I just knew it felt like home.)

It takes a good five minutes for me to gather up my nerve to go back into the bedroom. She's already got her stuff unpacked and her bullet journal spread out on the little desk tucked in the corner of the room. She even brought a blue plastic caddy of craft supplies with her. Brush pens and stamps and little ink pads and stickers.

"Making a timeline for tomorrow?" I ask her.

She scowls immediately.

"I'm not saying that like it's bad," I say hastily, before she can snap. Her shoulders relax.

"Sorry," she says. "I'm . . ." She just sighs.

"Me too."

It's so much easier to cross the room and sit in the chair across from hers, because the other option is to sit on the bed, and that's not happening. Nope.

(Not again.)

"Gran will be by in like twenty minutes," Penny says. "She wants us to pick out a restaurant."

"Like a treat?"

"Like we're nine again, yes."

"That's nice."

She sweeps her orange pen across the page before selecting a black felt tip from a hand-sewn pouch I recognize as Lottie's handiwork. "I know."

"She's amazing, your gran," I continue. I don't know anyone else who'd drop everything for months like this. I know she loves them. But Lottie has set herself up in an emotional minefield only Mom can cross, and Marion's wading into the thick of it willingly. You gotta admire that.

And I know she loves us. But Penny's her blood, and I'm just a straggler.

"I'd be doomed without her," Penny says, so matter-of-factly that it flips something in me. Like a rock you turn, and the ground below is grubs and worms, dead grass and pressed dirt, an imprint on the earth where something used to be.

"I'm glad you have her."

She doesn't pause in her drawing. The timeline fades from orange to a cool pink, and she's listed the steps: *intake, team check-in and questions, OR, ICU for recovery* alongside estimations for how long each will take. "I'm glad you have her, too."

Her phone buzzes next to her. She glances over at it. "Speak of the devil, as Gran would say." She shuts her bullet journal and begins to put away her array of pens.

Marion takes us to get Thai food, and we spend the entire time eating chicken satay and mee grob and not talking about what's going to happen in just twelve hours. I manage to text my mom only twice to check in on her, because the second time I do, she sends a video of her and Lottie singing along to "In Your Eyes" because they're watching *Say Anything....*

"There is not a shred of musical talent between those two," Marion tuts as I turn off the video before it ends.

"Or us." Penny points to her and me, and it shouldn't make my stomach squirm (to be an *us*, even for a second, with her). But it does.

"Tate played the recorder in elementary school," Marion says. "I remember your concert."

"Oh, I remember that." Penny grins. "You wanted to play drums and they wouldn't let you."

"Isn't that the class you got kicked out of for hiding in the supply closet?"

"Tate," Marion scolds, even though we're, like, ten years away from this.

"I didn't want to take music! I wanted to take art. But it was filled up by the time Mom signed me up."

"That's no excuse," Marion says, as they bring us the check.

She drives us back to the hotel, taking complete control of the radio. She plays us the Beatles the entire way home, and Penny pretends to be annoyed while Marion sings "Yellow Submarine" at her, but I don't even bother to hide my smile.

"I'm off to bed," Marion says as we climb the motel stairs. She hugs Penny, then me, and for a second I just want to stay there, held and safe with her, because she's never broken under anything I've seen thrown at her. She's the only person I know who I can say that about, and I want to know the secret . . . because I feel like breaking. So badly.

"Try to get some sleep." Marion says it like she knows it's impossible.

"I'm gonna go check on my mom," I say. (Anything to avoid that room and that bed.)

Penny just shrugs and heads away from me down the hall. I tell myself that's what I want (it has to be) and walk in the opposite direction to my mom's room. I can hear the buzz of the TV through the paper-thin walls, so I knock lightly.

Lottie's already in her pajamas—blue-gray tie-dyed silk that I know she made herself because she made Mom a pair for Christmas one year—and Mom's in bed, her back to me. Lottie's battered laptop is on the bed, too, frozen on what looks like *Legally Blonde*, if I've gotten my Reese Witherspoon movies right.

She awake? I mouth at Lottie, who nods.

I walk over to the bed as Lottie gets back in it. "Hey, Mama," I murmur, stroking her hair off her forehead. She blinks sleepily at me, turning from her side onto her back and smiling at me.

"Hey, sweets. Did you have a good dinner?"

"Mm-hmm. Marion took us to get Thai. I just wanted to say good night."

Her hand finds mine. Three squeezes. *I love you.* "Big day tomorrow."

"Biggest day," I say. "I'm gonna let you rest, though. I gotta sleep off the Thai food anyway."

"We have to be at the hospital early tomorrow," she reminds me.

"I know." I kiss her on the forehead, trying not to linger, trying not to worry that it's one of the last times. And then I walk over to the other side of the bed.

"Night, Lottie," I say, and—I think to her surprise—I bend over and brush a kiss over her cheek, too. "Thank you," I whisper in her ear. She takes in a shaky breath, squeezing my arm before I pull away. Her eyes are bright with the emotion I'm always searching for in her, wondering why it's not directed at Penny.

"Night," I say again, with a smile that doesn't reach my eyes.

I close the door behind me, the hall stretching in front of me. I look to my right, at the room Penny and I share. And then I look down at the kidney-shaped pool that's not even close to twenty-five meters . . . but beggars can't be choosers.

(And I can't share that bed with Penny. Not until I absolutely have to.)

27

Penny

JUNE 25

I STARE AT the timeline I've created in my bullet journal. The wash of orange to happy pink. From danger to safety.

Intake, team check-in and questions, OR, ICU for recovery. Mom's surgery starts before Anna's. Obviously. You don't really think these things through—the how of it all—until you have to. Mom's going to be under for, like, six hours as they take out half of her liver. And Anna's surgery will be even longer and more complicated, with way more recovery time.

I haven't even started the recovery timeline. I should. I should do that right now.

But as I stare at this one, the print begins to blur, and I blink furiously, trying to clear my vision . . . but it just makes my eyes spill tears. Maybe focusing on this is a bad thing. It's going to happen tomorrow no matter what. Maybe I should think about something else.

I walk over to my suitcase and pull out the little care package Meghan made for me. Inside are a few different face masks and a mini-bottle of the Apple-Grape Martinelli's. Mom loves sheet masks, so I grab one for her and one for Anna, plus the ice bucket and my keys. I can say good night to Mom and Anna on the way back from the ice machine.

There's something spooky about motels at night. It's like an in-between place. But I guess that's what a way station is. I scoop out the ice, climb the stairs, and head toward Mom's room. But before I can knock on the door, I hear them, their voices floating through the open window:

"You're hogging the blankets again," Anna says.

"I swear I'm not trying to!"

I hesitate, wondering if I should intrude. Because that's what I am in Mom's life, isn't it—an intrusion?

"Did Tate come in here?" Anna asks. "I didn't dream that?"

"Yeah, she came in when you were napping through the movie. She's probably off swimming."

"The pool's closed."

"Do you think that'll stop her? That girl is driven," Mom says, and the admiration in her words rankles.

"So is Penny," Anna says.

"Penny won't even talk to me about college. She shuts me down every time I try to talk about it."

"She's probably just nervous."

"Or she's following through on her threat."

"What threat?"

Mom sighs. "When I sold George's part of the business to Tim— remember how angry she was? And I told her I had to, for her future. For college. And she laughed and told me there was no way she was wasting her time with college. I'm hoping she was just emotional, but

158

it is Penny." Mom laughs, but there's no mirth. It's a mired sound, stuck in her throat, just as much as we're stuck in our pretending.

I'm scared it's all we have left of each other. That anything real is too much to acknowledge anymore.

"You keep telling me this is my new start," Anna says to Mom. "But it can be yours, too."

"I hope so" is all Mom says, and without seeing her, I can't tell if she means it . . . but if I move, they'll see me. So I'm stuck, again, wondering.

"Maybe a few weeks up in Salt Creek with Tate will be good for Penny," Anna says. Then she giggles. "It seems a little hypocritical, but I don't think I'd be this okay with them sleeping in the same bed if one of them was a boy."

Oh no. No. *No.* She's not going to—

Oh, but she is. She really, really is.

"Huh? What are you talking about?" Mom asks, as my dread builds.

Anna *cackles.* "Did I not mention that our girls are dating? I must have forgotten."

"What? They are *not!*" Mom's voice rises into a high-pitched squeak.

"Oh, I assure you, they are. I caught them sneaking into the house half dressed. There were some very interesting blanket togas happening."

"You're shitting me."

How can I stop this? I can't. I can't now. What in the world am I going to do?

"I was saving the news for a *really* good moment," Anna says. "I think they're keeping it under wraps right now, so don't say anything."

"Why would they hide it? They're both out to us."

"Who knows," Anna says. "Give them time to tell us properly."

"How long have you known about this?" Mom demands, sounding gleeful and outraged.

"Just since yesterday."

"Anna! You waited twenty-four whole hours? That is so unfair. You should've told me when you found out! I thought Penny was still heartbroken over Laurel."

I almost fumble with the ice bucket at the mention of my ex, suddenly aware of how the cold is leaking into my hands.

"I guess she's not anymore," Anna says.

"Oh my God." Mom's voice lowers to an excited whisper. "This is like a movie!"

"Remember when we were pregnant and used to joke that if we had one of each, they could get married? It didn't occur to me that if we both had girls, they'd date."

"Me either. Penny would say it was very heteronormative of us."

Because it is! I have to twist my mouth to keep from saying it.

Anna snorts. "I mean, it was."

"Oh my God. *This* must be why she's been sneaking out."

I lean against the stucco wall of the motel, trying to breathe but also not do it loudly, in case they hear me. She knows I've been sneaking out? *Shit.* This is going to ruin everything!

"Penny's been sneaking out?" Anna asks.

"She thinks I haven't noticed."

"You haven't tried to catch her?"

"So she'll get even cagier? Anyway, if she was just going out to meet Tate—"

"But Tate hasn't been sneaking out," Anna says firmly.

Mom laughs. "Are you sure?"

"Tate's up at five every morning. She may tease Penny about her schedules and bullet journals, but that girl thrives on routine just as much as Penny does."

"Oh, God, those bullet journals—she kills me with those," Mom groans. Anger flashes in me but dissipates as she continues: "The collages she's been doing in them? They're *so* good. But she won't let me look at them closely. There was one that was this rotted flower garden that was so gothic. I wanted to spend an hour looking at it. I got maybe five seconds before she slammed it shut."

"You do the same with *your* sketchbook," Anna points out gently.

Mom laughs. "Guilty," she admits.

"Like mother, like daughter."

"She's pure George, and you know it."

How long has it been since I heard her say his name? It used to be an ever-present part of my life. Mom calling for Dad. Laughing his name as he kissed her cheek. Murmuring it against his as they danced in the kitchen. And then she didn't say his name at all. Like the minute she got it engraved on that headstone, speaking it would summon her mistakes.

Tell your mother I love her.

"God, she really is sometimes," Anna agrees.

"The counselor they made me see to deem that I was mentally fit to give you ol' homeslice—"

"Is that what we're calling the piece of liver you're giving me?"

"I was going to call it Eunice, but I remember how critical you were of my baby name choices back in the day."

"Your preference for old-lady names is a bit odd. Penelope is a beautiful name. But *Gertrude*? That's going to get a child teased."

"Gertie and Trudie are adorable nicknames! *Anyway*, the counselor told me that I talk about Penny like she doesn't have half of me in her. And I told her that girl popped out asking *Where's Daddy?* followed by *Where's the river?*"

Anna laughs softly. "She was a daddy's girl all right. But she's got a lot of you, too. Especially when you were younger. She's got the rock-throwing side of you."

Mom snorts. "I was just thinking about that on the way down," Mom says, and I frown, because I've never heard a story about her throwing rocks. Throwing rocks at whom? "I still have a scar on my inner thigh from climbing those old oaks, waiting for them."

Waiting for whom? But it doesn't seem like I'm going to get an answer, because Anna continues:

"You saved me back then. And you're saving me now."

"Two times in almost thirty years isn't bad, considering how many times you've saved *my* ass," Mom says, and it's choked, a forced lightness that's determined.

"You're giving Tate and me a lot," Anna says. "I will never forget it."

"You promised you wouldn't get sappy on me," Mom says, but then she sniffs loudly. "You know I love you."

"You'd better," Anna says. "Because we might be in-laws someday."

"Shit, that would be something."

Mom laughs, loud and genuine and so rare near me that I revel in it for a second before I turn away and walk back to my room, the condensation from the ice bucket dripping on my fingers.

28

JUNE 25

Why do these things happen to me? P

M Is everything okay?

Anna told my mom about the whole dating mistake thing that she doesn't think is a mistake. P

M Shit. What are you going to do?

Deal with it tomorrow. Or the next day. Or maybe never. P

M Are you gonna tell Tate?

She's in the pool. P

M ?

M She won't be in there forever. You can tell her now.

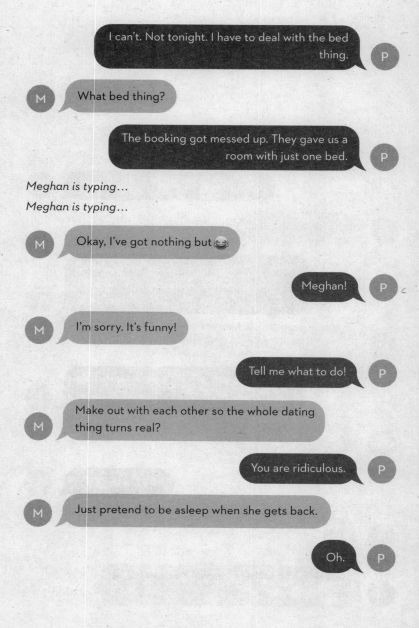

I can't. Not tonight. I have to deal with the bed thing. P

M What bed thing?

The booking got messed up. They gave us a room with just one bed. P

Meghan is typing…
Meghan is typing…

M Okay, I've got nothing but 😂

Meghan! P

M I'm sorry. It's funny!

Tell me what to do! P

M Make out with each other so the whole dating thing turns real?

You are ridiculous. P

M Just pretend to be asleep when she gets back.

Oh. P

29

TATE

JUNE 26

"YOU SLEEP OKAY?" Mom asks me.

I look over at her in the hospital bed. "I didn't sleep at all."

"Penny didn't keep you awake, did she?" Mom shuffles through her cards.

I'd spent the night curled up in the love seat in the motel room, but I wasn't about to tell my mom that.

"No, Penny was already asleep when I got back from the pool. I was just nervous."

"Well, thank goodness she doesn't snore like Lottie."

I laugh, staring down at my cards. It's a tradition to play while we wait. We've got the cards spread on the little serving table that swings over her bed.

When I was little, it was Go Fish and War. She expanded my repertoire the older I got. But today, it's a simple one again: Double Solitaire. We've already done a full game, with the nurses coming in and out, and Marion texting me every fifteen minutes.

"You could at least let me win," she says when I beat her for the second time.

"You could've asked to play a game you're better at."

"If we get into a poker match, I'll be thinking about it all the way into the OR."

I glance up at the clock. They took Lottie in a while ago. The surgery can take up to six hours. It was on the timeline in Penny's bullet journal. Mom's transplant will take up to twelve.

They'll be coming to prep her soon. And then it'll be time for me to sit in the lobby and do nothing but wait and hope for hours and hours.

"You look sad. Come here." She pushes the table away and beckons with her finger, crooking it like she's an evil witch in a fairy tale. She has the best witch cackle, my mom. It's quite the hit at the Haunted Beer Garden the brewery throws in Miller's Field each Halloween.

"I'm fine," I tell her, but it's only the IVs that are keeping me from crawling into bed with her.

"You smell like grapefruit," she says.

"I accidentally grabbed Penny's lotion this morning."

"I'm so glad you have her right now," she says, still holding my hand. I'm too afraid to grip her back as tight as she's holding me. (She'll know then, for sure, how scared I am.)

We've been here before. Not *here* exactly, of course. But we've been in that scary in-between space, where there's a light at the end of the tunnel, but it also might be snuffed out.

"It's gonna be time soon, sweets," she says.

"Mom—"

She has a rule. I'm not allowed to watch her get wheeled away. She had to watch her mom get wheeled away and never come back; my grandma died of ovarian cancer before I was born, when Mom was a teenager.

(God, she was around my age, wasn't she?)

We share this strange commonality of caretaking, I guess, though I've never considered it until this second. She took care of her mom, 'cause her dad left when her mom got sick. I try to take care of my mom, 'cause my sperm donor didn't even stick around for the lines to turn pink.

Are the women in my family just doomed to repeat themselves? Is that what being a daughter is? To either follow or break free of her mother's—and *her* mother's and *her* mother's—path? I don't know if I'll end up with someone who leaves, but I'm not going to lose her at seventeen like Mom did. (A spark of comfort in a fear that is too intense to control.)

We've been here enough times that there's a talk now. Just in case. I know all the points covered: where the passwords and papers are . . . and the emergency cash, stashed in the coffee can in the back of her closet, *I love you, Tate. You are the best thing I've ever made, do you hear me?*

I don't know if I can go through it again. And it's like she understands, because she says, "Did I ever tell you how Lottie and I became friends?"

I frown, looking at her IV. "Did they give you some drugs already? I know how you two met."

"*Meeting* is different than becoming friends," she says mysteriously. "Lottie always compares it to love at first sight."

"Lottie likes to romanticize things. First year we met, we didn't get along. I thought she was an annoying priss."

"I mean, you weren't wrong."

"She has her moments," Mom admits. "But then she did something that surprised me . . . that saved me."

"How?" I've *never* heard this story. Lottie always says they became friends when Mom shoplifted from the gas station and Lottie covered for her.

"When I was a kid, the county was a lot rougher, especially the Blue Basin side of the river. And there was a group of boys who ruled that stretch of it. Well, more like terrorized it. If you got cornered by them . . ." She shakes her head. "You'd get beat to hell and your stuff stolen, and there was one girl who . . ." She trails off again and the silence stretches as my brain starts to fill in the blanks.

Cold horror washes over me. "Are you—did they—"

She's not implying what I think she is, is she?

Mom looks back at me steadily. "There was a rumor about a girl who was assaulted. She moved away suddenly. We all heard about it. Traded the rumor among each other, like we traded makeup tips and the best times to get across Vollmer's bridge to avoid the boys."

"Mom, that's so *fucked*. Why didn't you tell someone? Or report them?"

"Partly because I wasn't raised like I raised you. It wouldn't have occurred to me to tell anyone. And if I had, I would've probably been told *boys will be boys*." Her mouth twists in disgust, just as mine does. For a second, we're twins, the few differences in our features disappearing in the unconscious mirroring.

"As for reporting it . . . to whom? Three of the boys were related to the sheriff's deputies. And the girl moved away and didn't report it." She shrugs. "You can't blame someone for not wanting to go through a system that isn't designed to help them. She did what she could at the time to warn the other girls."

"Did the boys go after you?"

She nods. "One of them kept snapping my bra strap in class. I got detention for shoving him." She rolls her eyes. "God, I hated my history teacher. But by the time I got out of school, they were waiting."

She's quiet for a long time, staring down at the IV in her hand. She has tricky veins, so they've run it through one on her hand, instead of on the inside of her wrist.

"You don't have to tell me," I say.

"I want to," she says. "I want you to understand, because I see it, sweets...the question in your head. Why Lottie and me are *Lottieandme*." She tucks a strand of hair behind her ear. They'll cover it under a blue cap for the transplant, but right now, it's just in a braid. "I got cornered. The boys took my bike and backpack. I thought maybe that'd be it. But after they got my stuff, it changed—the laughter, the way some of them looked at me—everything went sharp and heavy, like the air was going to cut me as bad as they would hurt me. And I was scared. I don't think I'd ever been that scared in my life before. Then the biggest one grabbed my arm."

Does she know she's rubbing that very same arm? It's involuntary, the way she touches it.

"I was going to fight. But before I could..." The smile that breaks across her face is so antithetical to this moment, it yanks me like a hook in the cheek. "Rocks just come flying down from the air on them. Like some vengeful god's arrived and is hell-bent on punishing them.

170

One smacks the ringleader—the one who snapped my bra—right in the head, and he's the one that goes down, not me. Just *bam*!" She snaps her fingers. "Clocked in the head and out cold on the ground. She really got him good." Her smile widens. "The boys scattered." Her lip curls as she says it. "I'm looking around, reeling, saved by someone, not knowing who . . . and then there she is, climbing down the tree: Lottie, in her baby doll tee and her Calvin's, with a whole JanSport full of rocks strapped to her back."

I can't picture it, but I also can. Because Penny is Lottie's daughter and Penny is the girl in the woods with an ax . . . just like, suddenly, her mother was the girl in the tree with the rocks. That adrenaline-high sort of recklessness? It's not something Penny inherited just from her dad.

It's Lottie, too. It manifested differently. Impulsively . . . and sometimes very badly.

But not this time. And not back then.

"She saved you."

"Lottie and the girl who moved away, they were friends," Mom says. "And when she left—"

"Lottie was left behind with the truth." I fill in.

"And she made sure the other girls knew to watch out for the boys," Mom continues.

"She spread the rumor?"

Mom nods.

"And stalked the woods. She was good at climbing trees at the time . . . and she was the star of the softball team."

"That's pretty badass," I say, and I hate how grudgingly it comes out.

"She risked herself for me," Mom says. "Just like she's doing now."

"I'm glad," I say. "For both times. Mom, you have no idea how glad. But—" I stop. I love Lottie. I do. But I hold warring feelings in my heart for her, and sometimes that weighs on me. It's like having to sift through sand to get to a fallen pearl. "But you've also gotta see it, Mom."

"See what?"

"That she didn't risk herself for Penny."

My mother looks away, her chin dipping to her chest, like it hurts to even hear it. But it's *true*. I was *there*. And if you can't talk about the true things even if they hurt, where does that leave you?

"I love Lottie. And I'm grateful for her. But . . ." I stop, unable to say it.

She reaches over and takes my hand and squeezes it. Once. Twice. Three times. *I love you.* A secret message of touch.

"But you love other people, too," Mom finishes.

I don't wrench my hand away—I have to be careful, it's her IV hand holding mine—but I want to. My heart thuds, a traitorous thing, heat climbing my cheeks.

"It's okay, you know," Mom continues softly. "To be on Penny's side."

My stomach clenches. And when my eyes meet hers, I don't try to hide the tears. "Mom," I say, and it's an echo of years ago, on that porch instead of at the funeral with Penny. "There shouldn't *be* sides."

"Oh, sweets," she says, and it's not sad; she's looking at me like I've hit her with a lightning bolt. "Damn," she says, shaking her head. "You're right. You're—you're absolutely right."

And then we can't talk anymore, because three nurses walk into the room.

"Today's the day, Anna," one of them says. "I'm Jessica. How are you feeling?"

Mom straightens up in the bed, picking at her hospital gown.

"Good . . . nervous. It's . . . it's a big day," she answers, and her voice shakes with the weight of it.

"Is this your daughter?" the nurse asks.

"This is Tate," Mom says, as one of the other nurses comes over and begins to check her IV drip.

"Hi." I give them a little wave.

"Okay, sweets," Mom says.

"No," I protest.

"Time to go," she insists. "Next time you see me, I'll be a whole new me."

"Look out, world."

She reaches out, careful with the IV and tubes, and holds my face in both her hands.

"You know what I love about you?" she asks me.

"My cutting wit?"

"Well, that first, of course," she deadpans right back to me. "I love how you fight for people. You stand up and you say, *This is wrong*. I want you to keep doing that, sweets—always telling the truth."

Her hands are gripping my face a little too tightly.

"I will."

I know if we continue down this road, we're both going to start crying. I don't want her to be tear-streaked for the doctors.

"I'll be right here waiting," I say, kissing her forehead, because hugging her might get us tangled. My other hand is still in hers.

"You know I wouldn't hate a *Judge Judy* recap when I wake up," Mom says.

"I'll keep that in mind." I don't want to let go of her, but I have to. "I love you."

"I love you, too, sweets. I'll be awake and with a functioning liver before you know it."

"Well, let's not rush them," I say. It makes her laugh, and I'm grateful that when I walk away, she's smiling—that this is my memory of her, of the hopeful part before the long climb.

Jessie points me toward the family lobby, and when I walk down the busy hall, the sounds fade in and out as my heart thuds, slow and steady, almost mocking. A reminder that I'm healthy and strong and always have been. It's not like a dream, walking down that hall. More like a painting: The closer you get, the more you see it's all just texture and smudges of color.

The lobby's small but nice, and when the door clicks open and I step inside, Penny's head flies up so fast, I'm surprised she doesn't knock it into the wall behind her.

Our eyes meet across the hallway. She's pale beneath her freckles, her hair pulled out of her ponytail since I last saw her. It's loose and haphazard around her face now. She's been chewing on her lower lip. I can see the red spots from here.

We stare at each other. I can't look away. All of a sudden, she's the only person who understands me. We are the only two people who have the same thing to lose for the same reason.

All we have to do is wait and wonder.

And worry.

Because some girls don't get some things.

And all girls lose their mothers or are lost to them, in the end.

30

TATE

JUNE 26

I UNDERSTAND EVERYTHING about waiting, you know.

Those thirty seconds or so when you're clinging to a starting block, your body tight and furled, waiting to unleash.

Those hours after Mommy collapsed at work and Marion picked me up, trying to say everything but the word *cancer* because, even at eight, I knew cancer is one of the bad ones.

Those days after she was diagnosed, a cloud of confusion as George took over school drop-offs, and Lottie took Mom back and forth to the doctors, and I slept in Penny's room, trying not to cry at night.

Those months after they removed her ovaries trying to get ahead of it.

Those weeks of chemo when I was nine, when she dwindled and I was old enough to understand not just how hard it was, but how it was the only thing standing between her and the cancer getting worse.

Those years—more than two of them—that everyone waited to hear the word *remission*.

We slowly built a shaky sort of foundation, only to have it shatter with a whole new disease.

I've waited for her to get better.

(I've waited for her to die, if I'm being honest with myself, but that's hard. A scared nine-year-old is more honest than a terrified seventeen-year-old. Sometimes I wish I was still nine, but I know I wouldn't be here if I hadn't become me instead. Sometimes you have to rise to the occasion. And you rise when the occasion is life or death.)

I've waited for so many things. Some that are almost in my grasp; some that aren't. (Those scratchy motel sheets in the Yreka heat, Penny's hand turning, fingers curling into mine, pressed shoulder to shoulder, our bodies twinning but not twining.)

I wish I could say I was good at it—but I just make it look like I am. *Your stoic child*, Lottie said to Mom once, and that's when I knew I had everyone fooled about the storm inside me.

We wait. Marion tries to get both of us to eat, and we both turn her down. Every time someone walks past the lounge windows, Penny's head flies up and she tracks them like they're standing between her and survival.

I pull out the pack of cards I brought with me, trying not to look at the clock as I lay them out in seven neat piles. I lose myself in the order of it: descending numbers, alternating colors.

We wait. I keep my focus on the cards: black, red, black, red.

Penny chews on her lips and then her nails, ruining her black-and-gold manicure. She stares at the clock like that'll make it go faster.

"Penny, why don't you take this and get some food from the machines at least," Marion says, holding out a five-dollar bill.

Penny barely glances at her—just enough to be polite, because you can't be rude to Marion. "I'm fine, Gran," she says vaguely, eyes snapping back to the clock.

Red. Black. Red. Black. The soft *thwick* of the cards is punctuated by the *click* of the clock.

"Ouch." My thumb snags against one of the cards at the wrong angle. Penny's head snaps to me as I suck at the paper cut, trying to ignore the sting.

"Here," she says, digging in her purse and handing me an old Altoid tin.

"Is my breath that bad?" I ask, but I open it to see she's made the tin into a tiny first-aid kit with Band-Aids and Neosporin and a packet of aspirin.

"Girl Scout," I say, just to see her eyes flare.

"You're just mad at how many more cookies I sold than you."

"And you're still mad there wasn't a 'Survived in the woods with an ax' badge."

"I'll have you know I sent in a letter about—" She stops abruptly, all the fight and blood draining out of her face as a surgeon heads toward the lobby, her head covered in a scrub cap.

"Oh God, that's her surgeon," she mutters, and my hand finds hers, and she grips it so tight, it would hurt if I had any sense.

(But I've never had any when it comes to her.)

Especially not with those twenty steps between the surgeon and us. An eternity. A gaping maw of space, wanting to swallow us.

Ten steps.

Five.

Three.

Two.

She opens the lobby door, and it closes behind her.

31

JUNE 26

Mom's out of surgery and in the ICU recovering! P

M YAY!!!

M 🎉🎉🎉🎉🎉🎉

Oh my God, I thought I was going to throw up when the surgeon came in. P

Like, vomit all over her shoes. P

Thank God I didn't. P

She said it went really well. P

Also that Mom has a "very nice" liver. P

Not sure what that means. P

M I am SO relieved.

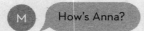
How's Anna?

No news yet.

I gotta get back to Tate. My signal sucks inside the lobby so I had to come outside to make sure my texts came through.

It's gonna keep going great! Just a few more hours!

32

Penny

JUNE 27

THE LONGER THE hours stretch, the more horrible it becomes. It's like the three of us are being crushed by the weight of time, trapped in that lobby.

My eyes are gritty from too little sleep, and I should have thought to pack Visine, but I didn't, and the gift shop downstairs closed hours ago. It's past midnight.

It's been too long. Anna's surgery started at noon. It's supposed to take *up to* twelve hours. Not *more than* twelve hours.

They'd checked in three hours ago. Or was it four? They said things were going well.

Did something go wrong after that? That's the question we're all thinking, I know it has to be, but Tate keeps playing solitaire, and I'm just sitting here quiet, watching her play, because it seems to be what she wants. God forbid we talk.

What would I say?

What will we do if Anna—

Don't think about it. God, don't think about it in this room, in this place, where she's just a few walls away, maybe fighting for her life.

But Anna's a fighter. Through and through. It's not inspiring in the way they talk about sick people—it's inspiring because she's the kind of woman you want to grow up to be.

The kind of mother you hope to be, if you didn't get one like her and want to break the cycle.

"It's going to be fine," Gran says out of nowhere, but Tate doesn't even stop shifting the cards into the right order. King of spades. Queen of hearts. Jack of clubs. Ten of diamonds. Nine of clubs.

The quiet of the hospital late at night—offset by the occasional beep and pages on the intercom—presses in on all sides until I'm dizzy from it. I try to focus on the gentle sounds of Tate shuffling the cards for yet another game.

"Gillian," Gran says, and Tate's first name jerks me up just as fast as it does her. Tate drops the cards and rises before she even looks up.

They've come through the double doors. Two of them. A woman and a man who's pulling his scrub cap off as they walk toward us.

"I'm right here," Gran says, taking Tate's hand. But it's me she looks at.

I know what it is to be untethered. And I know what it is to be tugged back to the ground by gentle hands. I've never been gentle, but I'm here. I'm willing. I will keep her here if the worst has happened.

They walk into the room, and when the surgeon beams at Tate, the knot in my throat starts to unravel.

"Dr. Rhodes?" Tate croaks out.

"The transplant went wonderfully," she says, still smiling.

"Anna's in the ICU, recovering. You'll probably be able to see her this afternoon if all continues as we expect."

"She's going to be fine?" Her voice doesn't shake. It flattens. Deadens like she has to kill something inside her to level the tone. "She's okay?"

"She is doing very well. We were lucky here. Alpha-1 can be hard to diagnose, and there aren't many living donors out there. To get a transplant before the cirrhosis got worse or turned cancerous is a very positive step toward long-term healing."

Tate stares at her, silent, and the doctor leans forward, her voice softening: "You can breathe, Tate."

Tate nods, but she doesn't take the prompt. Instead, she steps forward and throws her arms around Dr. Rhodes, a brief, fierce hug from a girl who isn't a hugger. "Thank you," she whispers.

Then, suddenly, she moves away from the doctors and then past them, out of the lobby, and down the hall, disappearing into the hospital without another word.

"Oh, dear," Marion says.

"She's not going to try to find her mom, is she?" Dr. Rhodes asks. "Anna can't have visitors yet."

"No, she's not. She's—" Gran sighs. "She doesn't like public displays of emotion."

"I understand." Dr. Rhodes smiles gently. "There are some things we need to go over with you."

"Of course," Gran says. "Penny, can you go find Tate?"

"Yes," I say, as if I'm not already halfway out the door.

I can try to go off in the direction Tate went in, hoping I'll catch up, but instead I gamble that I know her. She's been cooped up all day, like a lobster in a slow-boiling pot. Now she's free.

She'll go outside.

I take the elevator down to the lobby, expecting her to be by the fountain.

But she's not there.

My phone buzzes in my pocket. When I pull it out, I see her text:

Headed back to the motel. Tell Marion for me?

"Shit," I say. I have to get Gran's keys.

33

THE TIME IN THE POOL

Penny

JUNE 27

SHE'S IN THE pool when I get to the motel, even though it's almost two in the morning. She probably bribed the clerk.

The water glows in the night. It's all noise and light pollution. Nothing like home, where you can stand in the meadow and see stars you'd never spot here. I won't be able to sleep well until I'm back on our road where maybe twenty trucks drive past on a busy day. I open the pool gate and step inside. She doesn't notice. I kick off my flip-flops and sit down on the edge of the pool, dangling my feet in the water. She's half a foot away, midstroke, when she realizes she isn't alone.

She hasn't bothered with a swim cap, just goggles over her double braids, her dark blue racing suit cutting into her shoulders. She never wears suits with patterns on them. The other girls on her team do, but Tate's all black and dark blue, sometimes burgundy, if she's feeling wild.

Is she trying to hide? Because she always stands out. She's prettier and she's taller and she's faster than everyone else, and when she looks at you, all blue-gray serious, the world doesn't fade, it sharpens. Like you never knew it was there until her.

"Go away, Penny."

"If you get to use the pool, so do I," I tell her, because there's no way I'm going to leave her alone after she bolted like that.

Tate doesn't run away. She's stalwart. It's admirable and annoying all at once.

She swishes the water back and forth with her hands.

She's shaking. I can see it now, the vibrations in the water, her shoulders trembling in the pool light.

"Tate," I say slowly. "Are you okay?"

She nods, a jerky movement, but as I speak, she wraps her arms around herself like she needs a shield. From me. The flash of hurt I feel isn't new, but it's new because she's causing it. Sometimes the things she does gnaw at me, but they rarely hurt. Not like this.

"Your mom's okay," I say, just to remind her, and Tate nods again. "Everyone's good. Everything went just like it was supposed to."

She keeps nodding, but then she starts talking. I almost don't catch it at first. A low kind of mutter that slowly becomes clearer: "*Fuck. Fuck. Fuck.*" Over and over.

I don't really know what to do. I'm probably not the best person for this. But I'm the one who's here. And she was the one who was there when I needed her.

So I do the only thing I can think of. I slip into the pool. The skirt of my dress, flimsy rayon that clings when wet, floats up, and I push it down. My feet skim along the bottom until they don't, until I either have to tread water or grab on to her.

My hands slide up her shoulders, and she just stops. Stops trembling. Stops swearing. Stops moving.

It's just her and me. No looking away. No more careful lies.

Just the truth.

I wait, my breath caught in my throat.

"Penny, I thought she was dead. When they took so long—I was *sure* of it."

And there it is.

Her body shudders so hard I feel it through mine.

"I know I kept saying it'd be fine. Positive thoughts only. But I thought—oh, fuck, when they took so long to come out, I thought she was dead. I just kept thinking: *This is it*. My entire being was prepared for it, so when they came in all smiles, like they hadn't made us wait, like I hadn't spent every minute more and more convinced . . ."

She pushes back in the water like she can't keep still, and my fingers start to trail off her shoulders until her hand comes up, covers them. She pulls me farther into the deep end, our legs tangling, hips bumping, until her shoulders settle against the cement edge of the pool.

We're so close I can feel the warmth coming off her body—she's always run hot, like the speed her body's capable of is radiating out of her.

My chin dips in and out of the water as it ripples around us.

Water trickles down her face—or maybe it's tears, and I can't bear the thought.

"We all made it through," I say.

She shakes her head, and when her lips press together, I know she's crying.

"This is just the start."

She's right. It's step one of many. But it's a step a lot of people don't make, and Anna has. I want Tate to revel in it as much as I understand why it's so hard for her to.

I reach out and wipe the tears up her cheekbone and away from her face, the moisture gathering on my own fingers, on the ridge of one of my scars.

Long-held pain against long-faded pain. Fitting, I guess.

Does she think it through? What she does next? Because before I can fully pull back, her hand covers mine. I know the shape of her cheek against the cup of my palm like I know the scars that seam across my skin. They both haunt me in different ways.

We brush length to length in the water, my toes against her ankles, so close that when her arm hooks around my waist, anchoring me, bringing me *thatmuch* closer, it's no surprise.

It's inevitable.

My skin remembers hers—from the hay shed and from the lake parking lot, from the motel in Yreka, early morning light and my cheek pressed against her shoulder—and my nerves sigh into something like *finally*, every inch of me needing. My eyes flutter shut. There's almost no space between us. I can feel it. I can feel *her*.

It's such a relief. Like I finally fit.

"Hey! What are you two doing in there?!"

A man's voice rings out, startling me so much that I bite my tongue, jerking backward. Blood bursts in my mouth.

The flashlight beam hits us, and I squint in the sudden light as Tate twists away. I blink, trying to clear the spots as she pulls herself out of the pool to talk to the security guard.

"We gotta go," she says when she walks back to the edge, holding out her towel for me. "I showed him our key, but he told us to stay out of the pool."

I swim over to the ladder and pull myself out, trying to smooth my dress down and just . . . failing.

Tate wraps her towel around my shoulders and looks down, like she hadn't pulled me into her as if we were in a romance novel and my head is spinning—how is she acting so normal? We were about to . . .

I was about to . . .

I'm still about to . . .

Oh my God, I'm going to die if this is all in my head. It's not . . . is it?

It can't be.

It never has been.

"We've been up for like twenty-two hours," Tate says. "We've gotta be up in a few hours."

And I just follow her. I don't know what else to do. Next thing I know, we're in that room and there's that bed and I keep dripping on the carpet, so I say, "I'm gonna shower."

Then I go into the bathroom and *completely* freak out.

PART FOUR

Alone

(or: the time at Damnation Peak)

34

TATE

JUNE 27

IT'S THREE A.M., and there's a girl in my bed.

It's three a.m., and *the* girl is in my bed.

Not my bed technically. Not my girl at all. But hope?

Hope is a cruel bitch.

Mom's going to survive. I believe it now. I *know* it.

I know hope. I know dread. I have no idea what to do with relief.

If I hadn't gotten into that pool and started swimming, I would've sunk to the bottom and started screaming.

But then she was there.

I couldn't sleep in the love seat like last night. Not this late.

She's not asleep. I know how Penny sleeps—all loose-limbed and sprawled across the bed like she owns it. She's curled up like a pill bug right now.

There are little sheep frolicking on her blue sleep set. Even from here, on the very edge of the other side of the bed, I can see how soft the material must feel. Almost fuzzy.

We've put as much space as we can between us, and it's no use.

(If that security guard hadn't interrupted . . .)

My hands clench the sheets. All I can smell is the sharp-sweetness of her grapefruit lotion. My braids keep seeping water into the pillow because I didn't bother to undo them or even towel dry my hair. I just dove into my pajamas while she was in the shower and pretended to be asleep when she came out.

Now we're both pretending. Exhaustion and adrenaline swirl inside me. I am so tired. I've been up for . . . how many hours now?

I screw my eyes shut tight. *Sleep*, I tell myself. *Sleep*.

Penny shifts a little across the bed. There's too much room. There's not enough.

She is forever my contradiction. My downfall.

(She fit against me in that pool like it was where we both belonged.)

"Tate? Are you asleep?"

I keep breathing, slow and steady, even when she rustles a little closer to see.

Sleep. Just sleep.

She flops back on the pillows, and I keep breathing, slow and steady, until pretending to sleep becomes real.

I can't move. My phone on the nightstand buzzes me awake. A long line of heat is pressed against my side, and I blink in the crack of light that's streaming in from the curtains. Soft air brushes against my neck, and when I turn my head . . .

There Penny is. Inches away. Breathing gently against my neck.

She starfished across the bed in the night. No more carefully maintained space between us. Her arm's slung around my stomach, and her leg is slotted between mine. I can feel how smooth her legs are against the prickle of mine.

I try to pull away, but she makes a face, and I just . . . I freeze.

She's warm where I'm cold and I'm sharp where she's soft and pulling away seems impossible. Futile.

(Like in the pool when she sighed into me, and all I could think was *finally*.)

My phone buzzes again. This time it's not my alarm. It's a text. I have to grab it. If it's from Mom—

"Mmph," she groans as I shift under her, reaching for it. Her cheek smashes against my chest, and if I had a lot of cleavage, her face would be dangerously close to it. I'm trying very hard not to think about that when I see Marion's text: Everything's going great! More later.

Now that I've stopped moving, Penny's settled back into the crook of my neck, her lips fluttering with each breath.

Why couldn't she be a light sleeper? If I have to wake her up . . .

Fuck. I'm going to have to wake her up.

Count of three, Tate. One. Two.

Fuck. I hate my life.

Three.

"Penny." I tug at her arm, slipping my legs out from under hers. "Come on, Pen. Wake up." I shake her shoulder a little, and she flails awake, rapidly blinking at me.

Because my face is still, like, an inch away from hers. If I just lean forward . . .

(We'd have morning breath and it'd be terrible and wonderful, and it's just a little dip of movement, it's just a monumental choice . . . it's just that some girls don't get some things.)

She snaps away from me like a rubber band. "Morning!" she squeaks from the other side of the bed, total deer in the headlights, which is so not flattering to my ego, let me tell you.

We've been here before, after all. Once is a mistake, twice is a coincidence. I don't need to get to three times to know it's a pattern.

I know the pattern. All too well.

"Your gran texted me," I tell her. "Everything's going good."

She nods, clutching the sheets to her chest. "Tate, did I—"

"I'm gonna shower," I interrupt her. "You wanna go down to the complimentary breakfast after?"

I don't even wait for her to nod. I just get up and go run the shower.

Even more impressive: I don't scream into the towels. (But I want to.)

196

35

JUNE 27

Penny has invited Tate and Marion to group chat
TEAM SACRAMENTO—> HOME.
Tate has joined the group.
Marion has joined the group.

Morning, Gran! P

M Penny, I don't like to text.

I know, Gran! But this will be more organized. P

T This way you only have to type things once,
instead of to both of us.

We're getting ready to check out. Have you
seen them yet? P

M Not yet. Dr. Rhodes said soon.

Okay. Then I'll share the information I
gathered yesterday: P

The next 7-10 Days (Hospital Recovery)
The Transplant Wing Nurses

JESSICA: Head nurse. This is who we need to go to if we need anything big.

YOLANDA: She's got major seniority. The doctors fear her. The nurses obey her. Will also give you the heads-up when they change out the candy in the vending machine.

LILAH: New hire. Last resort option if you need something found or need something fast.

DIANE: Sweetest person you ever did see. Described to me as a secret weapon.

Do I want to know how you acquired this information?

I talked to Grace in pediatrics. We know each other from when I was here.

You had an insider this entire time?

I just went to say hi and bring her a coffee when they first took Mom in. The woman probably prevented me from getting septic. It was the least I could do.

Is she the one who turned you on to the terrible lime Jell-O?

My superior palate turned me on to the lime Jell-O. P

M Everyone knows the best Jell-O flavor is lemon.

T Marion coming in with a brand-new contender out of left field.

Are you a sports commentator now? Lemon, Gran, really? P

M How else do you think I get my lemon cake to taste so lemony?

WHAT?! P

You told me the secret was the fresh lemon zest! P

M The secret to the icing is zest.

M But the cake is Betty Crocker mix, extra eggs, and a whole lot of lemon Jell-O water.

!!!! P

T Mm, lemon cake. We should make some when we get back.

M: Recipe's in the little wooden box in the top cupboard in my trailer.

P: See, this is why you set up group chats. You find out family betrayals easier.

M: 🍋 RIP Lemon Cake.

P: We're gonna check out, Gran. See you in an hour.

36

TATE

JUNE 27

I HOVER IN the doorway of Mom's room, unsure she's awake, but her head turns toward me and she smiles, wide enough to make me know they gave her the *really* good drugs.

"Hey, sweets," she says when she sees me. She's hooked up to a lot of tubes and machines and stuff, but she's awake in that groggy, drugged-to-the-gills sort of way.

"Hi," I croak out.

"Gonna tell me what happened on *Judge Judy*?"

"I forget" is all I can say before I rush over to her bed. I can't hug her, of course, but I grip the plastic safety bar of the hospital bed and stare down at her, drinking her in.

She looks better. It's not my imagination, is it? Maybe it is. But she looks better to me. She looks perfect.

Her room is full of flowers—another thing I didn't think about and should have. I should have brought some. But luckily, everyone at the brewery really pulled through. Graham and the line cooks sent flowers, and the servers delivered cupcakes for the nurses. Meghan's parents sent a bonsai tree and Remi's mom sent tulips, and weirdly, the manager of Sentry Market where Remi works sent a ham—an expensive Italian one I wasn't sure Mom could actually eat, considering her post-op diet restrictions. I didn't even know Mom knew Remi's boss, but maybe they shared ordering sometimes. Getting stuff up the mountain is expensive.

She drifts off almost as soon as I get settled, and a nurse walks in—Jessica, the head nurse from Penny's medical reconnaissance list—and checks her machines and urine bag.

"She's doing very well," Jessica says in a quiet voice.

I nod. "Thank you for everything."

Jessica shoots me a quick smile before continuing her rounds.

I play solitaire. There's a kind of peace to it, the soft shuffle of the cards and the beeps of the machines, Mom's soft breathing (she's breathing, she's going to live, she made it she made it she made it).

Now that I've seen her, I am content in a way that is almost unsettling, because I don't know how to be this way. It's such a big feeling. I don't know how to collect it into small enough pieces to slip it under my skin to keep.

"Do you have my phone, sweets?" Mom murmurs.

I look up from the cards. "Hey, do you want some water or ice chips or something?"

She shakes her head. "My phone—I want to see how things went in the kitchen last night. Drew promised he'd text me."

"Mom." I prop my hands on my hips. "Drew is not going to text you about work on the night you had a liver transplant. He just said he would to appease you, because you're a control freak."

"That's mean!" But she grins all loopily. "What if they burned my kitchen down? Louisa's always playing fast and loose with the fryer."

"I promise, the line cooks did not burn down the brewery. They were all too busy texting to see how you were. Same with pretty much everyone who works or regularly goes to the brewery. Thus the garden surrounding us."

"I *love* the tiny tree," Mom says. "Did Lottie get a tiny tree? I don't want to share mine."

I wonder if I should have asked Jessica just how much morphine they're giving her.

"I'm not sure," I say. "I'll check."

"Good," she says, her eyes closing again. "I haven't forgotten, you know," she murmurs.

"About what, Mom?"

"About sides," she says. "We'll talk more about that when I'm home, okay?" Her eyes open like it's a struggle, like she needs to look at me while she says it, because it makes it a promise, and my mom doesn't break promises.

"Okay" is all I say. But I am steeped in skepticism, a pot of tea left too long and gone bitter. I can't imagine what it's like on the inside for Penny, when it's like this on the outside for me.

She drifts off again, and I curl up in the uncomfortable chair and make the most of the hours I have left.

37

Penny

JUNE 27

SHE'S OUT OF it. My mom. She sleeps almost the full four hours I'm allowed to visit, and when she's awake, it's hard for her to focus. She keeps asking for Anna.

"Anna's recovering," I remind her, and it makes her face squinch up in confusion before it smooths out and she remembers.

Gran's gone to the motel to shower and change, her last chance before Tate and I go home and she's pulling double-duty, checking on Mom and Anna. So I ask the nurse, Diane, "Should she be like this?" when she comes to check in on Mom.

"It's a major surgery," Diane says. "Her pain will lessen over the next week, and by the time she's discharged, it'll be much more manageable. I wouldn't worry too much."

But it's hard not to when Mom's in pain. My mom is not stoic. It all shows on her face, even when she's asleep.

"It's okay, Mama," I whisper when she whimpers, trying to shift in the bed.

"It hurts," she says.

"I know," I tell her. "But you're being so brave."

"I really didn't do much but just lie there," she says, and it's a joke she'd make with Anna, not me.

"Well, let's keep you lying *here*," I say. "And it won't hurt as much soon."

"Mm. Never liked morphine. S'itchy." She turns her head on her pillow—flops it really—so she's facing me. "You doing okay?"

My mouth goes dry, because I'm not sure when she last asked me that. "I'm good," I say, because even if I told her the truth, she wouldn't remember.

"You look so much like your Daddy," and fuck, it's a spear out of nowhere.

I suddenly don't like morphine either, even though I was thanking the universe for it a few years ago.

"I wish he was here." Her eyes close and then open, a struggle against the drugs dragging her under. "It was so much easier when he was here."

"Yeah," I say quietly, because it's the truth, and she won't remember. "It was."

The clock ticks and time is up.

Leaving her behind is so easy it frightens me.

Like mother, like daughter, I guess.

38

Penny

JUNE 27

"I WANT YOU girls to drive safely," Gran says, closing the back of my car in the hospital parking lot. "Call me as soon as you get in—I don't care what time is it."

"We will," I say.

She hugs me, kissing the top of my head in the process. And then she hooks Tate in with her other arm, squishing us together in her embrace, and it's hard not to get goose bumps from the warm press of Tate's skin against mine.

"I am so proud of you both," Gran says fiercely. "The next few weeks are going to be tough—the next few months, too. But I know you both are up for it now."

"I love you." It's not me who says it first—it's Tate. Muffled into Gran's shoulder, I can barely make it out, but it's like I know the shape of those words in the air when she says them.

"I love you, too," Gran says. "Both of you."

"Thank you," Tate whispers. "You're always there. For me. For my mom."

"And I always will be," Gran promises.

She watches us buckle into the station wagon with the kind of hawkish concern only a grandma can have. "Drive safe," she directs us again.

"Bye, Gran."

After she heads back into the hospital, I look over at Tate.

"Should we go straight to the apartment to pack?"

Tate groans. "We've got what, three days?"

"More like two and a half, 'cause I've gotta work in the mornings."

This is just the start.

"Let's go," she says.

It's nearly five when we get to town. We'd loaded up on bagels and Danishes from the breakfast bar at the motel, so we don't even stop to eat. We just start packing.

"You have a list, don't you?" she asks me as she unlocks the apartment door.

"Maybe."

"I'm still putting my clothes in garbage bags" is all she says after I pull out my bullet journal, and when I roll my eyes, she gets that pleased look.

"Why don't you do your room—I'll finish the kitchen," I say.

"Yep." She disappears into her room after grabbing a box of trash bags, even though the packing boxes are right there.

I go into the kitchen, opening my bullet journal to my packing checklist.

Anna has a ton of cooking things, for obvious reasons, and I

don't want to miss or break anything. Mom doesn't cook, so most of
our stuff at home is Gran's. She and Anna will have to figure out what
goes into the garage and what doesn't, because I'm not gonna get in
the middle of what cast-iron pan goes where. Cooks are scarily pro-
tective of those things. The seasoning, or something.

I check my phone, but there aren't any texts. I didn't really expect
any—Mom was pretty out of it—but I wonder . . .

Does she actually want a new start? Or was she just being sappy
with Anna when I overheard them?

Music thumps from Tate's closed door—something with a rapid
beat and words I can't make out. I clear my throat and grab my ear-
buds, turning on my rain sounds app.

It doesn't drown her out completely, but I find I don't mind so
much.

By the time my phone starts buzzing with a text from Meghan,
I've got all the cupboards empty.

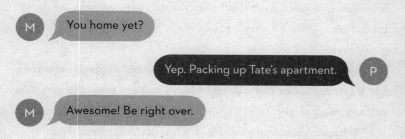

M You home yet?

Yep. Packing up Tate's apartment. P

M Awesome! Be right over.

"Hey, Tate?" I call, going down the hall to tap on her door.
"Yeah?"

I open the door. There's a tied garbage bag and a swim bag full of
clothes sitting next to the tiny, doorless closet.

"Meghan's coming over. She just texted me."

"Yeah? Remi too. They must be together."

I frown. "Since when do they hang out together?"

Tate shrugs. "I dunno. I guess lately. He mentioned it."

"Well, Meghan didn't."

"Will you help me get these stuffed in the bag?" She pokes at her extra blankets.

I grab the garbage bag and shake it out, holding it open for her.

"What did Remi say exactly?" I ask her.

"He said something about teaching her how to barbecue."

"What?"

"If they are hanging out or whatever, we should stay out of it."

"Wait, you think they might be *whatever*-ing?"

"I dunno. Are you going to act like this when they're here?"

"I'm just trying to get a handle on the situation!" I think about Remi and Meghan together. "They'd be kinda cute. He's not secretly evil, is he?"

"Do you think I'd hang out with a guy who's an ass? Or that some misogynistic jerk would put up with *me*?" Tate asks.

I try not to laugh, but when she arches her eyebrow, I have to. "I just wanted to be sure! I wanted to stone Meghan's last boyfriend to death, all medieval-like."

"You and your mom," she mutters.

"What does that mean?"

"Apparently your mom used to hang around in the woods by the river and throw rocks at would-be rapists."

"Excuse me?" I think my jaw dislocates with how hard it drops.

"My mom was in a sharing mood before surgery," Tate explains.

"No way. She must've been loopy on pain meds."

Tate shakes her head. "Made a lot of sense to me."

"*How?*" I demand.

"Trauma breaks or bonds you."

It's like a shadow passes through my heart at her words. How is she always able to do that? Just . . . gut me, so simply, so easily?

How can one person hold all of you in the palm of their hand and not know it?

"Yeah," I say. "It does."

My phone buzzes again. They're here.

"I've got food!" Meghan says, holding out a canvas bag.

"And drinks," Remi adds from behind her.

Meghan swishes inside. Her paisley skirt has a drawstring that has bells at the ends, so she jingles a little with each step.

"I've got tri-tip, stuff for sandwiches, chips—Tate, I didn't know what kind you liked, and Remi apparently has food amnesia about his own best friend—"

"Hey!" he interjects, but he shoots her a smile as he sets the drinks down on the kitchen counter.

"—so I got a bunch of different kinds," Meghan finishes, not even missing a beat. "Also, we brought more boxes and the trailer, so we can move some of the furniture. How are you two doing?"

"We're fine," I say quickly when Tate kind of just looks at her, trying to absorb all the information. Meghan is very detail-oriented, and she talks fast on top of that.

"And the moms?"

"Going strong. Gran texted me a picture on the drive here." I show it to her. "Apparently my mom is already complaining about not being able to room with Anna."

"This looks great," Tate tells Meghan, looking down at the spread she's neatly laid out. "Did you make all this?"

"I'm teaching Meghan," Remi says.

"That sounds like fun," I say carefully. I *want* to shoot Meghan a significant *what the hell is going on* look, but she won't meet my eyes.

"Eat up," she encourages. "You've been living on hospital food!"

"You really made this?" I ask after demolishing half of my sandwich.

"I even added my own little spin on the dry rub. Remi doubted me, but I was right, wasn't I?"

"You were," he agrees.

"We do actually have a reason why Remi's teaching me," Meghan tells me.

Tate glances up from her sandwich, eyebrows quirking. I want to mouth *I told you so!* at her, but I don't.

She nudges him with her foot, and he taps it back, so gently that I know: They're not just hanging out. Even if they think that's what they're doing.

"We have something to tell you," Meghan says. She is sitting *awfully* close to Remi.

"Oh?" I ask, trying not to sound smug.

"Meghan and I have been working on something together," Remi adds.

"Voila!" Meghan whips out a flyer from the depths of her swishy skirts and places it on the table between us.

TRI-TIP FUNDRAISER
SANDWICHES! RAFFLES! PRIZES!
WIN YOUR OWN BLACKBERRY BEAR!

"We got all the supplies and prizes donated," Remi explains. "And we're using the big grills from the store and the brewery."

"Thus the grilling lessons," Meghan adds.

"Meghan's really good." Remi smiles fondly.

"We took a page out of Lottie's book with the food fundraising idea," Meghan says. "But we figured we could raise enough money to at least pay off the cost of the Sacramento rental."

I stare down at the flyer, not knowing what to say.

"This is . . ." I press my hand against a heart that's beating so fast my ears roar. "You two . . . you planned all this? How? When?"

"Just over the last few days," Meghan says, like that's even remotely easy or normal.

"This is what happens when you give people my phone number," Remi tells Tate, and she actually laughs and then kicks him. Which just makes him laugh and kick her back.

"Meghan," I say, and then I can't say anything else because my throat's all tight. "I can't believe . . ."

"You all deserve a lot more," Meghan says earnestly. "But this . . ."

"This we can do," Remi finishes for her when her eyes shimmer.

"I just . . ." Tears trickle down my cheeks, and then I'm up and hugging her. "Thank you," I whisper in her ear.

I pull back. "Okay." I sniff, trying to get some control. "I want to hear about all the logistics here. Do you have a spreadsheet?"

"Of course I have a spreadsheet," Meghan says, pulling out her phone as Remi groans.

"Let's move the couch or something," he tells Tate, who eagerly follows him without another word.

39

TATE

JUNE 27

IT'S NEARLY TEN by the time we get the first load of furniture and boxes up the mountain, and Remi and Meghan head home.

Penny collapses on the pink couch. There are two couches now, Lottie's and Mom's, set across from each other like they're about to go to battle: Lottie's pink couch from the thirties she reupholstered herself versus Mom's beige one we bought at the thrift store.

"We've gotta go through all this stuff," Penny says, waving her hand toward the kitchen, filled with a maze of boxes. "Rearrange the furniture. Put some stuff in the garage."

"Is there any room in the garage?" I ask. "I thought the whole thing was Lottie's studio?"

"Half studio, half garage. Dad built a wall separating them." She blinks, like she's just surprised herself by mentioning him.

It's my in and I take it, because it's weird being in this house and realizing how much Lottie erased George from the downstairs. That little corner upstairs is the only reminder in a house he grew up in, and it's just . . .

Does Lottie think if she avoids his memory, he won't haunt her for what she's done? Because if there are ghosts and justice, he'll find a way.

"Can I ask you something?"

She nods, but she does it so warily I almost don't ask.

"Does your mom just never talk about him with you?"

Penny doesn't look away, but her gaze turns into a challenge the longer it goes on, until I can't look away either, cheeks burning under her scrutiny and maybe a little at my audacity.

"Did she talk about him when she lived with you?" Penny asks.

My heart skips, because the answer is yes, but probably not in the way she thinks.

"Did she?"

"She talked about a lot of things. Some days. And then some days, she didn't talk at all."

Just like there are some things you can't unsay, there are some things you can't unhear. (Lottie begging my mother to give her the pills, to let her go . . .)

I will never forget.

"She doesn't talk about anything with me," Penny says. "Especially him."

"You can talk about him with me," I offer.

Her face softens. "That's—thanks."

"He taught me a lot, too," I say with a shrug, because it's true. He was the one who took us camping when we were kids. I know how to build a fire and use a chain saw because of him. He was a good dad . . . a good man.

Maybe the better you are, the bigger hole you leave. George left a crater behind.

She smiles softly and then clears her throat. "Something is definitely up between Remi and Meghan," she declares.

"They told us what was up," I say, taking the hint that she wants to stop talking about her Dad. "They're putting together a fundraiser."

"I can't believe they did that."

"I can."

She looks questioningly at me.

"Remi and Meghan are, like, cinnamon-roll good," I explain. "And cinnamon-roll kind of people like to spread that good."

She sits up. "What does that make *us*?"

"People who immediately got more work and sold valuables as soon as it got hard, because who else takes care of your family but you?"

"But it's not like that," she protests.

"But we reacted like that."

That silences her, because she knows it's true. We reacted like it was up to just us and Marion to clear the moms' hurdles. We didn't react like we had a village.

And Remi and Meghan proved to us that we had one all along.

"What does that make us, do you think?" she asks suddenly.

It takes me some time to answer, even though I have one.

"I think it makes us wounded."

She doesn't say anything after that. Not even when I get up and say, "I'll see you in the morning?"

She just nods, and I go creaking up the stairs, into a room that's my room but not. When I hear her follow a few minutes later, the click of her door just across from mine, the closeness, the possibility—those few steps it would take to cross the hall are almost worse than being in the bed with her.

When my alarm goes off at four, my entire body protests. But I drag myself out of bed instead of hitting snooze. I use the bathroom and then do twenty minutes of yoga. When I'm done and guzzling from my water bottle, I can hear the persistent beep of Penny's alarm across the hall.

I shower at the pool, so I get dressed and braid my hair. By then I can't ignore the beeping anymore. "Penny? You awake?"

Dead silence, punctuated by beeping.

I open the door, stepping inside. Her calendar has the weeks the moms will be gone blocked out in orange, and the ever-growing collage behind her bed has sprouted from a flower garden into a tangle of moody forests.

"Penny?" She doesn't move when I call her name, so I creep farther into the room, careful not to trip on the rag rug she has spread out on the wood floor, covering years of chipped paint. I sit down on the edge of the bed, press my hand against her shoulder, and shake her a little. "You gotta wake up, Pen."

"Hmph." She moves a little under my touch, and then rolls over toward me, her eyes blinking open. The smile she shoots me, sleepy and satisfied and just so relaxed, more relaxed than I've seen her in months, makes my entire body jolt like I've missed a stair.

"There you are," she says, eyes drifting shut as she burrows back into her pillows.

"Time to get up."

"Mm." She frowns. "No. Come back to bed."

"Wha—"

She grabs my arm, her fingers closing around my biceps and tugging, and I'm so surprised, I bend into her, resisting only at the last possible second.

Her eyes snap open.

"Tate?!"

Penny drops my arm, popping up from the tangle of blankets and pillows like she's a windup toy. "Sorry!" she squeaks. "I thought—" And then her mouth snaps shut.

I stare at her, my heart doing that twisting thing in my chest that it only does around her.

"Oh, God, it's so early," Penny moans, burying her head in her hands.

"Sorry," I say. "I've got to go for my run."

She frowns. "On the road?"

I nod.

She groans, shoving herself upright. "I'll come with you."

"You don't have to—"

"Tate, there are bears. Also, if a logging truck sideswipes you into a gully where no one can find you, your mom will kill me. Do you know where Gran keeps the bear spray, or where the blind spots on the road are?"

I hate it when she has good points. "Okay, you can come."

"Just give me five minutes."

I try to pretend to not hear her softly mutter "fuck" as I leave her room.

(But it's kind of hard.)

40

TATE

JUNE 28

TEXT FROM MOM. I load the video of her in the hospital bed, giving a little wave.

Feeling good! is all she writes, but I play the video four times in the pool parking lot even though I'm running late. I'm rushing by the time I get out of my car, hoping I can still get a lane.

When I see the three girls from swim team hanging around the pool, it's too late to back up. They've spotted me. *She's* spotted me. I know she has, because Laurel's eyes are narrowing, the way they always do when she has to endure my presence.

Penny's ex and I have never gotten along. Even before she was Penny's ex.

It's one of the reasons I swim in the morning. They never swim in the morning.

So I just keep going, dumping my net bag down on the lane farthest from them. But even with that hint, Evie doesn't take it. She wouldn't. She's like the nicest golden retriever in the world—and I mean that as a compliment. The girl is sweet. And the only one who's been even barely nice to me since last year. But I don't want to deal right now. I don't want to think about the past when my present has suddenly become everything I hoped.

She's going to survive. My mother is sitting down in Sacramento with a working liver.

"Tate! Hi!" Evie bounces toward me, her white-blond hair damp around her face, cap in hand.

"Hi, Evie. Theresa. Laurel."

"How's your mom?" Evie asks.

"She's doing really good, thanks. She's getting out of the hospital soon."

Evie smiles, and it's not forced. "That's great!"

"We're really happy for you, Tate," Theresa says.

"Thanks. I appreciate it. So does Mom. Anyway. I should—" I jerk my thumb toward the locker room.

"Of course," Evie says. "Let me just." She steps forward. "Can I?" She extends her hands.

Oh, God, I think she wants to *hug* me. "Sure?"

She embraces me lightly, like I'm made of glass. "I'm really happy for your family," she whispers. "You've been through a lot."

I can't relax into her embrace. Her words make me breathe a little harder. Have I been that bad at hiding it?

"Thanks, Evie," I say, when we pull apart. "I'll see you around."

"Text me; we can hang out."

"Sure," I say, knowing I won't.

Some things you can't take back.

Some things you don't want to.

The shelter and emptiness of the locker room are welcome after

220

being surprised by that lot. I hadn't thought about how to navigate this part—the swimming part of my life—with Penny driving me and picking me up. Thank goodness I'd dropped her off, not the other way around.

I take off my clothes and am pulling on my suit when the clang of a metal door echoes through the rows of lockers.

"Hello?" I look over my shoulder, and when I see who it is, I just turn back to my duffel and pull out my towel, wrapping it around my waist. Without a word, I shoulder my bag and head out.

"You reek," Laurel tells me as I walk past her.

I hate that it's probably true after my run. I hate that it makes me stop. I hate that it pisses me off.

(But I kind of hate Laurel, so there we are.)

I don't say anything; I just stare at her and wait.

Laurel shifts. She never could keep still. She's a sprinter, good at the beginning of a relay, but she pushes too hard, doesn't save any energy for the end. We're opposites in that way. Start strong, finish strong, with no slow middle—that's what I strive for.

It's why I beat her, and she hates it. Almost as much as she hates me.

The only commonality we have.

(Well, other than Penny.)

It's like thinking that conjures it out of her mouth, because she asks, "How is Penny?" like she has to break her jaw to say it.

I want to walk away, just leave her at the question, but if I put off dealing with Laurel, Penny could get hurt. And I don't want that again. Laurel and I are on the same team. Which means it'll be harder for Penny to avoid her.

"You and I are going to make an agreement."

"Oh, really?" Laurel asks. "Did someone appoint you Queen of the Pool?"

"We're living together. Penny and me."

She flushes at my phrasing. "You're living with your *moms*."

"Right now, it's just her and me," I say, and then I let it sit there between us, all the what-ifs and implications that make her cheeks go scarlet with anger.

"That means, if you try to stop by, it's more than barbed wire that's gonna keep you out."

She huffs out a breath that tries to be a laugh. "You are always such a fucking drama queen."

"And you don't know when to leave a girl alone. Penny's been very clear about not wanting to talk to you after you broke up."

"I know that," Laurel snaps, so loudly it echoes between the *drip-drips* of the leaky showers. "You must be so happy," she mutters.

"I am," I say, and the smile that spreads across my lips is totally real and true, because *it's* true. " 'Sad, stoic Tate's sick mom' isn't so sick anymore."

She flinches when I quote her to her face.

"You'll see Penny around outside of school when she picks me up from practice and stuff. You're going to leave her alone."

"And if she doesn't leave *me* alone?" Laurel asks.

"Penny can do whatever she wants." I shrug. "Leave her alone unless she comes up and talks to you. But I wouldn't bet on that happening after what you did."

"You have no idea about Penny and me."

I shrug again, because I know it infuriates her. "If you say so."

222

"I'm not agreeing to anything. You can't stop me from talking to her."

"No, I can't. But she can. And I can help her. Guess we'll see how it goes."

I walk away, and Laurel's voice echoes when she calls out to me: "She's never going to love you, Tate."

I turn around to face her, still moving, backward this time, no hesitation as I shrug. "That's not why I'm doing it."

When I turn away, she has nothing left.

(But neither do I.)

41

TATE

JUNE 29

"THIS IS THE last day before we turn the keys in," Penny reminds me as I scrub at the grease spatters in the oven.

"I know," I say for the third time. "You don't need to keep saying it."

She's perched on the sink, using a microfiber cloth to clean each individual slat of the cursed and dated venetian blinds that hang in each room. It's a thankless task, and she hasn't complained once, but I can tell it's getting to her because she keeps reminding me of the ticking clock every twenty minutes or so. It's like she's got an alarm in her head.

"Sorry," she says. "I'm just—" She lets out a long breath and then holds it for a few beats, then breathes in. "I just want to get it all done."

"We will," I say. "Think about something else."

"What?" she asks hopelessly.

"My mom said they might be discharging Lottie tomorrow."

"Hopefully your mom, too."

"She might be a few days behind Lottie."

"Oh, God—that means Gran and Mom are going to be in the same apartment alone?" Penny's eyes widen. "I definitely wouldn't want to be there for that cage match."

"It's really that bad between them?" I ask.

"You saw how it was when I brought up the bills," Penny says.

I nod.

"It's like that."

"They used to get along."

"Well, I used to have a dad, and Gran used to have a son, and Mom used to have a husband." She can't look at me as she says it, focusing on the dust.

"Okay," I say, because I can't bear the droop of her shoulders, how she can't even meet my eyes when she's acknowledging the hole in her family.

It's like Lottie thought erasing him would fill it faster.

"Change of subject. Tell me about the rafting business."

"My plans with Meghan?"

I nod, wiping away the foamy oven cleaner and grease.

"Well, Meghan's come up with this weeklong guided camping tour of the river. There's two versions: one more backcountry, one that's more refined."

"Refined? How do you make it refined?"

"More trailers, fewer tents," she explains, as I finish up the oven and move to the sink. "But that'll require us sourcing four teardrop trailers and renovating them how we need them."

"Do you know how to do that?"

"Meghan loves that stuff, and I can learn. And once we tell her dad our plans, he'll want to help. He has a whole workshop, which means we won't need to invest in a lot of expensive tools."

"You've got it all figured out." Of course she does.

(God, Lottie's going to be furious.)

"We'll have to cut deals with some private landowners so we can camp along certain stretches, but I think it's doable. Dad had a lot of relationships with people that I think I can continue. And then there's the big trip."

"What's that?"

"I have a lot of setup to do to make it work, but eventually, I want to do trips down the whole river. From the start to the sea."

"You want to raft the entire river?"

"Technically kayak, but yes."

"Can you even do that? There are dams and stuff."

"Yeah, you have to go around those on foot. But people do it."

"How long would it take?"

"Three weeks or so to get to San Francisco."

"That's—wow."

She hops off the counter to move on to the next task on her list. "Do you think it's a bad idea?"

"No," I say. "It's cool. Just ... hard-core."

"I want to make it more than that, though. Make it not just about the physicality of the trip. Make it about the river. What it means to different people."

(Oh, yeah, Lottie's gonna lose her shit over this.)

She's looking up at me like she needs my stamp of approval, and it's strange to feel like she needs anything from me.

"That makes it a lot more than a trip—it's a whole learning experience. That's great," I tell her, and she beams at me in relief.

Knowing Penny, she'll do her homework. By the time Lottie finds out, it'll all be arranged, and things will be so far in motion that Lottie can't stop it.

"It's nice to get another opinion," she says. "Meghan's such an optimist. Sometimes I need someone to worry at."

"You can worry at me. But we should take out the trash," I say, gesturing to the stack of bags we've got set near the door.

"Good idea. I need to stretch a little."

We gather the garbage and head down the cement stairs. She stumbles at the bottom, nearly dropping her bag, and when she rights herself, I turn to look at what caught her attention.

Ronnie's leaning against his doorway, not taking his eyes off us.

"Who is that?" Penny asks.

"Landlord," I say.

"He's stared at me every time I've taken stuff out to the dumpster," Penny says.

A prickle goes down my spine.

"Was he creeping on you?"

"Just watching. Creepily. But he didn't say anything."

"Let's hope it stays that way," I say.

"Is he that bad?" Penny asks quietly as I follow her up the stairs, trying not to look down at him where he's still staring at us, drinking his coffee.

I follow her inside the apartment and close the door. "He's definitely creepy. He's also one of those asses who'll do everything he can to keep your deposit. There was a really nice girl who lived next door a few years ago, and her apartment was so clean when she left, but he said he had to steam clean her carpets because they 'smelled musty' and he took half of her deposit."

227

"Jerk," Penny says.

"Exactly. And we need the deposit back, so . . ."

"Don't worry, I'll behave," she says. "We've just got the bathroom and the floors left."

My phone is buzzing on the counter, and I pick it up. A text from Mom.

I know you start shifts at the brewery tomorrow. Can you film Drew making the pretzel dough for me? I need to figure out what he's doing wrong.

"Look at this," I tell Penny, showing her the text.

Penny laughs. "She's still on that?"

"Apparently he's only taken two of her six calls a day, because, like any rational person, he wants her to rest."

"He's so going to pay for that when she gets back in that kitchen." I smile, but it strains at the edges.

"It's gonna be forever until she's back working," I say. "The recovery . . ."

"It's a lot longer than my mom's," Penny finishes. "I know."

"You did me a favor talking to Graham about covering some shifts at the brewery," I told her. "We're gonna need that money. Hopefully he can keep me on when school starts. Or I can find another job."

"We've got a lot of winter expenses." Penny shakes her head. "My mom—she just doesn't pay attention to that stuff. My dad always did the finances and now . . ."

"You do."

"Even with both of us working and me picking up a lot more tutoring jobs when school starts, it's gonna be tight. Something breaking or one unexpected bill . . ."

228

"I can ask Coach about teaching swim lessons when she gets back," I say. "I can probably fit it in between training and school and brewery shifts."

"We'll figure it out," Penny says.

"Now who's the optimist?"

She laughs.

"I'm so glad your mom's getting out of the hospital," I tell her.

"I know," Penny says. "They'll *both* be home soon. Okay—not exactly soon, but . . ."

"Soon-ish."

"Soon-ish," she agrees, nodding. She shoots me a shaky smile, and then we get back to work.

It takes both of us and most of our Thursday, but when we're done, the apartment is spotless. Penny does a final walk-through as I drag the remaining garbage bags out of the apartment and down the death-trap stairs and across the parking lot to the dumpster. There are already flies swarming and a whiff of rotted eggs coming off it, so I try to make it fast.

Which, of course, is when Ronnie saunters out of his apartment and toward me.

"Whatcha doing out here?"

Even the sound of his voice pricks at the back of my neck.

"Just cleaning up the place, Ronnie," I tell our almost-former landlord. "I'll turn in the keys at the office."

"Saw some other girl dumping a lot of garbage in the dumpster. Almost called the sheriff about illegal dumping until I saw her going up to the apartment."

"That's just my friend who's helping me. Nothing illegal about it."

229

"Good thing I figured that out before I called anyone, huh?"

"Good thing," I grit out.

We've lived here six years, since I was eleven. And it wasn't much—Ronnie made sure of that by reluctantly fixing only the most urgent things—but it had been ours. It had also been tenuous, like all things in life are when you never have enough money. Being late on rent with Ronnie was hell. With the medical bills, it was always one thing or another, sometimes all things at once.

"Gonna miss your mom around here," he says with that creepy smile that says too much. "I'll have to go to the brewery to check her out."

You need the deposit, Tate. Do not engage.

(But, oh, I want to.)

"She's going to be on leave for a while. We really like our new place," I say, fighting to keep it bland, hoping he'll just *go away*. I've spent years of interactions with him feeling the same exact way, but I guess my hope is too much, because he stays put.

"Your mom's classier than you," he says, and it's a warning, and one I usually would heed. "You should take a page out of her book. Or there could be consequences."

"I'm not doing anything but cleaning out the apartment," I say, trying hard to make my face stone and probably failing because, fuck, I hate this guy. All I can think of is Mom's strained smile and the way she'd try to time dropping off the rental check when he wasn't home, and her shaking her head tightly when I offered to do it myself and making sure I always had my keychain pepper spray on me.

"You're using a lot of the dumpster. That's not fair to my other tenants. The ones who are actually sticking around."

I stare at him, incredulous. There are maybe eight bags of trash from our place in the dumpster.

"A little class will go a long way," he tells me.

And then he licks his lips.

I'm a teakettle boiling over, because the next thing out of my mouth is: "*Fuck. You.*"

I step forward instead of back. "You have blatantly stared at my mom's ass every time you've seen her for *years*, and somewhere down the line, you started staring at mine, too. You don't get shit from me, you power-tripping perv."

"You—" He steps toward me, and I tense, waiting for a fist or a grab or something.

"Hey, what's going on?"

Penny's voice.

Penny's here. Standing right there behind him. Relief floods through me as Ronnie leaps away, his hands clenching as his gaze darts between us.

Penny's eyes narrow, and her head tilts, ponytail swinging like an omen as she takes me in, and I can tell she knows. (Knows the way my nerves had shrieked, gut instinct we all have clawing to the surface: *Run, just in case he's really bad instead of just kinda bad.*)

Ronnie doesn't seem to notice the storm brewing. He latches onto his only power move left: "You girls are filling up my dumpster."

"Tate's a tenant until midnight," Penny says. "She has use of the facilities until then."

"Not if you're gonna fill up the dumpster with your moving trash. I'll have to charge you a fee."

"You can't do that," Penny says.

"I can do anything I want," Ronnie tells her. "This is my place."

How many times have I heard that line? Too many to count. Ronnie's really that kind of asshole. And he has power because his apartments are the cheapest, and you'll put up with a lot when something's the cheapest.

"I'm gonna have to look really closely at your apartment for damage, too," he says.

"Oh! Well, you'll *love* this, then!" Penny chirps, whipping her phone out. "I've recorded the entire cleaning process. Would you like to watch it in real time or sped up? I have both versions as I'm planning on uploading them as soon as I get home. I have a whole cleaning channel. I call it Shiny as a Penny. Have you seen it?"

She presses play, and there's Penny, wiping down the walls in Mom's bedroom.

Ronnie scowls.

"I took plenty of before-and-after photos, too," she continues. "We've recorded the whole thing, haven't we, Tate?"

She looks at me, expectant that I play along.

"Your audience is clamoring for more cleaning content," I say.

"They are," Penny agrees. "Positively *clamoring*."

He's turned angry-tomato red. "Get your trash out of my dumpster, or I'm going to haul it out and dump it back in that apartment."

The blood drains from my face, and Penny's smile snaps away.

Her eyes light up viciously.

"Fine," she says. She stalks past him and toward the dumpster. With great drama, she flings the top open and then her arm toward me. "Tate?" she asks imperiously. "Some help up?"

Not sure she's serious, I walk toward her and make a step with my hand. She hefts herself into the dumpster and begins pulling all our trash bags out, tossing them one by one onto the cement. When she's done, she's stinky and she's the most perfect thing I've ever seen.

She climbs out of the dumpster and collects the bags, two in each fist, marches over to her station wagon and starts dumping them inside. I scramble to do the same, and in a few minutes, the car's stuffed and Ronnie's turned from tomato-red to rage-purple.

"Problem solved," Penny snarls at him.

"Like I said before: I'll turn the keys into the office," I tell Ronnie.

"And if you come up with any more 'problems' "—Penny actually air-quotes at him—"I'll solve those, too. So just stop, appreciate what a good tenant you had in Anna, and wish her the best of health, because that's what any decent human being would do."

"Penny," I say, mock seriously. "You know he can't be decent; he's a *landlord*."

Penny presses her lips together, trying not to laugh.

"You little—" he snarls.

I cut him right off. "The apartment is spotless. We have photographs of everything. You're gonna give my mom back her full deposit. Or I'll *classily* take you to court."

"I love technology," Penny says, turning to me with a grin. "We should get going. We have to take a trip to the dump now. Bye, Ronnie!"

Her ponytail bounces right out of there, and after I lock up the apartment, I follow, hopping into the passenger side of her station wagon stuffed full of garbage, breathing through my mouth while I roll down the window.

"Okay," Penny says, getting into the car and clicking her seatbelt shut. "Look in my glove box; there's a Ziploc full of loose change.

233

There might be enough in there to take this all to the dump, because if we take it home, the bears will be all over it."

I just stare at her, breathing through my mouth, sick with it.

Not with the garbage smell.

But with *it*.

Some girls don't get some things.

And I do not get Penelope Conner.

(But, oh, do I want her.)

42

Penny

"THE LOOK ON his face," Tate says, shaking her head. "I can't believe you did that."

"I can't believe you had to live under that jerk's thumb for so long," I fume.

"You gotta take what you can get." Tate shrugs.

"It's bullshit."

"I'm sorry we had to use all your change," she tells me. "I'll pay you back."

"Tate, no. You don't have to."

"It was *my* garbage from *my* apartment—"

"Just shut up. Okay?"

She does that almost-smile of hers. "Fine."

Tate stretches out on the hood of my car as I change in the back seat and get out to join her.

Below us, the county sprawls, Salt Creek and Blue Basin bisected by the river. You can see everything from up here, and when she'd suggested driving up here after the dump, I'd agreed.

I smooth my pants, the ones she gave me to change into, over my legs. The material is shiny and waterproof, an unfamiliar rustle against my skin. I'm swimming in her swimming clothes, the hoodie she shoved at me at least a size too big on her, so it's like three sizes too big on me.

"What?" I ask as she watches me fold up the sleeves.

"Nothing," she says, but her mouth quirks up as she stares down at the towns.

"It is not my fault I'm small."

She laughs. It lifts her a little off the hood as I clamber up next to her. "I didn't say anything!" she protests.

"You tall people. You have such superiority," I mutter.

"I just didn't want you to have to wear your dirty dress," she protests.

"I do appreciate that. It was gross. But I'll wash it; it'll be fine." I check my phone, but no texts from Mom. Just updates from Gran.

Mom texted once. The morning after I left, she texted me a thumbs-up emoji.

But nothing since. Every time Gran calls me, Mom's asleep. I don't want to think it's on purpose, but I can't help but think exactly that.

It's happening again. Mom's pulling away—but there's no *us* to pull away from anymore. It should hurt less because of that, but it doesn't.

It almost hurts more.

"You can see everything from here," Tate says.

"Yeah."

"I haven't been up here since—" She stops, even though we both know exactly how to finish that sentence.

I haven't been up here since the last time we were up here.

Me either. But if I say that . . .

I can't say that. Can I?

"Penny, what am I getting into here?"

It startles me into looking at her, my heart in my throat, thinking one thing, until she continues: "I thought when your mom moved back in with you, it was because things were better."

"*She* is better," I say. "She's as happy as she can get, I think. Especially now that your mom's going to be okay."

"The house—it's like you divided it. The upstairs is yours and downstairs is hers."

"That's exactly what we did," I say, and her mouth snaps shut, her dark brows drawing together like I'm crazy or something. "Don't look at me like that. It's not like she banished me to a tower or anything. We didn't plan it out. She just . . . she avoids Gran and me, okay? She spends all the time she can in her studio when she's not at work. Her bedroom's downstairs, and there's no reason to check on me."

"Does she ever go upstairs?"

"Last time she did, she tried to take his pictures away, and I cut myself wrestling one of the photos back. The blood's the only thing that made her stop. But that was . . . that was early on. She's better now."

"Are *you*?" she asks. "Are you better? Are you happy?"

I can't answer her. It's not like if I say the truth, it'll be real. It's always been real.

That's why I've run from it.

"Do you at least get to talk about stuff in therapy?" Tate asks finally, as I just keep staring out at the towns instead of at her.

"She made me stop."

"What?"

"Mom made me stop therapy."

I look at her then, because she's staring so hard at me that I can't help it.

"When did she do that?"

"The night you found me up here," I mutter. "We had a fight. That's why I was so upset."

"I thought your fight was about her selling the rafting business."

"That was the consequence of the fight about therapy."

She's looking at me like I'm a constellation she's trying to make out. "What are you talking about?"

I sit cross-legged on the hood, so I can lean my elbows on my knees. I need some kind of support if I'm gonna tell her.

"I fucked up," I say. "I asked her to come to one of my therapy sessions. And as soon as Jane, my therapist, started talking about sending me to a psychiatrist and discussing medication and how there might be some diagnosis that fit me beyond the PTSD from the accident, Mom started spiraling. And when Jane suggested I start rafting again—"

"Oh, shit," Tate says.

"Yeah. She exploded. Took me straight out of there and told me I was never going back. And when we got home . . ." I stop.

Her hand covers mine, her thumb rubbing over the scar on my own.

"You don't have to tell me."

My hand turns in hers, so we're palm to palm.

That's what my mother wants. For me to be quiet. For me to push things down and hope they'll never bubble up.

It's killing me.

"No," I say. "You were there after. I want you to understand the before."

THE TIME AT DAMNATION PEAK

Penny

A YEAR AGO

MOM DOESN'T SPEAK the entire ride from Jane's office. But when we get home, she goes into the house instead of storming off into her studio like I expect.

I watch her go, staying in the car for as long as I dare, but after about five minutes, I have to get out. If I wait too long, she might come back, she might be even angrier that I didn't follow.

Gran's trailer lights are on. I could go up there, I could hide.

I want to.

Tell your mother I love her.

I don't go up to Gran's trailer.

She's in the living room on the phone when I come in.

"That sounds good," she's saying as I creep inside, hoping I can make it to the stairs.

She snaps her fingers at me, and I freeze. No way out now. I reluctantly go into the living room, standing at the edge of the rug as she says, "Great. Thanks, Tim. I'll see you on Monday to iron out the rest of the details."

Mom sets her phone down and crosses her arms.

"Sit," she says.

I don't move from my spot.

"Penelope, *sit down*."

I take my time. I don't care if it makes her madder.

"Why were you talking to Tim?" I ask.

"I was checking something," she says. "I wanted to make sure he hadn't been letting you take any of the rafting equipment out."

"He hasn't."

"Have you been on the water?" she demands.

"No."

She gets up. Paces in tight little circles in front of me. She starts and stops a sentence twice. She's *wringing* her hands. I didn't even know people did that outside of the movies, but there it is. It's like she can't stop moving in nervous little bursts of energy that make me uneasy.

"Are you lying to me?" *Pace, pace, pace.* "Have you been on the river at all? That therapist—" *Wring, wring, wring.*

My eyes dart from her hands to her face, and I don't know why, but everything in me screams *run*.

"Jane was trying to explain coping mechanisms to you, and you just blew up instead of listening," I say, trying to keep my voice as steady as possible.

Pace, pace, pace. "That woman wants to put you on medication you don't need." *Wring, wring, wring.* "She's trying to diagnose you. With things you don't have. Utter madness. All on top of encouraging you to put yourself in danger! I'm going to report her."

"You're going to report her for doing her job?" I ask incredulously. "Mom, you're talking crazy—"

"I am *not* crazy!" Her entire face changes as she says it, a Jekyll-and-Hyde transformation that jerks me back in my chair.

"I didn't say you were. I said you were talking—"

"I'm not doing this," she declares. *Pace, pace, pace.* "You're going to listen to me. You're *fine*. We're both fine."

"Mom—" Because I'm not fine and she's not fine. How could we be?

"I made sure of it," she says, nodding her head, and then she keeps nodding, her eyes going steely. "I made sure of it."

"What are you talking about?"

"I'm making sure you have a future," Mom tells me, and then she smiles, and it chills me, how blank it is. "It solves everything. You'll have to follow the rules now."

"What did you do?"

"I'm selling Tim the business," Mom says, so casually, like she's not killing every dream I've ever had. Everything Dad worked for.

I want to scream. But if I do, I'm pretty sure she'll start, too, and if we both break, I think that's it.

No going back. No repair.

It scares me enough to breathe through the panic. "You can't sell the business," I say. "Dad always meant for me to run it with him. It's supposed to be mine."

If anything, it makes it worse, staying calm. She just keeps *pacing*.

"It is not yours," she snarls. "It's mine to do what I want. And I'm selling it. Every fucking piece of it. I'd burn it to the ground if it wasn't worth something."

"Mom—"

"I will not let you continue this insanity," she says. "*You* are the one who's talking crazy. You are not going to be some drugged-up zombie. You are not going back on the river. You are going to have a *life*. A safe one. Not some adrenaline ride that mangles you even more than you are."

As soon as it's out of her mouth, her eyes widen, like she's just realized what she said.

"Well, fuck, Mom," I say. "Tell me how you really feel."

"Penny, I—" She freezes. Caught.

"I'm not *mangled*," I tell her, and I sound strong, but my throat burns. "That's a shitty, ableist thing to say."

"Penny, I'm sorry. But you need to listen to me. I have your best interests at heart. You need money for college—"

"I'm not going to college," I tell her. "You can tell yourself anything you want about why you're destroying everything Dad left behind. But you're not doing it for me."

"You are *not* dying!" She stabs her finger at me. "You're not," she says again. "And neither is Anna. No one else is dying!"

Tears well up in my eyes, and the sharp pang inside me is all regret. I should have gone to Gran. I should have just hidden.

"No one else is dying," she says again. *Wring, wring, wring.* "No one else is dying." *Pace, pace, pace.*

I get up slowly as she just keeps repeating it like she's on a loop. *Pace, pace, pace.* "No one else is dying." *Wring, wring, wring.* "No one else is dying."

There's something dreadful building in my stomach. I don't even have a name for this growing, sick worry.

I reach out to grab her arm, and she smacks it away.

243

"Lottie? Who's yelling?"

Mom whirls on Gran, who's standing bewildered in the entryway as I run to her. Her arm wraps around me automatically as Mom rounds on her.

"You!" Mom shrieks. "You're the one who took her to that therapist in the first place."

"Lottie, what are you—"

"Do you want her to die, too?"

"What are you talking about?" Gran demands. "Penny, why don't you go to your room?"

"Don't tell my child what to do!"

"Lottie, did you take your pills?" Gran asks.

"I'm not on those anymore. I don't need them. Have you heard what nonsense this therapist is filling her head with?"

Gran's grip on me tightens. "Penny, go to your room."

"I—"

"She wants to drug her! She thinks it's a good idea for her to go back to rafting! Just put her on drugs and have her risk herself, go back to the thing that took everything—"

"Penny, *go*," Gran says, and my mother lets out this primal sort of scream at Gran's words that scares me so bad that I just *move*.

But I don't go upstairs. I go into the hall, and when Gran's and Mom's voices begin to rise, I take a right instead of a left, and then I'm out the door, their voices are fading, blissfully fading, and I'm running, running away, and I'm so grateful that I just keep going.

And then I'm gone.

44

THE TIME AT DAMNATION PEAK

TATE

A YEAR AGO

M Tate, I need a huge favor.

Who is this? T

M It's Meghan.

For a second, I blink at my phone. Why the hell would Meghan be texting me?

What's up? T

M Can you please go up to Damnation Peak and make sure Penny doesn't drive home? I'm pretty sure she's drunk up there.

Scratch that. I'm positive she's drunk. She never makes this many typos when she's sober.

Is she okay?

She had a big fight with her mom.

Lottie moving back in has been tough.

I'm so sorry. I know things are intense rn with your own mom's health.

I'm with my grandparents in Sacramento. I wouldn't bother you otherwise.

I just don't want her to drive. She's not texting back.

And if I ask Laurel...

My stomach twists even seeing Penny's girlfriend's name.

Well.

I think you're the better choice here.

Laurel would probably just start drinking with her.

I'm on my way. T

M I owe you.

Don't worry about it. T

· · ·

She's not singing when I pull up to the lookout at Damnation Peak, where you can see all the lights of town and the dark glisten of the river snaking through it. She's drunk-humming, leaning against her car, a bottle of vodka in her hand.

It's not a tiny one. It's one of those cheap gallon jugs that Marion uses to steep herbs in for tinctures.

"Christ, Penny, that's got to taste like paint thinner," I tell her when I get out of the car, slamming the door.

Her entire face lights up when she sees me. "Tate!"

"Penny. Where are your keys?"

"In the car," she says. "Where did you come from?"

"Meghan didn't want you driving off a cliff or killing someone."

Penny frowns. "I wasn't going to drive," she protests.

"It's like ten o'clock. What—"

"I'm gonna sleep in my car."

I stare at her.

"I have blankets! They're cozy."

"Penny . . ."

"You want some?" She pushes off the car and holds out the vodka.

I take the bottle and then empty it onto the dirt.

247

"Hey!" She scowls at me but just keeps swaying a little, not bothering to stop me.

"You've had enough."

"You don't know how much I've had!"

"I can guess." I grab her keys out of the ignition and make sure her parking brake is pulled. "You wanna go home now?"

"Mom's there, so *no*, I do not."

"Okay," I say, leaning against her car. "We can stay out here. But you can't sleep in your car, Pen."

"I told you I had blankets," she says. She goes over to her station wagon and flings the door open, her movements even more dramatic in her drunkenness. She brandishes the fleece blankets. "See?" She wraps one around herself like a cape, flapping it at me.

I can't help it. She's so cute, even this drunk and sad. I laugh.

Her eyes widen. "Oh my God! Did I make Ms. Serious laugh?"

She bounds over to me, kicking over the empty vodka bottle, sending it skittering down the sloped ground. "Whoops."

"You never laugh," she tells me. "You're always so sad."

"I'm not—"

I can't finish, because she reaches out and presses her finger between my eyebrows. She's in my space, too tipsy to be aware of it, to keep the distance she usually does.

(We look. We don't touch. Because when we do . . .)

"You've got a little furrow," she tells me. "Right here. 'Cause you're sad."

"I think you're the one who's sad right now," I tell her, gently pulling her hand away.

(She doesn't let me let go.)

"What happened?" I ask her.

She drops my wrist then, tucking her hair behind her ears. "Nothing," she says. "Nothing. Mom just destroyed my entire life. That's all."

"Penny . . . what—"

She spins away from me, suddenly agitated. The blanket flares out at the movement, and she clutches it tighter to her.

"What was she doing that entire time she was living with you and your mom?' Penny asks.

"I think you should ask her that," I say carefully.

Her stare has always been able to slice right into me. Sharper than any knife.

"I'm asking you."

I bite my tongue. There's so much to say. Too much.

There's a light in her eyes, gleaming in my headlights. She looks almost feral. A girl on edge. One wrong move, and I'll lose her.

"Did you have to lock up her pills?" Penny asks, and when I take too long to answer (because *yes*), she shrugs and says, "Gran had to lock up mine."

She doesn't look away; she stares at me like it's a dare instead of just a fucking heartbreak.

(If I woke up some morning and she wasn't here . . .)

I don't even hesitate. I cross the space between us, four steps and a shuffle, and then she's tight in my arms, burying her head in my shoulder. Her nose is a pinpoint of cold against me.

She stiffens for a breath, and then she's grabbing me back, her arms around my waist so tight as her tears trickle down my chest.

"Every time I think I've got a little bit back, she takes it away," Penny cries. "Why can't she just leave me alone? She blames me still. She wishes it would've been me, not him. I wish it, too."

I pull back so she can see my eyes. So she can see the truth on my face. "Well, *I* don't," I say quickly as she blinks, dazed at the ferocity in my voice. "Your dad didn't wish that. He saved you. You're here right now, with me, because he loved you so much that the last thing he ever did was save you. She can't take that from you—no one can."

Tears carve out little paths down her face as she stares up at me with wet eyes.

"No one can take him away from you," I say.

"She keeps trying," Penny says, her voice thick. "It'd be easier if I just gave in."

"Penny, you are the most stubborn person I've ever met," I say. "It wouldn't be easier if you caved to your mom's shittiness. Forget about her. Just for a minute. Look at me. Calm down. Feel your heart. Here. Breathe with me."

I take her hand and press it against her chest, my own covering it. Her heart thunders through her skin and mine, but breath by breath, it starts to slow.

It's not like meditation, even though that's where I got the idea. It's nothing like that when it's her and me and this. When my fingers are pressed against hers and the slope of her breast is just below my palm, and her eyes, those endless dark eyes, shimmer, barely blinking as she stares into mine like I'm a drawing that's missing something.

"Why did you come?" Penny asks.

"I told you, Meghan texted me."

"You could've texted Gran. Or Laurel."

Laurel's name brings everything into focus. Like this has been a fuzzy fairy tale until now. Back to cold, hard reality.

"Do you *want* me to text Laurel?"

She's shaking her head as soon as the words are out, and it's so sweet (I'm so selfish) that I don't even try to pull away.

(I tell myself I will. I *will*.)

"Why did you come?" she asks again.

"You're drunk," I warn her.

"You always show up," she says. "Why?"

"Penny..."

"Why?" And I hate it, how confused she sounds. It makes me want to actually answer. "Is Laurel right?"

Ice in my veins. My hand drops away from hers (my skin aches at the loss of her heartbeat).

"What are you talking about?" I ask shakily.

"She didn't believe me when I said we never..."

My stomach sinks.

"She said there had to be something...." Penny lets out a nervous laugh. "She said it was *obvious* we'd..." Penny rolls her eyes. "She was kind of bitchy about it, really."

"Laurel's always kind of bitchy," I say, and a giggle burbles to her lips, so suddenly she claps her hand over her mouth.

"Is she right?" Penny asks through her fingers.

"I'm not getting into Laurel's paranoia," I say, trying to fully pull away, but she's drunk too much vodka, clearly, because she says, "I wonder if I just—" and she reaches out and *taps* my lips, feather-light, and then she just kind of hesitates and her fingers trace my lips, and I'm just...

Gone. So fucking gone.

(But I *can't* be. There are so many reasons why, and so few to stay still . . . but here I am, staying still.)

"I wonder all the time what would make you happy," Penny says. "You only smile when you're with your mom."

"Penny." My words buzz against her skin. If she just tipped up . . .

(If I just bent down . . .)

"What would it take?" she asks.

(Her thumb is on my lower lip. Just . . . rubbing. Back and forth. I didn't know you could be touched so gently. So wonderingly.)

I wish the answer was as simple as *you*. But it's not. For either of us. We're too fucking broken. Our timing is never right. She does this only when she's drinking.

(I want to give in. I want to sink into her mouth. I want to be weak and take and take and take.)

But I can't. Too much has been taken from her. I'm not gonna fuck up her relationship, even if I don't like Laurel.

My hand wraps around hers, pulling it away from my lips. Her eyes flicker—hurt or relief? I don't know.

"I'll be happy if you let me drive, and you drink some water, and next time, text your girlfriend for a ride."

Her lips press together, and if I wasn't so angry, I'd shrink under the fury of her gaze.

"Coward," she says, and then she stalks past me toward my truck.

252

PART FIVE

Truth

(or: the time in the diner parking lot)

45

JULY 11

> The bear statue for the raffle just got delivered to my house. **R**

> **M** Great! I've picked up the gift certificates from Talbot's Bakery, the hardware store, and the antiques store so far.

> Meghan, you didn't tell me the bear was six feet tall! **R**

> **M** Whoops. Sorry! I thought I was clear.

> It's sitting in the middle of the driveway. I could barely get it off the truck with the delivery guy. It's that heavy. **R**

> **M** Do you need help moving it?

> Yes, I need help moving it. It's a six-foot bear statue carved out of a single log of heavy-as-fuck oak. **R**

M Someone's cranky.

R My neighbor's dog is going ballistic. He thinks Barry is a real bear.

M You mean Berry.

R Meghan.

M Admit it, you're laughing.

M You're at least smiling.

Remi is typing…
Remi is typing…

R You got me.

M Yeah?

R Yeah.

M Be there in a half hour.

46

TATE

JULY 18

"YOU AND DREW are conspiring against me," Mom complains as I put the finishing touches on my hair for work during our video call. I slide the final pin into the braid wrapped around my head. After almost three weeks of working at the brewery, Penny and I have fallen into a routine. Up at four, running by five, at the pool by seven, Penny to work at ten, and then my shift starts at eleven.

It hasn't been all smooth sailing at home. There are boxes everywhere still, because I don't know where to put anything without asking the moms. Penny is not a morning person and she hogs the coffee—but she never complains that breakfast is always steel-cut oatmeal and that I'm dragging her on a four-mile run five days a week.

We eat dinner at the kitchen table instead of in the dining room, and neither of us says it, but I think we both know that the dining room feels strange with just the two of us there. Sometimes as we eat whatever meal the line cooks at the brewery have given us, like we don't know how to feed ourselves, she works on her bullet journal, and sometimes I grab whatever mystery novel Marion has sitting around. But other times, we talk instead.

Sometimes it's like we can't stop, now that we've got no one else in the house but each other.

"I can't believe my own child is betraying me for the enemy," Mom says dramatically, jerking me back from the thought of Penny to focus on my phone.

"How is Drew your enemy when he's your right-hand person?"

"He keeps bragging to me via text about your knife skills—as if I didn't give them to you!"

I snort. "Mom, I can't walk inside that kitchen and *breathe* without him or Louisa being like, 'Oh, she's just like Anna.' So I think your legacy of instilling knife skills in me is secure."

"It better be," she mock-grouches.

"Tell me what the doctors said," I encourage her, grabbing my lip balm from my bag and applying it. The brewery bathroom is tiny, but it's clean. Partly because that's one of my jobs.

"Everything's good," she says, vague as ever. "Lottie's last checkup might be next week."

"Already?"

"It'll be three weeks," Mom says.

"Do you think you can come home then, too?"

"I'll probably be down here the full four," she says. "But don't distract me from my mission: I want to know how long Drew is leaving the yeast in the warm water—"

"Mom." I shoot her a look.

"I'm bored," she says, shifting in her bed.

"Marion not keeping you amused with card games?"

258

"She won my candy! All of it! I'm going to have to start writing her IOUs."

"Building up candy debt is the way to ruin, Mom."

She laughs. "Oh, sweets, I miss you."

"Me too," I say, my throat tight.

Someone taps on the bathroom door.

"I gotta go," I tell her.

"Remember to watch Drew make the dough!"

I turn my phone off and head to work.

When I finally get off my shift, I smell like ketchup and beer, and Penny's been sitting in the parking lot for three hours, waiting for me.

"Long day?" she asks when I open the door and get inside.

"Mom's still obsessed with what's wrong with the pretzel dough," I say, just to make her laugh.

But it only makes her smile, tight and fleeting. She's got her bullet journal spread out on the folding wooden desk she's rigged to fit around the steering wheel.

"Where did you get that?"

"Meghan made it for me," Penny says. "I told you, she loves DIY stuff."

She doesn't pack up her pens and journal. Instead, she fiddles with the cap of her blue pen, staring down at the page.

It's the house budget, with little snowflakes decorating the page.

"You planning for winter?"

She nods.

I scan the categories on the grid she's made, the expected costs versus the money in the bank. There's a lot more costs than money.

"I'm worried about heating the house," Penny admits. "Wood's expensive, but propane's even more. And my mom puts a space heater out in the garage while she works, and it makes the electric bill spike."

"My mom's gotta stay warm," I say. "She can't get sick."

"That's why I want to make sure we've got everything we need, but I've got no idea how to pull it off with our new budget."

"Can we cut down a tree or something, chop our own firewood so we don't have to buy it?"

She frowns, twirling the pen in her hand. "If you cut down a fresh tree, you've got to season it. But there is a tree that fell last winter. Back of the property. It didn't smash any of the fences, so Gran just left it."

"Is it a pine?"

"Yeah."

"Pine burns fast," I say.

"Oak's better," she agrees. "But it's a big tree. Lots of wood," she says. "You'll have to help me. I can't use the chain saw for a long time. My hands—"

"Of course," I say quickly.

She smiles. "Thanks."

"What is that?" I ask when we pull up to the front gate. Beyond it, in the driveway, is Remi's truck and next to it is a giant statue of a bear.

Penny drives up and parks behind the truck.

The bear towers over both of us on his hind legs, with a giant wooden blackberry settled on his shoulder, his paw clutching it like a sack of flour.

"That's a Blackberry Bear," Penny declares, standing in front of it, hands on her hips.

She's right—it looks like one of the statues outside of the diner. All the Blackberry Diners have at least three of them. It's probably a franchise rule or something.

"What in the world is it doing here? *Meghan!*" Her voice rises to a call on Meghan's name.

"We're in the meadow!"

I follow Penny past the house and toward the expanse of yellow grass that really needs to be cut. I should ask Penny to put it on whatever to-do list she has in her bullet journal.

Meghan's got a blanket spread out, and Remi's lying on his back, hand cradling his head as he stares up at the sky.

"I made pasta salad," Meghan declares when she sees us.

"What's with the Blackberry Bear?" Penny asks, plopping down next to her, taking a bowl of pasta salad when Meghan offers it.

"That's our big raffle prize for the fundraiser," Meghan explains.

"Meghan named it Berry," Remi says.

"How did you get them to donate it?" Penny asks incredulously. "The couple who makes them only does them for the diner."

"Fortuitous timing and charm," Meghan says. "We'll have to provide transport of the bear for whoever wins her, though, if they're local."

"You need two people to move Berry," Remi says. "Meghan and I managed—"

"I almost dropped Berry on your foot!"

"I was being nice, not mentioning that."

"I nearly broke his bones," Meghan says cheerfully. "But we wanted to get Berry out of Remi's driveway."

"One of the neighbor's dogs did not like Berry," he adds.

"So can we keep it here until Saturday?" Meghan asks.

"Sure," Penny says. "This is great," she tells Meghan, pointing her fork at the bowl.

Meghan beams. "Good, because I'm making it to serve alongside the tri-tip."

"Do you have a date when the moms are coming back?" Remi asks.

"Doctors said my mom could come home next Wednesday," Penny says.

My stomach drops. "What? When?"

Penny puts her fork down. "Gran texted me when I was getting off work. Mom's still trying to decide if she wants to come home or wait until Anna can."

"Are you going to go pick her up?"

"If she wants to come home, yeah," Penny says. "She's driving Gran crazy. It'd probably be better if she came back. Give them some space."

"She's gonna try to overdo it when she gets home. You know it," I warn.

"I'm thinking of switching the locks out on her studio so she can't get inside."

"That's brilliant," I say sincerely.

"Penny!" Meghan protests, and Remi snickers as I lie on my back next to him, staring up at the sky and losing myself in the chatter.

(With Lottie coming back, there'd only be so much peace to be had.)

47

Penny

JULY 20

ON MY ONE day off, I get to sleep in until nine, which is glorious. Tate's not back from the pool yet, so I go outside to the garage to prep the chain saw.

I walk past the door that leads to Gran's part of the garage—Mom's weird about her workspace. She worked out here even before Dad died, a courtesy extended to her by Gran that makes me shudder now—because Mom hasn't fallen far from just me. She and Gran used to not be . . .

So quietly mad at each other, I guess.

I worry it's getting even worse. They haven't had to share a house *ever*. Gran moved out to the trailer the day Mom moved in here, and they're good at avoiding each other, even when Gran's in and out of the kitchen and garden.

But they can't do that in Sacramento. I can hear it in the strain in Gran's voice when we talk, and in the silences in Mom's rare calls. Gran can't wait to get home, I can tell.

I pull the chain on the light and look around for the chain saw.

It's stored under the worktable, in a green plastic case. I lug it out carefully, setting it outside before going back inside to the pegboard where Gran hangs her tools. I select the handsaw, the clippers, and the ax. I also dig out a can of gas and a fire extinguisher.

The sun's bright as I set it all outside, just as I see my car coming up the drive.

"Good swim?" I ask Tate as she pulls a pink bakery box out of the car.

"Yep. I got you donuts."

I take the box from her, flipping it open. There are half a dozen perfect cinnamon crumb-cake donuts inside. "Did you forgo the oatmeal today?" I ask, even though I know the answer: She didn't. She ate her oats mixed with peanut butter and ran four miles and then swam all those laps and came back with donuts for me because . . . why?

Because she knew I'd like them? My cheeks burn at the thought.

"You need fuel for today. Don't want you wearing out."

"Do you need to rest before we get to work?"

"Nope," she says. "I'm good."

She pulls off her flannel shirt, exposing her white Turkey Trot T-shirt that she's not only cut the neck out of, but has also turned into a tank top and frayed the hem. The T-shirt fringe dances along her waist, and I keep getting distracted by the strips of skin I can see through it.

I clear my throat and shove a donut in my mouth to distract myself.

"If we load the chain saw and the tools and stuff in the wheelbarrow, it'll be easier," Tate says.

I nod around my mouthful of deliciousness.

Gran's property is terraced, with the house and the meadow next to it on one level, the access road behind the house, and then a slow incline of forest beyond. The fallen pine is near the property line and the old barbed-wire fence that uses pieces of telephone poles as fence posts—a hack of my grandpa's back when he had just married my gran. He apparently cut a deal for the poles, then cut the poles into posts for the fence so the dog Gran wanted wouldn't run off.

Tate and I get the wheelbarrow up the dirt road and past Gran's trailer. But that's as far as it'll go, so I grab the tools and the extinguisher and she grabs the chain saw and the can of gas, and we hike off the road and toward the fence line together.

"Did your mom decide?" Tate asks.

"Yeah," I say. "I'm gonna pick her up the day after the fundraiser."

I trudge behind her through the pines, our feet crunching through the too-dry pine needles and branches that make up the forest floor. We're heading into the worst of fire season the next few months, which is why I brought the extinguisher. One spark from a chain saw in the wrong place could be a hundred-acre inferno out here.

"You good with her coming home?"

"Better than Mom losing it on Gran," I say. "They need space or it's gonna be a shit show. Your mom doesn't need the stress . . . and she gets along with Gran. It's better this way."

"We gotta get the kitchen and living room cleared, then," Tate says.

"Are you gonna come with me to Sacramento? You can see your mom."

"If I can trade shifts with someone, yeah. Careful—squirrel nest!" She skirts around the bundle of leaves and stray dog fur.

265

"Please try to trade your shift," I practically beg. "I do not want to spend hours in the car with my mom alone."

"So I'm your buffer?"

"*Please?* I'm not above using puppy-dog eyes."

She side-eyes me. "Is this what it's gonna be like, living with a gaggle of Conners?"

"We are not a gaggle. We should at least be an unkindness of Conners. Like ravens. Or a murder, like crows. Crows are so smart. They form complex bonds and have transactional relationships, just like humans."

"They're basically feathered dinosaurs."

"Lots of dinosaurs had feathers. The way we picture them from the skeletons and fossils is likely inaccurate. But I guess we won't know until someone pulls a real-life *Jurassic Park*."

"Or we could learn from the movies and *never* do that," Tate says. "I'm concerned at how you say that like it's a given."

I smirk, thinking of all those hours I spent watching and talking about those movies with my dad. "I'm just saying I'd be first in line."

"I'm now going to be creeped out this entire day in the woods, waiting for a raptor attack," Tate declares, and I laugh as we come to a stop at the top of the fallen pine, the branches spread across the ground, the pine needles browning from all this time dead.

A fallen tree is chaotic. You don't really think about how huge they are until they're on the ground. When they fall, they're out of place, but also not, because really, *we're* out of place here. The tree belongs, both upright and fallen.

"What's the plan?" Tate asks.

"Strip it of the branches, set them aside to cut into kindling. Then use the chain saw to cut rounds. We'll set up a chopping station in a flat area and then bring pieces down to the road with the wheelbarrow."

I pick up the ax, pleased that my hand doesn't hurt too bad gripping it.

"Sounds good," Tate says. Her head tilts, taking me in.

"What?" I ask. My fingers flex around the handle, and I look down. Is she staring at my scars?

"Do you remember that book we read in elementary school?"

"What book?"

She picks up the handsaw and goes over to the tree, fifty feet of fallen pine in front of her, picking her way through the branches to get to the trunk.

"The one that inspired you to go off into the woods with an ax."

"*Hatchet*?"

"Yeah. That one."

The smile on my lips, it's unfamiliar. Because I don't get to talk about memories involving him a lot. She keeps drawing them out of me, though.

"My dad spent every night I was out there camping a hundred yards away, where I couldn't see him."

She smiles—one of those slow, hard-earned smiles that makes you feel like you've grasped starlight in your hand. "That sounds like him."

"You teased me about doing it at the time," I point out, climbing into the mess of branches with her.

"Because I thought it was cool and didn't want you to know."

"She finally admits it," I say to the sky, and it startles a laugh out of her.

"Caught," she says. She almost sparkles at me . . . and Tate doesn't sparkle. She simmers, but maybe not as much anymore. Maybe now, she gets to spark instead. Maybe the weight of worry has lifted, just a little. I hope so. She deserves it.

We get to work, falling into a rhythm as she saws and I swing. I have to stop every ten strokes or so to stretch the fingers of my right hand, but she doesn't comment on it, and I try not to let my eyes catch on her in those moments when I've stopped and she's still in motion.

But Tate in motion . . .

She is all strength and capability, the fringed hem of her shirt dancing as she breaks the half-sawed branch, snapping it with one swift, stomach-jolting stamp of her boot.

Sweat trickles down my back, and it's not because it's hot outside. It's her. It's remembering.

It's knowing what her thighs feel like against mine, the memory of the strong slope of her stomach and the Luna moth–like span of her rib cage imprinted in my mind and hands.

"You okay?" She rips me from my thoughts, and I should be thankful for it, but all my body wants to do is protest.

"Yeah." I look away from her. "Just stretching my hands."

"Let me know when you need to take a break."

"I'm fine," I insist.

"Okay. Then I'll let you know when *I* need a break," she says serenely.

I roll my eyes and get back to work.

"So what's *your* plan?" I ask her, fifteen minutes later, when the silence gets to be too much for me. I should've brought my phone to play music.

"Hmm?"

"You know all about my plan for after school. For better or worse."

"Trying to gather blackmail material on me?"

"Please. You are tediously honest. I bet you a hundred dollars your mom knows all your plans."

She's quiet. "Not gonna take that bet."

"Ha! See? I was right. So what's the plan? It's got to have morphed from 'just get out of here.'"

She keeps sawing. Back and forth, and I think maybe she'd be content with the rhythmic scraping of it forever, but she's strong and sure, and she cuts through the branch so it snaps free of the trunk.

"It's more than just 'get out of here' now," she admits.

"What is it?"

She leans back on her heels, looking down the tree at me. Are her hands as sticky with sap as mine? If I stepped forward, lumbered over the pile of pine branches, I could reach out and see.

"Get some college to pay my way because they want me to swim. Get a degree. Get a job that pays and is steady enough that Mom doesn't have to worry about money or insurance anymore."

She ticks them off her fingers, and I wonder, does she remember? That night in the shed when I told her about my thirty-five-step plan for life? I'd told myself for years she had more to drink than I did— that's why she held so still and unguarded when I cupped her face. She probably doesn't remember that like I do. Not that moment in the hay shed. Not the one on the porch or at the Peak.

But now . . . the way she's looking at me, almost daring, makes me wonder.

"What kind of degree? What kind of job?"

"Accounting or something, I think."

It's not what I expected. "Really?"

She shrugs, setting the saw onto a thick branch. "I'm good with numbers and people's bullshit."

"Good point." I drag another set of branches away from the trunk, adding them to the growing pile I'm making ten feet down from the very top of the fallen tree. "Is that what you really want, though?" I ask.

I can't help it, because she talked about her mom; she didn't talk about herself . . . and if she's on my side, doesn't that mean I should be on hers?

"I think it could be cool" is all she says. I try her tactic and wait her out. After at least a minute of sawing, she finally continues. "I thought about maybe going to L.A., see if I could work for people who manage athletes' money and stuff. If I get into the right school."

The picture becomes clearer as she paints it. "So you want to, like, manage *major* money."

"Lots of people in all kinds of pro sports start from families like ours," Tate says. "It's sink or swim."

"You're gonna be the money lifeguard?"

She ducks her head, and I know she's trying to hide her smile, but she can't—I know the angle of her neck and the curve of her cheek when she's smiling and not.

"I don't think I'll be putting that on the business cards."

"I'm very hurt."

"I can tell."

"You'd be good at that," I tell her. I can see it.

"Yeah?"

If her earnestness was a dagger, I'd be dead right now.

"Yeah. Really good. Because you're hard to rile."

She lets out a huff—her almost-laugh—and turns back to the branch. "I wouldn't say that," she mutters, and it's so soft I wonder if I wasn't supposed to hear it.

So I pretend I didn't, grabbing the ax again and getting to work.

48

TATE

JULY 22

THE DAY OF the fundraiser, loading Berry into Remi's truck takes the three of us, even with the ramp. Meghan's already at the grocery store, setting up the grills and tables.

"Here, this is your end," Remi says, tossing the rope across the truck bed.

Penny hesitates next to me, not picking it up.

Fuck. The accident.

"Here," I say, grabbing the rope. "I'll do it."

She looks up, the relief palpable. "Thanks," she whispers, casting a glance at Remi. He hasn't noticed anything, or at least he's not acting like he has.

"I think we're good," I tell Remi, giving a final tug and then a quick push against Berry's knee. The statue doesn't even budge.

We follow behind Remi's truck all the way to town, Berry rocking a little back and forth against the ropes as Remi takes the curves of the road.

Meghan's a multitasking genius, because the tables are all set up and the grills are lit by the time we get to the store. The parking lot's empty this early, but in time, it'll be full.

Remi's already hopped out of the truck and is loping over to talk to Meghan.

"Oh my God, they have matching aprons," Penny says in awed horror as Meghan holds out the apron and Remi puts it on. She says something, and he laughs. "Only twins and twee couples wear matching outfits, Tate," she continues.

I snort so hard that it makes her giggle.

"Come on," I say. "Let's go help."

My mom calls as I'm setting up the folding chairs, and I put her on video so she can see everything.

"You've taken over the whole lot!" she exclaims.

"Meghan got a lot of donations," I say, turning in a slow circle with my phone so she can see everything.

Mom beams, but in the background, I can hear voices and then a door slamming. Her smile fades for a second as she looks over her shoulder.

"You okay?" I ask, determinedly cheerful. Are Marion and Lottie arguing again?

"Yep," Mom says. "I'll let you go."

"Okay, but—"

"Kisses!" She blows me a kiss and is gone.

I pocket my phone, looking up from the bag of napkins I was about to set out on the condiment table. Remi and Meghan are grilling away, but Penny's at the far end of the lot, bending down every few seconds.

I tuck the napkins under the jar of ketchup and cross over to her.

"What are you doing?" I ask.

"I love these!" She bends down, her ponytail spilling over her shoulder as she plucks the bright pink sweet peas. "We can use them as centerpieces."

She's got a whole bouquet of them tucked into the pockets of her dress.

"Am I supposed to pick flowers, too? We've gotta get everything set up."

"So cranky." Her nose wrinkles, and I tell myself it's not adorable. (It is.) "I can fix that."

She reaches out unexpectedly, and I stand still, static in her presence (in anticipation of her touch). Her lips curve up as she tucks sweet peas into the elastics tied around the ends of my braids. "There." She smirks. "Since you're lacking sweetness."

"Oh my God," I say. I laugh it. "You are so fucking corny."

She smiles brilliantly at me, and I'm beaming at her like a fool (I am foolish, always, when it comes to her).

"You love it," she says, and then her smile falters and her eyes sweep down, and I can't help but wonder—is it because she knows? Or because she feels it, too? Because I swear, she steps away too fast for it to be meaningless.

"Come help me with the plates and stuff," I say, and she follows, her shoulders slumping like she's grateful to have an out.

Meghan has everything organized by the time people start arriving: she and Remi at the grills, Penny making sandwiches, and me taking money while selling drinks and raffle tickets. When noon rolls around, we're a well-oiled machine, with a steady line of people going

274

from the grill to the field next door to eat, watched over benevolently by Berry, whom everyone keeps taking selfies with.

I think everyone I've ever met comes by. It's so many people, so much caring, it puts me a little on edge. When Mrs. Kellogg, my second grade teacher, stops by and almost starts crying when she talks about my mom volunteering for the PTA, it makes three women in line behind her cry. Everyone wants to talk and ask questions, and I didn't think about this part of it until Penny starts stepping in when I take too long to answer.

When Remi's parents take over for a little bit so we can eat, he sits down next to me.

"You okay?" Remi asks me under his breath.

"This is great," I say, and he accepts my overwhelmed dodge because he's my best friend.

When we're done, we head back toward the lot. Meghan's beat us there, already back at the grill. Penny's nowhere to be seen.

"I gotta get more raffle tickets out of my car," Remi says. "Help Meghan, will you?"

"I dunno. Do I get to borrow your apron so she and I can match?"

He shoots me a scathing look. "I know better than to turn down a gift from a girl. Especially one I like. Plus, it has lots of pockets."

"So you *do* like her."

"I never said I didn't."

"You were so annoyed when I gave her your number at the start of the summer."

"I was wrong," he says simply.

"Wow."

He grins, his eyes hooking over my shoulder for a second, on Meghan. "Yeah," he agrees. "Wow."

And then he turns around and walks toward his truck, like it's that easy.

(Is it?)

"Hey, Tate!" Meghan grins at me when I jog over to the grill to help her.

"I'm spelling Remi for a sec," I tell her. "But you gotta tell me what to do."

"Oh, great, just take this spray bottle and spritz the farthest row of meat." She thrusts it into my hands. "This is working out better than I expected," she says as she wraps up another whole tri-tip. "There's so many people here!"

"We've already gone through that big roll of raffle tickets."

"Really? That's awesome!" She flips the tri-tips with tongs in both hands at a truly dizzying speed. "I never thought I'd like standing and cooking so much," she tells me with a grin. "Cooking over a live fire is way more fun than in a kitchen on a stove."

"New hobby, huh?"

"I owe it to Remi."

"You two are getting along."

She arches an eyebrow at me. "Is this the part where you tell me if I hurt him, you'll kill me?"

That almost makes me laugh. "No," I say. "This is the part where I tell you that he seems happier lately, and I think it's probably because of you."

Her teasing smile fades from her face, something vulnerable replacing it. "You really think so?"

"I do."

The smile that comes now isn't teasing. There's a softness to it that makes me think that maybe it's reserved just for him. (I know about those smiles that are reserved just for one person.)

"Thanks, Tate."

I keep scanning the crowd, but I don't see her. "Have you seen Penny?"

"She's taking a break inside for a second."

I nod, spritzing the meat like she told me. But she doesn't turn back to the grill.

"Can I ask you something?" Meghan asks.

"Sure," I say, thinking she's gonna ask about my mom or something.

"Are you ever going to make a move?"

I drop the tongs with a clatter. "What?!"

"Not on me." Meghan laughs at my shocked look. "Come on, Tate. You know what I mean."

"I don't—" I start.

"She lets you touch her hands," Meghan says.

I just stare at her, wondering what the hell she's talking about. "Huh?"

"Penny. She doesn't like it when people touch her hands. She pulls away. Have you never noticed?"

"I—" I don't know what to say. I guess I haven't.

(Because Penny lets me touch her hands. Not anyone else. Me.)

"You and I, we're friends, right, Tate?" Meghan asks. "I know we're not close, but—"

"Of course we're friends."

"Okay. Then I'm gonna say this. As *your* friend. It means something when a girl who doesn't let people even see her wounds inside lets you touch the scars on the outside."

I have to fight the words in my throat for a second, because I'm too scared to ask, but I need to.

"I've known you both for like seven years," Meghan says. "And between the sniping and the arguing and the mutual insistence you just tolerate each other for your moms, there's one thing I always noticed."

"What?"

"That when it comes down to it, you show up for Penny, and Penny shows up for you. To the point where it's not just a pattern. It's a given."

And there it is (the truth we can't seem to run from).

I have your back. You have mine.

"You know what I would call that?" Meghan asks.

"What?"

"Love." She shrugs when she says it and then reaches out and squeezes my shoulder, before turning back to the grill.

When we start packing up for the night, I go to the car alone. I take out the sweet pea blossoms Penny tucked into my hair. For a moment, I hold the two sprigs in my hands, the deep pink against my skin, and the idea of tossing them is unfathomable. But all flowers fade and die, even when they aren't cut.

I look around the car, trying to think. The only book I have in my bag is last year's math book, so I press the flowers between the pages of that. I tell myself as I hurry back to help pack up the tables that it's because the flowers will look pretty.

(It's not.)

But it's not a reminder either.

I'll remember long after the dried, pressed petals crumble, because some things grow brittle with age.

But not this feeling.

(*Love.*)

49

THE TIME IN THE DINER PARKING LOT

TATE

JULY 22

"KEEP IT LEVEL! Are you sure you don't want me to walk backward?" Penny asks me.

"I'm fine," I insist. "Just two more, right? Then we're all done."

"Well, we have to deliver Berry to their new owner next week."

I adjust my grip on one of the tables we borrowed, looking over my shoulder to carry it across the Blackberry's parking lot. They're not the flimsy plastic kind, so they're heavier than you'd expect.

We lean it against the back wall of the diner next to the others. I'm digging in my pocket for my work keys when I hear a car door slam, followed by Penny's quick intake of breath.

I look up and all I can think is *fuck* and then I say it, because—

"Fuck."

Laurel strides across the lot like she's leading herself into battle, blond curls swinging around her shoulders. Penny stiffens next to me, stepping back until she hits the wall.

"This is the back door, Laurel," I say.

"I'm aware," she says, like I'm an idiot. "Can't a girl say hi?" She swings her keys on her finger, back and forth. "I heard about your fundraiser. I was gonna stop by, but I lost track of time."

Penny and Laurel stare at each other, and I'm between them (*fuck*—once again, I'm between them).

Should I move? (I am forever moving out of my own way, aren't I?)

"I've been texting you," Laurel says to Penny. "Ever since I heard your mom was in the hospital."

"I know." Penny's chin juts out as she says it. I want to be mad, but I didn't exactly tell her about Laurel confronting me in the locker room, so I'd just be a hypocrite.

"Then you didn't block me." There's something triumphant about the way Laurel plays with her curls. "I wish you would've answered. My mom wanted to send flowers. I ended up having to call Lottie myself to figure out where to send them."

"When did you call my—" Penny's mouth shuts so hard I think she clamps down on her tongue. I want to wince in sympathy.

"I was worried," Laurel continues. "I really like your mom."

"She *really* doesn't like you," I mutter, and Laurel's eyes narrow at me. "What?" I ask her innocently. "Were you under the impression that Lottie did?"

"So it is true," Laurel says, her brown eyes skittering between the two of us. "Lottie told me about it, but I thought maybe it was just the morphine."

"What are you—" Penny starts to say, and then *her* eyes get all big, and she turns bright pink. "Oh."

Laurel rolls her eyes and flicks her hair over her shoulder in the kind of movement that has me begrudgingly admiring the smoothness of it. "Yeah, she told me all about you two."

I frown. What is she talking about?

"How did she put it?" Her keys swing as her fingers tap her hip. " 'They finally came to their senses and got together,' I believe it was. I'm sure you all laughed about it." She rolls her eyes. "But really, who's laughing when it was *me* who was right all along?" She stares hard at Penny, not meanly, but searchingly. "You gonna say something, Pen?"

There's a beat of screeching silence as I try to understand and just . . . don't. I'm caught between Penny and Laurel, and it's so familiar (too fucking familiar)—but last time, I knew what to do.

Now I don't know anything at all.

"Yeah," Penny says. "Front door's that way."

Laurel doesn't move.

"I knew this would happen. I predicted it," Laurel tells her. "You're a liar if you say I didn't. I told you she—"

"—and you were wrong then," Penny says firmly.

When? What is she even talking about?

Laurel's arched eyebrow is what really gets me before she sneers. "I don't believe that for a second."

"Oh, fuck you," I say, because, really, *fuck her* with her dodges and justifications. She's been full of them since the start.

"Forever the protector," Laurel says, and then she seems to take Penny's dismissal to heart, because she turns around and stalks off toward the diner, shaking her head like she can shake us off.

"Oh my God." Penny startles like a deer across a highway, heading to the car. I follow her, my entire body numb except for my heart, beating terribly loud in my chest.

282

"I'm gonna be sick," Penny says, bending down next to her car and breathing hard. "I managed to avoid her all semester last year."

"Penny."

"Seriously, don't look at me if I start throwing up," she warns, breathing deep as she leans against the driver's door of her station wagon.

"Penny!"

She flinches, looking up at me.

"What is Laurel talking about?" I ask slowly.

Penny looks like she swallowed a cup of rusty nails. "I—I was going to tell you."

"Tell me *what*?"

"Our moms kind of think we're dating."

"What?" The confirmation out of her mouth is so staggering that my knees might buckle. I want to lean against the car, but that's weakness, and I'm mad enough not to show any of that to her right now. (Maybe ever. Tate, you should've learned your damn lesson the first time.)

"Remember that night you found me on the lake? And your mom caught us coming back wrapped in blankets?"

I'm silent, my mind churning. That was over a month ago. That was before the transplant. I would've known if my mom thought—

Oh my God. Is this why Mom's been so weird and sappy? I thought it was the transplant, but if she thought Penny and I—

(My head is going to explode. Just . . . shatter into brain pulp.)

"Your mom made an assumption," Penny continues, tugging at the end of her ponytail nervously. "She asked me—" She turns scarlet.

"What?"

"I mean, she just . . . she said something that made me realize she thought we were dating."

"What did she say?"

"Tate . . ."

"She's my mom!" I burst out. "*My* mom, *my* business. It's in the freaking truce." I slap the hood of the car so hard my palm stings.

"She asked me if we were being safe, okay?" Penny snaps. "She assumed we'd snuck out to have sex, which I still don't understand, because we have two perfectly good beds at home and they're right across the hall from each other. And she started talking about sex ed, so I just told her, yes, we were being safe, before she could whip out a condom and demonstrate how to turn it into a DIY dental dam, because it was *that* awkward. I panicked about correcting her, because if she found out I'd been kayaking, she'd have told my mom. If you wanna throw down the truce, we weren't going to upset the moms, were we? And she seemed really pleased. I was going to tell her after the transplant, but by then, she'd told *my* mom and they were both like, in their rom-com happy place about it and I just . . . I thought I could figure out how to explain."

"To whom? Me or them?"

"Both," Penny says, without a lick of hesitation, which tells me it's probably the truth.

(It doesn't matter. She's been playing a game this whole time. Foolish fucking girl.)

"I made a whole plan in my bullet journal about it," she says, because *of course* she did.

"You've been fucking with me for the moms' benefit," I say out

284

loud, because I need to hear it out loud. I need her to hear it, what she's done.

Her eyes widen, horror floods. "What? No. God, no. That doesn't even make sense. They're not even here!"

"I don't believe you. Why should I?"

Her eyes aren't horrified anymore. Now they flash. Anger spills, and there she is, the Penny who's all fearless instead of fears, because it wrenches out of her mouth, maddening and biting:

"I don't know, Tate, maybe because *this*"—and she flings her fingers at me, into the space between us (into that spark and simmer that is her and me and our history)—"it isn't *new*. Maybe you should believe me because we've spent almost half our lives ignoring the *thing* between us. I don't need to make it up to fuck with you or fake it for anyone else. It's there. It's *always* there. The *thing*."

I laugh. Scornful bubbles of noise that I'd never dreamed of wanting to aim at her (until now). "You can't even say it."

And maybe I do it to goad her. Maybe I do it to see what she'll do.

"What do you want me to call it? Meghan would call it 'energy.' " Oh, God, she's doing air quotes again, and I shouldn't find it cute, but it's there, under the layer of anger.

(She let my mom think we were *dating*. . . . What the fuck?)

Penny steps forward, and I fight the urge to retreat, only to fail because I'm already against her station wagon.

"Is *tension* a better word?" she asks.

Another step.

I really, really need to get out of here. She's got the look in her eye. The look from the hay shed. From Damnation Peak. All dare, no fear.

"Shared history?"

"I didn't ask to share your history," I croak out.

She's right in front of me now.

"I know," she says quietly.

She places her hand on the station wagon, right over my slumped shoulder, and then lifts the other hand as well, until her arms bracket me. When I straighten, slow and steady in the space between, we make a slanted *H* against the car, her arms linking our bodies into the letter, and I never loved a shape more than in that moment, her face and breath so close.

"What would you call it, Tate?" she asks.

Remi had been right at the beginning of the summer. And I'd run away from it. I'd denied it. But here I am, in the thick of her thorns.

Here she is, reaching inside my rib cage and squeezing my heart into a wreck.

"Please," she whispers, so close I can feel her breath on my lips. Her hands drop from my shoulders to my waist, two of her fingers hooking into my belt loops, and I think I might die if she tugs me forward, but she doesn't. She just watches me, wide-eyed and earnest and closer than she should be, and I sway forward, captured by her for a moment.

"What would you call it?"

Love.

"Trouble." The word tears out of my mouth, right from my pulpy mess of a heart. A truth I can't run from.

And then I tear away from her. Soft skin above rough denim, her fingers slipping from my belt loops . . . *Go back, go back.*

But I don't.

I run.

PART SIX

Break

(or: the time in Yreka)

JULY 22

Tate **P**

Are you coming back? **P**

Penny is typing…

Penny is typing…

Please. **P**

I'm sorry. **P**

. . .

Do you know what the hell just happened? **R**

M ???

Tate's here. She's crying all over my bed. **R**

M Oh, God. Did something happen with the moms?

No. R

Something happened with Penny. R

M Oh shit.

M Something bad, you think?

She's crying!! R

Tate doesn't cry. R

M Fuck. Let me text Penny and see what's up.

. . .

M You okay?

Do you know where she is? P

Is she with Remi? P

M Penny, what the hell happened?

M You two were great all day at the fundraiser!

M Do you need me to come get you? Where are you?

I fucked up. **P**

Oh, Meghan. **P**

I fucked up so bad. **P**

51

Tate, P

I'm sorry. I should never have let your mom's assumption lie. I should have corrected her in the moment, even if it meant telling her the truth about me kayaking again. P

I didn't mean to use you as a human shield for my secrets, but I did, and it was wrong and I'm sorry. P

I will do whatever you want. I will group chat the moms right now and tell them everything. I'll call them and admit I lied. I'll tell my mom everything—about Meghan and my plans after school. Whatever you want. I don't care. P

I care that I hurt you. P

I don't want to hurt you. P

I never want to hurt you. P

That's like the opposite of what I want to do. P

I thought… P

The last few weeks, I thought… P

I thought maybe I made you a little happy. P

I just want to make you happy. P

Even if that means my head on a spike. P

Metaphorically, hopefully. P

But if you really want to go literal… P

I know I have more to apologize for than just this. P

You told me in Yreka that I was running, and you were right…and I just kept running. P

I shouldn't have. P

Please. Just talk to me. P

Tate is typing…

My heart leaps when I see the little bubble appear. And then when my phone buzzes and the image becomes clear, all my hope crashes to the ground.

She's sent me a photo of the Truce Agreement. She's underlined
the last edict:

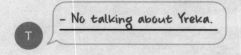

- No talking about Yreka.

THE TIME IN YREKA

TATE

5 MONTHS AGO

I'M IN YREKA for a swim meet with the whole team, and the day's been perfect. I won every single one of my events. I'm flying high, texting Mom my times and getting a gajillion emojis back, and then a video of her and Lottie dancing to "We Are the Champions" in the brewery kitchen, with Drew and Louisa accompanying on spoons and pots.

The motel we're at is cheap and cheesy and dated, with wagon wheels as the prime theme of the decor and seventies wood paneling on the walls. We're two to a room, and Theresa jokes she'll kick me out of the queen bed that takes up almost all of our small room if I steal the blankets.

"As long as you don't hog the bathroom."

"Don't worry; I'll be here only to sleep," she says.

I know Skylar's brought a bottle of vodka, because I overheard her talking about it at the meet. I don't really care that they're hiding it from me, since I'm looking at an early night of stretching and sleep.

"I'm gonna go to Skylar's room," Theresa tells me after we unpack, and without even looking in a mirror, she reapplies the fuchsia lip gloss she always wears. It's impressive as hell. I'd look like a clown if I tried to do that. She lightly smacks her lips together, pocketing the gloss. "You want to come?"

I collapse on the bed. "I'm kind of wiped. I'm just going to stay in."

She nods, like she's expecting it. "'Kay. I have my key, so just leave the deadbolt unlocked for me."

I nod. "Good job today on the relay."

She smiles "Thanks. You too."

Theresa leaves, and after I shower all the chlorine off, I get out my foam roller and turn the TV on, focusing on my aching shoulders. I always swim the butterfly part on the relay team—it's not my best stroke, but I'm faster than the other girls. And you want to start and finish strong.

When it gets to be nine and I've watched yet another episode of *Murder, She Wrote* on the motel TV that gets only eight channels, I text Theresa: Hey, just reminding you that curfew is at 10.

I text my mom good night, but I don't get an answer. She's probably starting to wind down the kitchen for the day. I watch the video of her and Lottie again, because it's ridiculous in that sweet way that makes you feel warm, even as you're laughing at how silly the two of them are.

It's almost curfew, and Theresa still hasn't shown up or answered my texts. I'm not her babysitter, so if she wants to spend her night sneaking behind Mrs. Rawlins's back and swimming tomorrow hungover, I'm not going to try to find her. But I'm annoyed that I can't deadbolt the door as I get ready for bed.

And even more annoyed when I hear her banging on the door. Did she lose her key?

I yank it open on a "What the hell, Theresa?"

But it's not Theresa.

It's Penny, standing there in the night, illuminated by the yellow motel light.

For a second, I stare at her, because she's so out of place and unexpected.

And then all that falls away when I realize she's crying, mascara-down-her-cheeks, lipstick-bitten-off sobbing, and it makes me reach out before I can think it through, grasping her wrist gently and pulling her inside.

"Penny, what are you doing here?" I ask her as I shut the door.

She throws herself on the bed—actually *throws* her body on it—and I don't think I've ever seen someone do that. "She told me she loved me" is all she says between tears, and I can feel little splinters of ice working their way under my skin, because Penny is not acting like a girl whose girlfriend has declared she loves her.

"Why would she do this? She kicked me out of her room! Like *I* was the problem. *They* were the ones who were undressed! Has it been going on this whole time?" Her eyes snap to mine, and there's a beat of horrified silence on her part and confusion on mine before she says, "Did *you* know?"

"Know what?" I ask, bewildered.

"Are you lying to me?" Her voice rises. "Am I the joke of the entire team? Oh, God, have I been a giant joke between all of you this whole time?"

"Penny." I cross the room and sit down on the bed next to her. "Breathe, okay?"

She lets out a breath that's more sob than air.

"Good. Now tell me what you're talking about. Why are you here? Why are you crying?"

More tears. I scramble for the box of tissues on the desk.

"I came up to surprise Laurel. Her roommate gave me her key. I had it all planned out, and I..." She dissolves into tears again, and before I can ask more, there's a banging on the door.

"Oh, God." She straightens at the sound. "Is that her?" She looks around frantically, like she's expecting a wardrobe to spring up so she can escape through it, portal-fantasy style. "Please don't let her in, Tate. Please. I know you couldn't care less, but—"

My heart twinges at that assumption. "Don't worry," I say. "Just... stay here." I go over to the door and peep through the hole. I pull the towel out of my hair, twisting the damp strands into a knot at the back of my neck.

"You're leaving?"

(The way her voice cracks breaks me.)

"I'll be right back, Pen. Okay?"

It takes her a few seconds to nod.

"There's more tissues in the bathroom" is all I can think to say before I open the door wide enough to just slip through it, letting it slam shut, automatically locking.

Laurel stands right outside, her curls a halo around her head, her eyes narrowed. She barely has enough time to step back before I'm in her space, just out of necessity to let the door close.

"Is she in there?" Laurel demands.

"Walk with me." I don't even wait to see if she follows, I just go—down the stairs and toward the parking lot.

"God, Tate," she says in disgust, but it works because she trails after me.

My sneakers hit asphalt, and I keep going, moving toward an empty corner, across the way from the smoking area that's made up of wagon-wheel halves stuck upright in the ground.

I turn around, folding my arms, and I wait. Guilt gets to you, if you have a smidge of good.

She shifts from foot to foot, her shoulders hunching.

Laurel really is so damn pretty. She and Penny together have been an assault of cuteness and kisses and crop tops. But there's something in the way Laurel's always looked at me, even before they started dating (like I held all the things she wanted in my palm easily).

"Did you bring me over here to fight me?" Laurel drawls, finally breaking the silence that I've let stretch between us.

"Did you do something that I should fight you about?"

"It's none of your business, Tate." She's clipped. Angry.

(Definitely guilty.)

"Like hell." I jerk my thumb toward the building. "She's crying in my motel room."

"I didn't know she was coming up here. She walked in on something, and before I could explain—"

"Explain what?"

Her mouth clicks shut. Her lips are shiny under the streetlight, and I blink, the sight of them tumbling around in my head.

Laurel doesn't wear that fuchsia-colored lip gloss.

Theresa does, though.

"Explain *what*, Laurel?" I am completely aware of stepping forward—that's no unconscious move on my part. Because I want to punch her right now. Did she actually do what I think she did? Did she really cheat on Penny?

"It was just a moment, Tate," she says. "A weak one. But it was just one kiss, I promise. I could have explained! I would have told her about it, I swear I would have. But Penny saw us and she ran."

Her eyes narrow. "She ran to you." She laughs. *"Of course."*

Something buzzes in my head like a warning. "Stop it."

She shakes her head. "No, I don't think I will. I don't have to play nice anymore. And I've been playing *so* nice when it comes to you."

She steps into my space this time, but she's still shorter; I still look down on her. And I'm not the flinching or retreating type.

"I tried to ignore you," Laurel says. "But you're always around, aren't you? Star of the swim team . . . I don't think there's one person who has a bad thing to say about you at school. Stoic, sad Tate, with the sick mom and everyone wanting to help her."

"Talk about my mom again, and we're going to have a bigger problem than we already do."

She lets out a laugh, but I can hear the fear under it.

"I couldn't get away from you at practice or at school, and when I met Penny, I thought, well, at least my love life is free of this girl. But then Penny . . ."

She looks away, like the memory hurts.

"What about Penny?" I hate myself for asking, but I want to know. She got to know Penny in a way I never will, and I hate her for that . . . and hate her even more for squandering it.

"Penny worked so hard to never talk about you. But I *knew*. I just knew." She smiles, but it's more of a grimace as she shakes her head, her face struggling against a total crumpling. "One of you was going to snap eventually. So I guess I did instead." She lets out a watery laugh. Her eyes shine, and I think it might be with tears.

Why would she fake this?

They must be real, and it makes my stomach twinge (because it means her feelings for Penny are—*were* real).

"You're just making stuff up in your head to make yourself feel better about cheating."

"I'm not. And if you don't really see it . . ." She shakes her head. "I don't believe it."

"Penny doesn't talk about me because she doesn't think about me. We're not friends."

"Yeah, you two are definitely *not* friends. Ask Remi. Or Meghan. Ask anyone either of you are *actually* friends with." Her smirk's back, and this time, it *is* mean. "Ask your moms."

"Ask them what?" I'm amazed I can keep my voice level. She's fucking with me, I know she is. But I can't help but walk right into it.

"You *know* what," she hisses. "You're smart. And you're sneaky. But you watch her when you're in a room together. And she watches you."

I don't deny it. (I can't, because it's totally true on my part and maybe a little on hers, because sometimes when I look for her across a room, she's already found me.)

"I'm out of here," I tell her.

"I can follow you back to your room, you know."

"You won't even get to the sidewalk."

"Oh my God." She jabs her finger at me. "*That*. Right there. Do you not hear yourself? You two may keep your distance when you can, but you and Penny are like your own personal wolf pack. You'll bite anyone who gets close to you."

My chin tilts up. "Penny came to me. She told me to not let you or anyone else in. I'm just listening to her."

"Why? She's apparently not even your friend. She's *my* girlfriend."

"If you cheated on her, I don't think that's true anymore."

Her lips snarl the word. "Bitch."

"Probably. But not when it comes to this."

"You can't hide her away forever," Laurel snaps. "She has to see me. We have school. She can't hide."

"Penny can do whatever she wants. And I'll help her. I'm done now."

"Well, I'm not!"

I shrug and turn around. I'll admit it: There's a part of me that wants her to go for me. But I'm not going to get into a fight unless I'm defending myself. Not when Penny's crying in that room alone. Also, my mom would be pissed.

But Laurel's a coward, and she lets me go. She probably runs right back to Theresa. I can't decide if I'm mad at her, too. Theresa and I have always gotten along. Maybe Laurel told Theresa she and Penny broke up before they . . . did whatever they were doing when Penny walked in.

Dread builds as I climb up the stairs, unlock the motel room, and step inside. Penny's spread out on my bed, bundled in the scratchy comforter like she's a badger who's found its burrow. Her entire head is covered in the blanket, but every few seconds I hear a sniff coming from it, so I know at least she's breathing and not suffocating beneath the polyester.

"Penny, you okay?"

She doesn't answer. Just more sniffling.

I check my phone for the time. Mrs. Rawlins is gonna be by to check on us any minute. All I can hope is that Theresa stays put with Laurel or something.

So I rustle around the room and pack my stuff for the next day's round of events and turn the lights out, so when Mrs. Rawlins knocks on the door ten minutes later, I can open it, and all she sees is the lump of blankets that is Penny and assumes it's Theresa.

"Everything good in here?" she asks when I open the door for her.

"All good," I say.

"Night, Tate. Theresa."

"Night."

I close the door before Penny has to fake an answer. I hear Mrs. Rawlins's footsteps down the hall, her knock on the door of the next room, and let out a sigh of relief.

In the dark, I look over at Penny, bundled in blankets, and I feel like sighing again. I walk over to the bed and tug on the top blankets.

"Penny, can I have one of these? I've gotta make a bed on the floor."

She lets out a huff, and I'm seriously wondering if I'm going to have to sleep in the tub with my swim parka, when she finally emerges, flinging the blankets off with a gesture that is definitely not butterfly-like. She switches on the light on the bedside table.

Her nose is red, and so are her eyes, and the running mascara makes her look like a very cute, very sad raccoon.

"You're not sleeping on the *floor*, Tate, honestly." She gets out of bed. "I'm going to shower."

She disappears into the bathroom, and I don't have any choice but to sit on the edge of the bed, trying to breathe. I hear her turn on the shower, and she stays in there for a while, long enough that I'm lying on the bed by the time she comes out wrapped in a towel. When she sees the extra pair of sweats and the T-shirt I've set on the edge of the bed, the look on her face is hard to puzzle out. But she picks them up and disappears back into the bathroom... and when she comes out, she's wearing my clothes. (It's stomach-dipping to see her in *my* shirt.)

Penny sits on the right side of the bed, her back to me as she finger-combs her wet hair and starts to braid it. The Earth Day T-shirt that I'd cut the neck out of slips off her smaller shoulder much farther than it does mine, and I want to carve the memory of her in my clothes into my brain so deep, it'll be the last thing I see before I die.

I swallow. Sleeping on the floor would be a better choice. Much, much better.

But I stay in the bed as she finishes braiding and slides in next to me.

(I am so fucking brainless sometimes.)

She switches off the light, and in the silence, I can hear her shuddery breath.

"Are you okay?"

Penny shakes her head. There's enough light coming from the bathroom that I can see the movement, the line of her profile.

"What did Laurel say?" she asks finally.

"She said it was just one kiss—"

Penny snorts. "Considering she was down to her panties, I don't think so."

304

"I hate that word."

That makes her laugh, and it actually has some humor in it. "Panties? Of course you do."

Penny shifts toward me, onto her side, and I mirror her so we're facing each other. "It wasn't just one kiss, Tate."

"I believe you."

"You do?"

"Of course. I didn't know she was messing around," I tell her again. "I really need you to believe that. If I'd known—"

"—you would've told me?"

"*Yes*," I say, hating the sarcastic edge to her voice. "Fuck, Penny, who do you take me for?"

"I dunno," she mutters.

"When have I ever lied to you?"

I don't realize it's the wrong thing to say, even after it's out of my mouth.

(I don't realize it's a lightning bolt between us.)

But she's quiet so long, staring at me in the dark, and the longer it goes on, the more I can't look away.

"You haven't," she says finally. "You always tell the truth. Even when it's uncomfortable as hell."

"I would've told you," I insist.

"Then I guess it sucks you didn't know," she says, her voice growing thick with tears.

"I'm sorry. I know you—" I don't want to say it. But I know it's true. It's not like with Jayden. She cared about her. Maybe even . . .

(I can't even think it, I hate it so much.)

"It doesn't matter," she says, so dully it's almost like she's said it a million times already . . . or maybe thought it. "I knew better. I did. I just thought—" She sniffs. "God, I'm so stupid."

My stomach twists at the self-loathing. "You are *not*," I say fiercely.

"What else would you call a girl who keeps trying to get people who obviously don't love her to love her?" Penny demands. "First my mom. Now Laurel. I need to accept it."

"Accept what?"

"That I just don't . . . I don't have *it*. That thing that makes people love you. I'm too much or too little, or something. I know I'm bossy and I can be annoying—"

"*Penny.*" My fingers find hers on the bed, in the dark, and her hand's close enough to her face that I can feel the hot splash of her tears on the back of mine.

"She said it once," Penny whispers, broken words that have me horrified. "That I was . . . that I was hard to love."

"*Fuck* Laurel," I growl.

"No," Penny says, and the horror sinks into something new, something so much worse, I'm not sure there's a word when she says what comes next: "Not Laurel. My mom."

And yes, I want to say *Fuck Lottie* in that moment, but I know I can't, because it's not that simple, which is even more enraging.

"No one's ever going to love me," she says hopelessly, so sure of it that I can't stand it, in that bed with her (and loving her . . . always, always loving her).

I'm doing it before I think it through, because if I think it through, I won't start, let alone follow through.

"Penny." I say her name quiet in the space between us, question and comfort wrapped into two syllables. "Come here." I tug lightly on

306

her hand, my other arm stretching out, offering my space to make into hers (ours).

And she does. She cuddles into me, tear-stained and grieving (always grieving) . . . and she *fits*. It's something I can never unknow. How she fits right under my chin, the top of her head and the crook of her part and the lay of her hair in the braid against my arm a new territory to learn. Her hand clasps mine to her chest between us, into the softness and slope of her, and my stomach throbs, my mind splitting in a million different directions.

But my body knows what to do. My free hand knows to stroke her hair, and the little sound she makes when I do tells me it's right, and there's not an inch between us, our arms and legs tangled, but we don't talk and we barely move. And slowly, inch by inch, I can feel her body relax and then sag into the heaviness of sleep.

I don't stop stroking her hair, even when I'm sure she's drifted off.

I don't say it until I'm sure she can't hear me.

(But I have to say it.)

"You're not hard to love," I whisper into the darkness, my words pressed into the top of her head above my fingers, like they'll be able to sink into her mind and body and heart . . . so she'll see herself like I do. "Yeah, you can be bossy, but you're also good at everything, so who cares? And everyone's annoying sometimes. But you've *never* been hard to love. And I know, Penny. Because I love you. I've loved you before I even understood what it was."

I close my eyes against it, the words I thought would be forever unspoken. It's the cruelest trick, the girl I want in my bed, in my arms, the words finally spoken . . . but nothing is like I'd dreamed when I let myself. Because she's heartbroken and I'm angry at everyone but her,

307

and we'll forever be these two comets in the sky. The crash would be galaxy-changing, but we're always going to miss each other in a mess of what-ifs.

My thumb runs along the ridge of her braid lying across her shoulder. And I remind myself: This, this is all I get. But it's hard to remember that, wrapped up in her, her hand at the small of my back, under my shirt.

(What if...

... you told her?

... you kissed her?

... it was okay?

... it was wanted?

... some girls do get some things?)

53

5 MONTHS AGO
1 A.M.

M How did it go?

M Was Laurel surprised?

M I want to know everything!

M I mean, not everything, obviously. But you know!

Meghan, this is Tate. T

I know it's really late. Can you text me back when you get this? T

M I'm here. Did something happen to Penny? Should I call you?

Penny's okay right now. T

M What happened?

She and Laurel had a fight. She's here with me in my room.

Can you drive up and get her before we have to check out?

I'll be there.

Thanks.

54

Penny

5 MONTHS AGO
6 A.M.

I'LL NEVER KNOW what wakes me. But I remember how it feels.

Warm. Not in that unbearably hot, sticky, I-need-to-tear-the-blankets-off-me sort of way. But warm like gold light spilling across a wood floor and gifted jewelry against beloved skin.

I blink in the fuzzy light and shift beneath the sheets, my toes brushing up against the long line of her leg. We're not spooning, but I almost wish we were; I wish my back were to her, because we're front to front, wrapped together, and that's so much worse—so much better—being tucked into her, enveloped by the shelter of her, her strong arms and shoulders and freckled skin against my scars.

Her hand's on my hip, the fingers stretched in a way that makes me want to press up into them just to see if they'll clench around me. My forehead's pressed against her collarbone, my head settled into the crook her neck and shoulder make, and I feel the length of my braid slip against the soft inside skin of both our arms.

I don't move. I should pull away now that I'm awake. I didn't come up here to sleep in Tate's bed—in Tate's arms. I came up here for Laurel, and now I'm here instead. Laurel would laugh at me. She'd call it revenge.

Fuck—she'd say she told me so.

How had I gotten here?

Why hadn't I just gone to the Denny's across from the motel? Why hadn't I just called Meghan to come back to get me last night? I hadn't even thought about texting her, even though she was the one who drove me up here. She'd helped me plan Laurel's surprise.

Why had I gone straight to Tate like my feet knew something I didn't?

My fingers twist at the ends of her sleep-shirt, the questions mounting in my head. I unclench them, but that just lays my hand against her back, and that . . . is an experience. I can feel her muscles through the fabric.

Her phone begins to buzz against the table, and she moves so suddenly, I know she's had to be awake this entire time—maybe even longer than I have. She pulls away from me, my hands falling away from her at the movement, but our legs still tangled. She turns her phone off, and then—

—she comes back.

She tilts right back into the warm space we made between us, and the only difference is she's scooted down enough so we're face-to-face, and her hands are resting between us, instead of on my hip.

"You okay?" Her voice is rusty in the morning, and it pulls at something deep in my stomach.

I nod, because I'm scared if I speak, she'll pull away, forever this time.

"Good," she continues, and I wonder if it's to fill the silence.

I wonder if she feels it, too—the breathless weight of being in the nonexistent space between her and me. I want to ease it, to lift it, and I know the way. Maybe I haven't always. Maybe I've flirted with it like a child who loves fire but hates getting burned. But right now, in this bed with her, I feel—

—like hers.

She loves me. She said it. It counts, even if she thought I was asleep.

Doesn't it?

Do I want it to?

"It's early," she says, and I know why she says it.

I'm supposed to agree, and one of us is supposed to pull away, and it's supposed to start all over again: The world crumbles, Tate is always there, and I'm always a coward. Especially when it matters.

What would it be like to be brave?

To see what she tastes like?

To know the shape of her lips?

To learn her body against mine?

"Penny?" she asks, because I'm not pulling away.

"Don't go," I say.

There's no space in this bed.

I never want there to be.

"Penny." She's not asking this time. She sighs it, her eyes closing when I reach out, tracing the line of her jaw, my finger pressing against the freckle that rests right below her ear.

"Don't you want to know?" I ask, because *I* do.

I want to know. I want to feel *something* more.

And she always makes me feel so much more.

She makes me feel everything.

I didn't even know you could touch someone so completely, and it spins through me, carving new knowledge into every nerve ending. The only parts of our bodies that aren't touching are our lips.

If she just leans forward . . .

If she just slips her hand into my hair, and pulls me in . . .

And then she does . . . and I go—willingly, gratefully, *finally*.

I'm finally going to know.

My eyes drift shut. It spikes in me, the anticipation, and then . . .

Nothing.

"Penny," she says softly, and my eyes drift open and the breath I suck in . . .

Oh, her eyes.

She's always so sad.

"I deserve more than this," Tate says. "More than you heartbroken over another girl. More than tearstains and running . . . because you *are* running, Penny. You're running from so many things."

She could have hurt me less by taking out a knife and stabbing me with it. Especially when she leans forward and presses a kiss to my forehead, and I gasp against it, against the intensity of her bleeding into me like we're one, just for a second.

"You deserve a lot more than this, too," she whispers fiercely in my ear. "*We* deserve it."

She gets up and disappears into the bathroom, leaving me lying there, as crumpled as those motel sheets.

When I hear the shower turn on, it jerks me out of a trance. My heart beats wildly, and I look down, frantic as I breathe faster and faster.

I manage to get to my phone and then to the door, and I'm bursting into the cold morning air, stumbling toward the parking lot, trying to breathe, as Meghan pulls up.

"Penny! Penny? What happened?"

Meghan rushes out of her car and to me, and I can't say anything; I just shake my head and start crying, and she doesn't say another word.

She just gets me out of there.

55

Penny

JULY 23

AFTER OUR FIGHT in the parking lot, Tate doesn't come home. The next morning when my alarm goes off, she's still gone.

I think about texting her. But her sending me the truce agreement last night kind of clinched it.

There's a part of me that thinks about it. Going over to Remi's. Grand-gesturing it.

But I know her—that's why I should've never let Anna think we were dating. Tate will just hate me more than she does if I push.

So when I get the call Mom's ready to come home, I drive to Sacramento and cry the whole way. Four and a half hours of tears and sad music and no texts, no calls—nothing from her. I have to stop twice at a gas station to get a cup of ice for my eyes, so I don't arrive at the apartment a giant puffy mess and all obvious about it.

I still look like crap when I knock on the door, though.

When Gran opens the door and sees me, the relief in her eyes is thick. "Oh, Penny," she says. "You're here."

I step inside and hug her. "That bad, huh?"

"Your mother..." Gran trails off because I can see Mom sitting on the couch in the living room, wrapped in a blanket.

"Hey, Mom," I call.

"Honey! Hi!" She beams at me, moving to get up.

"No, no, stay there," I tell her, hurrying over. When she puts her arms out, I almost hesitate, because when was the last time I hugged her? I don't even know. It's been too long to remember.

It feels weird. And not just because I'm scared to press too hard and hurt her. She's still in recovery.

"Where's Tate?" Gran asks from behind me.

"Oh, didn't she text? She had to work," I say, the lie like a teaspoon of cinnamon in my mouth—unbearable.

"Anna's resting," Gran adds. "I'll tell her in a bit."

"I'll tell her," Mom says, rolling her eyes, and Gran smiles determinedly.

"Of course," she says. "I'm gonna put your bags in Penny's car."

"Thank you," Mom says, and it's beyond begrudging. "Honey, come sit!" She pats the spot on the couch next to her, and I go, because there's no other real option.

"This is nice," I tell her, looking around the apartment. It's very modern, with sleek furniture and pops of color here and there, with one too many throw blankets with extravagant trim.

"I miss my studio," Mom says. "I can't wait to go back. To be free. Your grandmother is a *tyrant*. I don't know how you put up with her when you were recovering."

I stare at her, heat crawling from my chest up to my cheeks in nauseating inches as her comment thuds through me. My instinct is to brush it away. To hide in the lie and falseness of *I'm fine* instead of *You're killing me*.

But dodging the truth has gotten me nothing but trouble and pain and losing people I never even got to fully have.

I'm kind of done with it, I think.

"I wouldn't have the dexterity I do in my thumb if it weren't for Gran," I say. "She did all my exercises with me."

"Of course she did, honey," Mom says. "I just meant—it's different."

Yeah, you have me. I didn't have you.

"I'm gonna go check on Anna," Mom says. "Be right back."

She heads down the hall, and I lean back against the couch, trying to ignore the sick swirl of dread in my stomach.

Until just this second, I didn't realize what a relief it was, not having to tiptoe around her for these last few weeks.

I'm a terrible daughter.

She's a terrible mother. That's what Tate would say if she were here.

I pull my phone out, hoping I've missed a text . . . but nothing.

What am I going to say if Tate's not there when I get back home with Mom?

How am I supposed to come clean about the dating thing without having Mom destroy all my plans again?

I've got no answers and too many questions and a whole lot of anxiety and nowhere to spew any of it, so I sit there on the couch, pull out my bullet journal, and nervously flip through it. I land on one of the collage pages.

The garden one. Mom had said she liked it. An artistic compliment from her was . . . .

Well, it was really rare.

"Penny!"

I look up, forcing a smile when I see Anna moving slowly into the room, leaning on my mom.

"Hey. I'm sorry Tate couldn't make it."

"Don't worry, she texted," Anna assures me, kissing me on the cheek after sitting down next to me. Mom takes the other side, and I'm in the middle of them, my bullet journal still in my lap.

"Oh my gosh, is that one of your collages?" Anna asks. "Can I see?"

I can't really say no to her. "Yeah," I say, letting her take it from me.

"Such talent," Anna murmurs, tracing the garden gate I'd assembled out of pressed flower petals.

"You've gotten very impressionistic," Mom says.

The front door opens. Gran's back from putting Mom's luggage in the car.

"All set," she says, coming to settle into the tufted armchair across from the couch.

"Kicking me out already?" Mom asks, her voice light, her expression anything but.

"We should go," I say, when Gran doesn't answer. "We'll miss traffic if we do."

"Fine." Mom sighs. I get up, and she leans to hug Anna gently. She whispers something in her ear, and Anna laughs and nods.

"Give Tate a hug for me?" Anna asks, and I smile, though I don't even know if I'm gonna see Tate again until her mom's home.

She can't hide forever. But she can for a while, if she wants.

It's not like my mom would care or even notice, really. I know her too well.

Getting Mom to let go of Anna and walk to the car is kind of an ordeal, but I finally manage. Gran stands on the sidewalk as I close the passenger door and go over to her.

"Hey," I say. "You steady?"

She'd ask me that sometimes after physical therapy. A worry that became a habit and then a motto.

"I'm tired," Gran says, and it shakes me, because I guess we're both in the same place.

Unable to dance around the hard truths anymore.

Mom's really fucked, then. And so are we.

There's no winning in this. We've all lost. And we can't seem to find each other.

"I've got it from here," I tell her, and it's supposed to make her feel better, but her face falls.

"Oh, Penny," she says, and then she folds me into her. "Drive safe."

"I will."

Mom's already playing music when I get in the car, so I guess she's picking. At least she didn't choose a true crime podcast. She listens to those sometimes while she works.

I get all the way out of Sacramento and toward the long stretch of highway that's all rice fields and hay without her backseat driving too much, but every time a big rig passes by, she tenses up like she thinks it'll swerve right into us.

"Are you okay?"

I'm so startled, I flinch at Mom's question.

"I'm fine," I say, focusing on the road. It's a straight line, flat land good for growing rice, until we hit the mountains, and orchards become cliff and rugged pine.

"You've been crying."

"Allergies," I lie, hoping she'll take the excuse, even though I've never had allergies in my life.

But for once, she doesn't avoid. Of course, when I want her to leave me alone, she doesn't.

"Did something happen with Tate? Don't get mad," she adds hastily. "Anna told me that you two were— You know we're happy for you, right?"

"Mom, I'm not . . . Just drop it, okay?"

She stares at her hands, fiddling with her charm bracelet. She'd made it years ago, flattened pennies on train tracks and punched holes in them. When I was little, I used to play with it on her wrist, and she'd laugh and say she'd give it to me when I was older.

She's never been good at promises.

"Did you girls have a fight? Couples fight. It's perfectly normal, even if it feels like the end of the world."

"We're fine. I'm fine. That's what you want, so we're all fine."

She lets out a nervous laugh. "What does that mean?"

"Nothing," I say. "Did you get any sketching done while you were recovering?"

"I'll talk about my sketches if you talk about your collages," Mom says, and it's so childish, so her, that I can't even be mad.

"You just saw one of the collages. I showed it to you."

"You showed *Anna*," Mom says.

"You were sitting right next to her!"

My fingers flex around the steering wheel.

"Why don't you let *me* see them?" Mom asks. "You stopped drawing, and that bullet journal and the collages are the only artistic things you do anymore, and—"

"Oh my God," I burst out. "What is *wrong* with you?"

"Excuse me? *Penny!*"

She yells my name, because I swerve off the road and onto the shoulder. Skidding to a halt, the car kicking up gravel, I throw the parking brake and turn to look at her.

I thrust my hands out, angling them so she can't avoid seeing the scars like she usually does.

"I don't draw as much anymore because my fine motor skills kind of suck. I can't do the kind of detail I used to be able to. So I moved into collages. And yeah, the bullet journal's the only thing I do anymore. Because it's the only thing I *can* do without my fingers hurting after twenty minutes."

Horror washes over her face. I don't even care if it's sincere. I'm too mad.

"Penny . . . I'm sorry. I didn't think—"

"Yeah, you never do."

I slam the turn signal on and get back on the highway.

We don't talk for nearly two hundred miles.

56

TATE

JULY 23

I HEAR PENNY'S car pull up in the driveway, but I don't budge from my room, even when their voices float upstairs.

A big part of me didn't want to come back. Remi said I could stay as long as I wanted, and I was so tempted. But I knew Lottie would tell my mom, and then she'd worry.

So I'm here. And they're downstairs, and even this far away, I can hear the strain in Penny's voice as she gets her mom settled.

(I hate that, even now, I want to go to her.)

"Mom, no!"

I'm up on my feet, because I know that tone. My feet thunder down the stairs, dodging around the suitcases in the hall. I get to the living room to find Lottie on the ground, her face twisted in pain, and Penny struggling to help her up.

"Hey, hey," I say, hurrying over. "Wait a second. You've got to lift her right."

"I'm fine," Lottie says, batting at my hands.

"Lottie, please let me help you." I lift her up carefully, walking her back to the couch. She leans back with a sigh.

"What hurts?" I ask. "Have you eaten? Did your gran give you all her meds?" I ask Penny.

"They're in her bag. I'll get them," Penny says, hurrying into the hallway.

"Do you want something to drink?" I ask Lottie.

"I just want to get to my studio," Lottie says. "The sketchbook I need is in there. I can walk across the garden. I'm supposed to move around."

"Not after you've been in the car for hours! You need to rest," Penny insists, coming back with a plastic bag with the hospital logo stamped on it. "I've got all the pills and instructions."

"I need my sketchbook. The gallery in San Francisco wants me to ship the pieces in a few weeks," Lottie says. "They might want more if they do well."

"I'll go get it, Mom," Penny says. "You fell over when you got up. Look, I made you a little basket of snacks right here and I've got a bell." She picks up the bell on the end table near the pullout couch. "You can be very annoying and ring it instead of texting me."

Lottie takes the bell with a grin, because of course she does.

"I'm going to get you some water," I say, because that's the only thing that isn't stuffed in the little box of snacks Penny's prepared like Lottie's in a hotel.

Penny doesn't follow me at first, but as I'm pulling the water jug out of the fridge, I hear her footsteps in the hall.

"You came back."

I grab a glass from the cupboard. "Yeah, well, I live here."

"Tate, can we—"

"No, we can't," I say, pouring the water with such fury that I splash some on the counter.

"Tate."

"What?" I demand, whirling around to face her. "What do you want?"

"I want to apologize."

"Not necessary."

"Yes, it is."

"It's not," I insist, hating how that cold seed of doubt worms around in my gut. "We're not friends. We've never been friends."

"We've never been enemies either," Penny says.

She's right.

What we were . . . I used to think it was maybe undefinable. That a word to describe this constant crossing of paths and reluctantly entwined lives didn't exist.

I don't think that anymore.

I think there's a word for it.

I just think we both ran from it, and when we couldn't, we fought instead.

It was simpler.

And then she just fucked it all up by pushing it into complicated territory. All so my mom wouldn't rat her out about kayaking.

"Penny?" Lottie's voice rings out from the living room. "Were you going to get my sketchbook?"

Penny looks desperately at me, waiting for me to say something.

"Penny?" Lottie calls again.

"Just go," I tell her.

"I am sorry," Penny says again. Then she raises her voice. "I'm going, Mom!"

I don't return to the living room until I hear the front door open and shut and I'm sure she's gone.

57

Penny

JULY 23

WHEN I FLIP Mom's studio light on, the bulb flickers and goes out.

"Of course," I mutter, holding out my hands and zombie-walking forward, keeping to the right side of the room so I don't accidentally run into any glass pieces and knock them over.

I'd never hear the end of it if I ruined one of the pieces the gallery was waiting for.

It's hot as hell in here, the stale, intense kind of heat that fills your lungs with each breath.

My hands close around the end of her worktable, and I pull open the drawer, scrambling in the darkness for the flashlight. Finally, I find it.

The beam's weak, but it's better than nothing. I shine it on her table, scattered with tools and half-finished pieces. Her sketchbook, held together with rubber bands, is stacked in the corner. I grab it, turning to go when the flashlight hits the stained-glass piece set on the easel to my right.

I see them in the dim light—three pieces, two of them fully draped, the other half covered with a drop cloth.

It's like my mind's playing tricks at first. It can't be.

Because what I see—

It's like a dream.

A nightmare.

I walk toward it, creeping toward it like a wolf toward a trap, pulling the draping off slowly. Dust motes fly in the air, but I don't see them.

All I see is the glass.

All I see is what she's done.

I pull the second piece's draping free, and then the third, and when I stand back and see them all together—

I have never hated someone more than I have my mother.

They're abstracts, like all her work since Dad died. But they're also . . . not abstract. Not if you *know*.

It's a trio of stained glass panels. A story in three parts. A trilogy of pain. There's probably an art term for it, but I don't know it and I don't care because she—

The first one's all greens and blues. The forest and the river cutting through it. There are careful slices of gray—suggestions of people, of me and Dad—set in yellow and blue shards of glass that cradle the figures like a raft. It's serene, if you don't know.

It's sinister if you do.

The second one—the green's pushed out to the edges, the focus on the blue and white that's all storm and wave, so chaotic you have to look closely to find the gray glass people in the churn. But once you find them, you can't unsee the desperation.

The third piece is like an aerial view gone abstract: The greens and browns of the forest and cliffs, the snaking color of the river fades from blue to shattered yellow to bloodred.

I sink to the ground, my hand still clenched around the last drop cloth.

Did I know dread before this? Because I've never felt this before, a crash of too much, hurtling at me from all sides, that red blaring at me like a siren. My face contorts from it, my lips straining against the shriek that I want to let out.

I don't know how long I stay there, on my knees, staring up at what Mom's done.

At the art she's made out of my trauma.

All I know is the next noise I hear other than my own ragged breath is her.

Of course it's Tate.

Forever the witness to my worst moments.

"Penny, your mom sent me—" Tate cuts off abruptly. "What the fuck."

I look over my shoulder, but she's not looking at me. She's staring at the stained glass and the horror on her face—

—it's like a gift.

Validation.

I'm not crazy. She sees it, too. Doesn't she see it, too?

"You—you see it, too?" It tumbles out of my mouth, and it's so high-pitched, it doesn't even sound like me, and shit, am I breathing?

I need to breathe. Like Jane the therapist taught me.

I'm leaning back before I can think it through, and the cement floor of the garage is cool. I like it, I think I'll just stay here. But suddenly Tate's next to me, her hands pushing me up gently, her arms supporting me.

"Penny, look at me," she directs, as everything swims and fuzzes.

"I—"

I can't stop staring at the glass. I want a hammer. I want to *shatter* them.

"Hey," she says, and then she moves, blocking the pieces from my view. "Don't look at them. Look at me, okay?"

"She made art out of it." I force the words out.

"She did," Tate says simply.

Is this a betrayal? Can Mom betray me when she's let go of me so thoroughly? It feels like betrayal. Or maybe it's just confirmation that I shouldn't have hoped.

I lost them both that day. I was just kidding myself to think it'd ever change.

"This is fucked," Tate says, cutting down to the truth of it so simply. It's such a relief, I'm sagging into her warm skin and smooth shoulders as she wraps her arms around me, one of her hands hovering over the back of my head before she finally cups it. Her thumb strokes down where my neck meets my hairline and tears leak out of the corners of my eyes. Our bodies touch like a shudder, like that bracing quiver when you slip into water hotter than you, before the relaxation comes.

But I can't. Not here. Not with those so close.

"I can't be in here anymore," I say, and without another word, I pull out of her arms and walk out of there and toward the house. I hear Tate swear and follow me across the garden, but I don't look back.

I head straight inside the house, making a beeline for the living

330

room, where Mom's spread out on her bed. Her sketchbook's still clutched in my hands, and I think about throwing it at her. Paging through it to see if there are sketches of the stained glass out in the garage. I think about tearing it up. But instead I just stand at the end of the bed until she looks up at me.

"There it is," Mom says, making grabby hands toward it and then wincing a little. "Thanks, honey."

But I don't hand it over.

"Did you think I'd never find out?" I ask.

"Find out what?"

"One of the drapes on your pieces fell off."

She doesn't even look away from the sketchbook. "I hope you put it back. I want them in perfect condition for the gallery."

"No, Mom, I didn't put it *back*."

Her head tilts up. "You're mad."

She has the audacity to frown at me.

"You think?"

"Why would you be . . ."

She looks so confused. And it makes me shrivel, just for a second, at exactly the wrong time, and the words die in my throat. My entire body's shaking from trying to deal.

"Those pieces are incredibly fucked-up, Lottie."

It comes from behind me.

From Tate.

She's standing in the big dining room doorway, the one that has the rickety double doors we never draw close because they're always breaking. She seems to take up the wide space completely, like her broad shoulders can carry anything.

Once again, she's the witness to my worst.

The lifeline that I grasp on to.

"Excuse me?" Mom glares at her.

"You heard me," Tate says.

"You're on thin ice, young lady." Her voice sharpens but doesn't raise.

"Mom, you had no right—" I start.

"—to make my art?" This time, her voice does raise.

"To make art out of what happened."

"It happened to me, too, Penny."

"Fucking hell," Tate mutters, and Mom's head snaps to her again, slower this time.

"Gillian, stop it," she snarls.

I breathe in and out, trying to stay calm. This only works if I don't freak out, because then she'll just dismiss me as hysterical or run away again, like she did when she told me about selling Dad's business. And it's not even that I'm sick of the running. It's that I can't anymore, after seeing it laid out like that in colored glass.

Mom puts her hands together; it's a pleading gesture, but all I can see is placating. "We both lost your father, Penny," she says.

"No," I say, and it's not just bubbling in me, it's seething. The desire to break this invisible deal of silence between us. "You don't get to act like it's the same. And you don't get to make art out of that day when you weren't *there*."

"No one asked me to be there," she says. "Maybe if I'd been there—" Her face twists against what I realize is an old, old wound.

I blink, taken aback, because this line of thinking's never occurred to me, and maybe that's selfish. He and I had gone alone, a

332

dad-and-daughter trip, and we hadn't even asked her to come along. She never liked rapids.

"Mom," I say, being gentle and harsh at the same time, because that is what the truth is. "If you'd have come, we all would've died."

"I— No. No. That's not—" Mom claps her hand over her mouth, trying to stifle the choking sob.

"The extra weight . . . We would've sunk even faster. We would've never made it to that tree. And if you had *ever* asked me about what happened that day, you would've known that. But you never asked. Not once. You just ignored me and took me out of therapy and tortured yourself with what-ifs and made art out of your fantasies about what you *think* happened instead of actually dealing with it!"

"They are *not* fantasies—how dare you say that!" Tears flood her eyes.

"Fantasies. Metaphors. What else do you call a bloodred river?" I shake my head. "You don't get to make a metaphor out of a reality you *ran* from. You weren't there. You weren't there with him. You didn't hear him begging me to let him go. You don't know what happened. Because you never asked! You never asked *one question*. And you barely know what happened after, because you weren't there either."

"Penny—"

I've lost all focus and control. The words keep spilling out, finally, *finally*.

"Dad let go of me because he *had* to. I know that. I do. But you let go of me just because I was too hard to deal with, and I only had Gran, and she didn't even get to grieve because she was taking care of me. I know what it's like to be put first because *she* put me first. You didn't put me first. You got to grieve all you wanted, how you wanted.

And Gran and I are over here trying to make sure my hands actually work while you sell off the house and the business and erase him from Gran's house and act like it's all fine, swanning back after *months* of living with Anna. After all the hard stuff was done, after Gran did everything for me, you just invade Gran's house and what we built in the after, and I was supposed to act like it was fine. Like you were a *real* mother. And I did. Because it was easier. Because *you* are easier to deal with if you get your way. But you don't get his death. You don't get that day. You weren't there. It's *not yours.*"

"Penny." Her eyes fill with tears.

"Stop just saying my name! Say something that actually *means* something! All you ever do is fuck up my life and take me away from people who actually help me! You never say stuff that means anything!"

But she just keeps crying. And I know then that no matter how much I want it, I won't get answers or anything I want today.

None of this shit is solvable in a conversation or a day or a terrible moment of revelation.

But none of this is solvable without conversations over days and weeks and months and maybe years. And if she won't talk, even now, if she's still shutting me out . . .

What am I supposed to do when she won't even try?

I toss the sketchbook onto the coffee table.

"There you go," I say. Because there is nothing else to say.

"Penny, please," Mom says.

It's a plea, all right. A plea for me to go back to normal. To ignoring it all. To playing our avoidance game.

But I'm done.

No more games.

Just truth.

"You know, if you'd ever asked me about that day, I would've told you everything. How brave he was. How calm. How focused he was on saving me. And if you hadn't been so scared, then you'd know: the last thing he ever said, his last words? Were to beg me to tell you he loved you."

The sound she makes is not human.

It's familiar.

It's the same sound I made when he let go.

58

TATE

JULY 23

PENNY WALKS RIGHT out of the living room, and I don't try to stop her. I just stand there in the doorway as Lottie sobs on the couch.

Lottie's about to drown in her own snot, so I go over and place the box of tissues on her lap.

"Are you happy?" she demands, like she's five.

I stare at her, incredulous. Part of me wants to bite it back, the words I want to say. But I can't anymore. Not after this.

"This is your fault, Lottie. She was going to break eventually. And you're an idiot if you didn't think so."

Her breath sucks in, clogged and angry, but I'm distracted by a car starting up outside.

Shit! I run toward the front door, yanking it open, just in time to see Penny's taillights disappearing down the driveway and through the open gate.

"What the fuck!" I yell, the anger getting the better of me, only to be quickly replaced by fear.

She shouldn't be driving. Not when she's this upset. It isn't safe.

"Tate?" Lottie calls. "Was that—What's happening?"

I ignore her, slamming the front door closed.

"Tate?" she calls. "I'm getting up if you don't—"

"Please don't!" I stalk back into the living room. "You're not going to help anyone if you hurt yourself."

"Did she leave?" Lottie asks, her lower lip trembling. If she starts crying again...

"Did you really think those pieces weren't going to bother her?" I ask, unable to stop myself. How could she be this cruel?

"The counselor," Lottie says.

"What?"

"The counselor. The one I had to see before I became a donor. She asked why I wasn't fully channeling my grief through art, and I couldn't get it out of my head. I just—it was the only way to get her question out of my head. To get the images of that day out of my..." She fades off into another one of those horrible sobs.

All I can think is *fuck*. All I can feel is pissed. Because of course, *Lottie* got to have an epiphany in therapy, but Penny wasn't even allowed to go.

I have never loved and hated someone so much as I have Charlotte Conner. I don't know what to do with it; it's overwhelming, and I'm not even her child. What Penny must be feeling...

I need to find her.

But I can't leave Lottie.

"Stay there," I say, walking out of the living room and heading to the hallway. I sink to the bottom of the stairs and pull out my phone.

I need a plan. I need a solution. I need a goddamn miracle.

What I've got is Meghan and Remi. Which is close.

337

I send them the same text in a group chat:

I need help. Can one of you come here and stay with Lottie?

I need to go find Penny. They had a fight.

A big, big fight.

As I wait for one of them to text back, I get to my feet, heading up the stairs so Lottie can't overhear.

Every step is unsure. I don't know if this is the right call.

All I know is that this has to stop.

That sometimes, things are beyond us.

That sometimes we need help.

Lottie has put every obstacle in Penny's way. Making up ridiculous rules and dodging mentions of George like she's a moth fleeing shadows, making Penny suffer and smaller and sadder because it was easier than Lottie facing the loss head on.

Penny deserves more.

Penny deserves everything.

She deserves some goddamn help.

59

Penny

JULY 23

I'VE ALWAYS LIKED it up here at Damnation Peak. All the lights of town reflecting off the river that snakes down through the mountains. It's peaceful, even when you're anything but.

I can't get them out of my head. Those pieces Mom made. The idea of someone owning them . . . I don't even know how to feel about that.

She'd probably tell me I didn't deserve an opinion.

I never deserved one. Not about whether Dad's stuff should go into storage. Not about getting yanked out of therapy. Not about her coming back like she hadn't abandoned me, only to throw herself into saving Anna.

Tucking my legs under me, I lean back against my windshield, staring out at the lights.

Maybe I could just drive. Leave everything behind. Find a job somewhere and just never come back.

I don't ever want to go back home. Why would I? There's nothing left for me there.

I'm back right where I used to be. The only family who actually loves me is Gran.

My chest aches, thinking about her. She knew Dad the longest. It's funny to think of it that way, but it's true. She got to be alive for every second he was.

That had to make it hurt more, not less.

But she never blamed me. She never stopped trying for me. She never regretted me.

I wish she was here.

The night she locked all my pills up, she sat by my bed for hours. She couldn't hold my hands back then, obviously, but she laid hers next to mine so that I could feel their warmth.

She was just there. Existing with me. Making sure I kept existing.

I remember what that felt like. Not wanting to exist.

I don't want to feel like that ever again.

Laying my hands on top of each other, I close my eyes. But it's right there in my mind: those fucking pieces. That bloodred river. How *dare* she?

The sound of a truck driving up makes me sit up. I squint in the beam of the headlights, but I know as soon as I see Berry's silhouette, looming in the truck bed, waiting to be delivered to their new owner.

Tate always finds me.

Maybe I've always liked that about her.

"Driving around with that bear in the back is a safety hazard," she says as she climbs up on the hood next to me, leaning against the windshield.

"My mom?" I finally ask.

"I sicced Meghan on her," Tate says.

It almost makes me laugh. But I don't have it in me to make it all the way there.

"I'm sorry," I say.

"You're—"

"You came out here. You're mad at me for a lot of good reasons and you still came out here. You didn't need to."

"I needed to make sure you were okay."

"I don't think I'll ever be okay. I don't think I can go back," I say quietly. I can feel her gaze, but I can't bear to admit it to her face.

"Penny," she says softly. She straightens, crossing her legs so she's sitting facing me, her thighs butterflying out. "I did something. And you might be mad, but I'm mad at you, too, so we can just be mad at each other, if that's the way it falls."

"What did you do?"

She holds out her phone. I take it. It's open on the Notes app.

TATE'S PLAN TO HELP PENNY

1. Call Marion.
2. Get Penny's ex-therapist's number.
3. Issue ultimatum to Lottie.
4. Make emergency appointment with therapist.

I stare down at the plan. The words blur, tears dripping down my nose to splash onto her screen. I hastily wipe them away and hand it back to her.

"I haven't done anything on the list," she tells me. "I just—you liked the therapist, right?"

I nod.

"You wanted to keep seeing her? You wanted to see the psychiatrist and—"

"Yes." I breathe it out, because I can barely even support one word, my heart is beating so fast.

It's so simple, written down in black-and-white. Four steps to help.

Four steps back to someone who actually listens.

Four steps to answers and *knowing* myself.

"Penny, I can't do anything about your mom continually and monumentally fucking up. But I can make her let you go to the therapist."

"You didn't see how she reacted during that one session she came to," I protest, because having any kind of hope is so damn hard.

"It doesn't matter how she feels about it," Tate says. "If it's what *you* want, I will make it happen."

"How?"

"Your gran's going to tell her that if she doesn't let you go, she has to give up her studio."

I gape at her. "You can't—"

"It's Marion's house. Marion's garage. You think she won't agree? You think she doesn't want you happy and healthy?"

"She's my mom, Tate."

"She's hurting you," Tate says. "This is just as bad as if she kept you from having surgery or stopped your physical therapy halfway through. She's just getting away with it because the world's shitty about feelings and mental health stuff."

"I—" I can't argue with her.

Hard to argue with so many truths.

"She's not evil," Tate continues. "She's just dumb and selfish nd lost in a grief pit still. She needs a therapist, too, but that's not my job."

"But I am?"

I can't look away when she meets my eyes. We go from sad to electric in a breath, and I'm reeling from it.

"You're not my friend," Tate says. "And you've never been my enemy, Penny. You're...*you*. I am on your side. That means I don't give up on you. Especially when all you want is to go to a therapist who was helping you."

I want a lot more than that, but if I say it, it unlocks all sorts of doors that I've kept closed for so long.

"I will do what you want me to do," Tate says. "If you don't want it, I won't do it. But if you do, I will sit here and hold your hand as you call your gran. I will be there when Marion tells Lottie. I will drive you to the therapist myself. But if *you* don't change something, Penny, it's not going to change. Lottie won't let it."

She's right.

Tate is always right. It's very annoying most of the time, but now...

I'm so grateful.

I hold out my hand.

She takes it.

"Let's call Gran," I say.

60

Penny

AUGUST 2

JANE'S OFFICE IS like I remembered. Not exactly—she's gotten new throw pillows. But it smells the same. Walking inside was almost overwhelming, like a knot in my chest was finally loosened when I sat down on the couch.

"It's good to see you," Jane says.

I nod, pressing my lips together as I fight back tears.

I've been on edge all week, waiting for this. My mom had signed the forms as soon as Jane sent them.

I wish you understood how scared I am of losing you, Penny, she'd told me when she handed them back to me.

I wanted to scream at her: *You already lost me.* But I didn't.

Jane would've been proud.

She discreetly pushes the box of tissues toward me. I take it, holding the whole box instead of using one. Just for something to grab on to.

"I'm nervous," I confess.

"Last time we saw each other, it was very dramatic," Jane says with a gentle smile. "Your mom was really upset with the situation as she perceived it."

"She was wrong," I say.

"She was acting out of fear," Jane says. "Diagnosis makes things more real to some people. And having a negative attitude about medication is very common, but I admit I was discouraged by her reaction. It wasn't fair to you, Penny. It must've been very painful."

"I guess I can just add it to the list," I say, trying to go for a joke and failing miserably, because Jane just looks at me, waiting for the truth to surface.

"It's been bad," I confess in the silence and space she gives me.

"Your grandmother mentioned your mother's been in the hospital."

"Yeah, she up and donated a piece of her liver to her bestie."

"How did you feel about that?"

"I'm glad," I say. "I am. I'm so glad Anna's okay. But it's been . . . She didn't even warn me. They told us five days before they did it."

"That is really short notice," Jane says. "That seems to be a pattern with her."

"My life the last two years is her springing shit on me," I say. "Dad dies and she buries him instead of giving him what he wanted. She never comes home, just shoves me on Gran and lives with Anna. Tate has spent more time with my mom the past few years than I have. Do you know how fucked that is?" I don't even stop to let her answer. "And then she sells the rafting business. Because of you."

"Because of me?" Jane asks, frowning.

"Well, not because of you. Because of the session we had. She freaked out about the idea of me being back on the water and made a rule that I wasn't allowed in the water unless it was a pool, and she sold my dad's business, and I've gotten to watch his business partner run it into the ground the last year."

"That's a lot to deal with," Jane says.

"And then she gave her liver to Anna—well, part of her liver—and Tate and Anna moved in, because do you *know* how expensive anti-rejection meds are, Jane? It's criminal. This country fucking *sucks*. And so now I get to live across the hallway from a girl who—" I stop myself.

Finally. Wow, that was word vomit.

Emotion vomit.

Jane straightens a little in her chair.

"It's been bad," I say again. "And then it got worse."

"How?"

"I stopped pretending."

"Pretending..."

"Pretending that I was fine. My mom was in Sacramento for almost a whole month recovering. That entire time, I didn't have to tiptoe around my dad's death. I didn't have to worry about Mom catching me sneaking out to kayak. I didn't have to smile while she just walked past me with her dinner, heading to her studio instead of eating with me. It was like the entire house had been black and white, and as soon as she left, it was technicolor. The really gaudy, saturated kind from the 1950s musicals."

Jane chuckles. "I like those musicals, too."

"It was so nice, not pretending. It was so nice to be able to talk about my dad with Tate. With someone who had some of the same memories as I did. To eat dinner with someone every morning and night. So when Mom got back..."

"You had to start pretending again."

"I couldn't even last the ride home," I confess. "And then I saw..."

That bloodred river spins in my mind. Every time I've walked past her studio this week, I've thought about going inside and destroying them. When I got the nerve one time to try the doorknob, it was locked.

She'd locked me out.

Protected her precious death fantasies above all else.

I tell Jane about the stained glass trio and the confrontation after, and when I'm done, she's quiet for a long time.

"Art is something you and your mother have in common, isn't it?" she asks finally.

"Yeah. I guess."

"Have you been expressing yourself through art since the accident?"

I bristle. "Are you saying it's okay, what she did?"

"No," Jane said. "It was incredibly hurtful what she did. It crosses a lot of boundaries. She avoided talking with you about not just a tremendous loss in both your lives, but an enormous physical and mental trauma you underwent. And now she's making art to try to fill in the gaps of what she doesn't know about the accident and that day."

"I would've told her," I insist, "if she'd just asked."

"I know," Jane says. "And you deserve to tell her what happened just as much she deserves to know, instead of creating scenarios in her head."

"She wants to sell them," I whisper. "The art pieces."

"It might be that she hates looking at them as much as you do, Penny," Jane says softly.

It's something that didn't occur to me.

"Then why would she make them in the first place?"

"Art is her coping mechanism, I suspect," Jane says. "Like rafting is one of yours. Your mother reached into her toolbox and chose the most familiar tool. The safest. She buried herself in her work, in the stories she told herself of the accident, so she wouldn't have to face what came after. The choices she's made every day since. Because she's made some very bad choices, and your mother . . . she has a hard time with her emotions."

"Well, so do I, but she keeps making me handle mine and hers."

"And that's not fair. But we can work together to figure out ways to set up boundaries when she tries to do that. The difference between you two is that you're aware you're having a hard time with your emotions," Jane says. "You sought out help for it. And you have our work here to use in your toolbox."

"So it all comes down to me being a bigger person than her?" I ask.

"It comes down to knowing that you get to have a say in the kind of relationship you have with your mother," Jane says. "Or if you have a relationship at all. You get to set your boundaries. You talked about how hard it was to pretend when she got back. How freeing it was to be able to talk about your dad. What if you just . . . kept talking about your dad? What if you asked her to have family dinner? What if you told her you wanted to talk about the accident? What if you told her you were going to the lake to kayak because it was safe and you needed the outlet?"

"I don't know," I say quietly.

Jane leans forward. "Maybe it's time to find out."

PART SEVEN

Home

(or: the time we figure it out)

61

TATE

AUGUST 9

"DO YOU SEE them?" I ask, craning over the sink, looking toward the dark driveway. No headlights.

"They'll be here soon," Penny says. She stirs the pasta sauce on the stove. It's been slow-cooking all day.

She made the lemon cake this morning—complete with the secret Jell-O. It's sitting on top of the fridge, waiting for later.

"Should I go get your mom?" I ask.

"Yeah, probably," Penny says.

Lottie's made her way slowly but surely out to the studio for the past two days. I followed her out the first day, afraid she might fall, even though the doctor did want her to walk around. She still needed to take it easy. The second time, I just watched from the porch and checked on her every hour. I brought her lunch each day and helped her back into the house for dinner, which she took in her room.

I leave Penny in the kitchen, heading outside to the garage.

It's getting dark—Mom and Marion left late; the last doctor's appointment took longer than Mom expected, but the doctors gave her the all clear.

Any minute, Mom will be home.

It'll be over. It'll be beginning.

(The rest of our lives. Mom, healthy. Thriving. I don't even know how to picture it, and I can't wait to find out.)

I knock lightly on Lottie's studio door before trying the knob. It's surprisingly not locked this time, so I walk inside, because I don't want to make her get up until she's ready.

There they are: her trio of pain. The drop cloths are long gone.

Lottie looks up from her chair where she's slumped, staring at them.

"My mom and Marion should be home soon," I say. "We've got dinner up at the house. Do you want me to help you back?"

She nods, but she doesn't get up or look away from the stained glass.

Lottie takes a long sip of water. God, I *hope* it's water. If it's something else, we are so fucked.

"I'm supposed to pack them up," she says, gesturing with her water bottle toward the stained glass. "The gallery's waiting for them."

"Are you really going to send them?" I ask her.

If she does, I don't know if Penny will be able to take it.

Lottie's face is like flame appearing from the back of a piece of paper. Everything darkens before the light consumes.

"I was going to. I was. But now—"

She rubs the tears away. "The only right choice I've ever made was becoming friends with your mom."

I can't even disagree with her. Maybe it's true. She certainly has a shitty track record when it comes to choices.

352

"You could ask yourself what she would do here," I suggest.

Lottie's eyes shine as she considers it. It's almost creepy, the way they slide over the stained glass pieces like she's trying to memorize them.

She pitches the water bottle violently against the middle one. It happens so fast, a sudden movement that has me jumping in my flip-flops even before the bottle hits the churning river dead on.

The heavy glass splits on impact, the easel teetering.

Crash.

The easel falls, taking the other two pieces down.

They shatter on the ground, a mess of blue and green and red.

Lottie shakily rises to her feet, moving toward the glass, and I grab her, because she's just wearing slippers. She fights against me, weak, but I'm so worried about hurting her that my hold is totally ineffectual as she struggles.

"Tate?! Lottie!"

Weathered hands pull me away from Lottie, and I almost sag in relief when I see it's Marion.

"Mom?" I'm calling for her before I even see her. She's standing in the doorway of the studio, staring at Marion as she pushes Lottie as gently as she can into the chair so she doesn't cut herself.

"What's going on here?" Mom asks. "Tate? Are you okay?"

I nod.

"Lottie?"

Lottie shakes her head. "I fucked up," she mutters. "I fucked up so bad."

"We'll fix them—" Mom starts to say, but Lottie shakes her head.

"No, I shouldn't have made them. I should've talked to her. I shouldn't have fucked up."

"What is . . ." Anna trails off, looking at Marion searchingly.

"Later," Marion says.

"Have you been keeping things from me?" Anna asks.

"Yes," Marion says, no shame or apology at all. "You've got other things on your plate. Lottie, where are your shoes?"

"In the house," Lottie says. "I need to clean this up."

"You need to get some damn shoes on," Marion says. "And then you need to put your butt on a couch or in a bed and rest. You look like death warmed over."

"Mom, you need to go in the house, too," I tell her. "The drive—"

"I'm fine," Mom assures me. "Lottie, what's going on?"

Lottie shakes her head. "I'm fine," she insists, rising to her feet. "I just need to go to my room."

The idea of her holing up in there for another dinner while I watch every bit of hope dwindle inside Penny kills me.

"We made dinner. You should eat," I say.

"I don't—" Lottie starts to say.

"Penny would like it," I interrupt.

She looks at me.

It's like that light's been snapped back on inside her. "Yeah?"

"Yeah," I say.

"Let me help you girls," Gran says, settling herself between Mom and Lottie as they begin to walk toward the house.

I follow, moving to close the door to the studio behind me.

The broken glass shines dark against the gray cement floor, and I know it's not enough.

But it's a step toward the right choice.

62

Penny

AUGUST 9

DINNER IS ANYTHING but perfect.

The sauce I made is absolutely perfect. You can't go wrong with Gran's recipes. But as soon as everyone comes in from the driveway, the energy is instantly weird. My mom's eyes are all red, and Anna keeps frowning. Gran gets them both settled on the couch, and Tate stays with them while Gran comes into the kitchen and hugs me, long and hard.

"You steady?" she whispers in my ear.

"No," I say. "But I think I'm gonna get there. Thanks to you and Tate and Jane."

When she pulls back, she's smiling, the sad edge to it all regret. "I'm sorry I let things get so bad."

"You didn't."

"I should've stepped in more," Gran says. "I shouldn't have let your mother take you out of therapy. I promise that won't happen again."

"I'm not gonna let it happen again," I say, thinking about what

Jane said about boundaries. The pasta is nearly done, so I use a skimmer to transfer it to the saucepot, tossing the noodles to coat them perfectly.

"There's garlic bread in the oven," I tell her as I take the pot over to the counter so I can dish the pasta out.

"And you made lemon cake," Gran says, spotting it on the fridge.

"Tate helped," I say.

She's been nice, this whole hellish week where Mom hid from me and I crept around like going to see Jane was some kind of sin.

"She's been helping a lot," Gran comments as she pulls out the garlic bread and begins to cut it.

Tate's been endlessly helpful. Running interference between me and my mom. Taking her food so I don't have to. Checking on her every hour, just in case.

It's so unfair. I lied to her. To the moms. All so I wouldn't get caught in my other lie, but instead of just dropping me like she should, she got my gran to emotionally blackmail my mom into letting me go back to therapy. Tate's Plan to Help Penny. I have a screenshot of it on my phone. I look at it before I go to sleep. Like it's a talisman.

Four steps to the start of knowing.

Four steps to the start of healing.

How many steps would lead me to her?

The only Parmesan we have is in the little packets from the last time we got pizza, so I break one open over each bowl of pasta and layer the bowls on my arm, carrying all five of them with the ease of someone who knows how to survive the Sunday-morning rush at the Blackberry.

Gran follows me with the garlic bread, and I hand out plates, then drag the coffee table closer to Mom's couch so they can use it.

I sit down next to Tate, and that's when I realize we've divided ourselves: moms on Mom's couch, us on Anna's. Little opposing war councils, ready to hammer out a treaty.

"This looks great," Anna says. "Don't be offended if I just eat a little. That drive took it out of me."

"Do you want to go straight to bed?" Tate asks, getting to her feet instantly. She looks like she's ready to grab her mom and carry her to the bedroom.

"Nope," Anna says. "What I'd really like to know is what the hell is going on."

Dead silence in the living room. I stare down at my pasta.

Anna points to Lottie. "You've been crying."

Gran's next. "You've been positively cagey with me since that late-night phone call last week."

She gestures to Penny. "Penny is practically vibrating from nerves."

Mom levels me with a look.

"And, Tate, sweets, you get this little divot between your eyebrows when you're quietly freaking out. And that's on top of the absolutely destroyed stained glass in the studio. I'm betting that was not artistic temperament?"

My eyes fly up to stare at my mom. "You destroyed them?"

She can't even look at me. At first, I think it's anger, but when she says, "Yes," her eyes meet mine and it's not anger in them.

"I'm sorry," she says. "I should've never agreed to sell them. And

357

I should've never made them. Not without talking with you first. It should've stayed a sketch. Something just for me."

What if you stopped pretending?

"Yeah," I say. "It should've been just for you."

Anna's eyes dart between us, absorbing our conversation. Putting together the pieces.

"I don't want to hurt you, Penny," Mom tells me.

"Then stop," I say. Because it really is that simple. It *should* be that simple.

It isn't. It's a journey. Maybe a lifelong one.

"I'm really trying," Mom says.

It's only a lifelong journey if she can actually commit to it. I don't know if she can. I don't even know if I want her to. If it's better that we heal together, growing closer, instead of healing and growing apart. I think, sometimes, growing apart can be the healthiest option. There's a piece of me that hopes we won't, but there's another part that wonders if it's inevitable.

"Then get help, because you kind of suck at trying on your own," I tell her. It's a challenge, one I don't think she's ready to take. The only reason she saw that counselor before the transplant was because it was the only way she could give Anna her liver.

Her eyes flare, but I just stare back at her, unwilling to look away. Unable to bullshit anymore.

If she wants her daughter, she's going to have to take me as I am, not the husk as she strips the inside of me away.

"That's a big ask, Penny."

"It's not," I say. "If you can't do it for me or for yourself, then do it for Dad."

Her fingers curl around her napkin at his mention, like she needs something familiar to anchor her.

"He would've hated seeing you like this," I tell her, and it is the truth. It would've broken him, to see her so sad. So lost. So unwilling to reach out for help.

"I hate seeing myself like this, too, Penny," she whispers. It's all she can give me for now. An acknowledgment of misery. Maybe someday we'll get to the point where it grows so great she has no choice but to get help. I don't think it's today or even tomorrow or a week from now. She might surprise me. I want her to.

But if she does or if she doesn't, I guess Jane's right: It's up to me to decide if her changing is enough.

I do know Mom and I have one thing I didn't get with Dad: time to figure it out, if I choose.

Mom and I have time. Anna and Tate have time.

The only people I'm scared have run out of time are Tate and me.

63

Penny

AUGUST 11

"I THINK WE'RE lost," I say.

"We're not," Tate insists, as we hit a particularly nasty pothole and the truck rocks back and forth.

I look nervously behind us. Berry the Bear statue is secured in the truck bed with extra tie-downs, but it's been at least ten miles since the pavement faded to gravel, and ahead of us the gravel turns to dirt.

Delivering Berry has been an ordeal from the start. It took forever for both of us to get a day off to make it happen, and then Remi wasn't available to help, so it was just me and Tate carting the giant bear statue through the woods.

Berry's new owner lives deep in the backwoods of North County. A fitting place for a chainsaw bear, but a pain in the ass to drag the statue out that far.

"It says first right on South Fork Road," Tate says, pointing to the directions scribbled on a napkin that Remi had given me. "All the side roads have been on the left. It's just farther down the road than we thought."

"We should call to make sure," I say, picking up the napkin and pulling out my phone. But there's no signal. I don't know what I expected. This deep in the forest, we are truly in the land of no contact.

"There!" Tate points. "Right turn."

She flips the turn signal like a Girl Scout even though we haven't seen another car this entire time. Takes the turn and—*crack!* We suddenly tilt to the right, Tate's body sliding toward mine, jerked back by the seatbelt as the entire left side of the truck lifts into the air.

"Shit," Tate says.

"Did we just—what happened?" My shoulder's jammed against the door, the handle sticking uncomfortably into my side.

"Let me see," she says, unbuckling her belt with one hand as she grips the door handle and pushes. She climbs out, dropping onto the ground.

I can hear her swearing, but I can't see her, so I unbuckle and climb out. "Tate?"

"Under here."

I circle to the front of Gran's truck, where Tate's lying flat on her back, trying to get a good look underneath. Now that I'm out, I can see the Chevy's sagging to one side, the left wheel bent inward. In the back of the truck, Berry's leaning dangerously to the side, one of the tie-downs snapped free.

"Did we hit something?" I ask.

"That." Tate points ten feet behind us. A long, shallow ditch has been dug at the start of the turn. A makeshift speed bump. "I hit it at the wrong angle. Messed up the axle."

"Shit." I crouch down next to her, trying to get a good look. "With

Berry in the back, the weight's too much for us to jack it up safely to get a good look."

Tate wiggles out and gets to her feet, dusting dirt from her jeans. "It's not like it matters much. We can't fix it out here."

I look over my shoulder and then down the road. Nothing but forest.

"We're at least eight miles from the paved road. Maybe ten," I say.

Tate looks up at the sky through the trees. "It'll be dark in an hour."

"And we have no phone," I say. "Gran's going to freak when we don't come back."

"Someone might come by?" Tate suggests.

"Maybe," I say. "Hopefully."

"And the moms have the address," Tate points out. "If we don't show up, someone will come looking for us."

"It's gonna be a while before they start missing us," I say. "We should figure out what we've got on us."

"Good idea."

It's Gran's truck, so of course the toolbox is stocked. It's just harder to access because I have to scoot behind Berry. I wedge myself between the statue and the toolbox and hand Tate the stuff. There's a wool blanket, an emergency kit with first-aid stuff, a flashlight, bear spray, a gallon Ziploc full of snacks, two jugs of water, and three flares that I'm certainly not going to set off during fire season.

"Not bad," she says, laying it all out on the tailgate. "We won't starve."

"Gran and her candy, always coming through." I pluck a bag of peanut M&M's out of the Ziploc and open them. Sitting down on the tailgate next to the snacks, I kick my legs back and forth. "If we're stuck here, what are we gonna do all night?"

As soon as it's out of my mouth, I'm wincing, because holy shit, Penny. Awkward.

"There's a pack of cards in the emergency kit," Tate says.

"Yeah? You want to play?"

She nods, grabbing them from the kit, removing the rubber band, and shuffling. She deals me and herself ten cards each, and I divide the rest of the M&M's between us to use for bets.

We play until it gets dark and the crickets and other night noises of the forests swing into full gear. I get up and turn the hazards on. We're far enough on the side of the road that no one's going to run into us, but better safe than sorry. Tate packs up all the stuff we need and puts it in the cab, and then we climb inside.

It's not even ten and I'm wide awake, too many thoughts in my head.

"This week." I sigh, leaning back in the bench seat.

"This month," Tate agrees.

"This summer." I look at her when I say it, my head tilted, wishing hers would, too.

"It's almost done," she says.

She says it like it's supposed to be a good thing. A reassurance. But my entire body rejects the idea, like someone gave me cough medicine and said it was maple syrup.

Because somehow, some way, this summer made me.

I can't tear my eyes away from her determined profile. I don't want to. Maybe if I keep looking, she'll finally turn. She'll reward me with blue eyes and judgment.

"Tate, can we talk about it?" I ask.

"I don't know . . . ," she starts. "What are you talking about?"

"*It*. All of it," I interrupt. "I know I said I was sorry about lying to your mom a few times, but—"

"Penny, don't." Her words overlap mine, like she knows my thoughts before they're out of my mouth.

"I'm sorry, Tate. About Laurel and the diner parking lot. About letting your mom think—"

"I'm not doing this," she says, scrabbling for the door handle.

I follow her. This time, she can't go anywhere that I can't follow.

"I'm sorry I fucked up," I continue, marching right after her. She's ten feet from the truck, the only light's from the moon and the blinking red hazards, illuminating her back in crimson in a clicking rhythm. I hesitate, lingering by the tailgate. "I should've corrected your mom. I was selfish. It was easier than letting her know the real reason. But not for you, and I'm sorry."

"Fine," Tate says. "You're sorry. I get it."

"I'm sorry about other things," I continue, because I can feel it: time slipping through my fingers when it comes to her. "I'm sorry you had to put all your feelings to the side so you could help me."

"I'm not," she says fiercely. "I can, in fact, be mad at you and help you at the same time. It's called being emotionally nuanced."

I laugh, and it's maybe not the best time, but she's so weird sometimes. She always surprises me.

"There's more," I say. "In Yreka—"

"No." Her face turns stony. "I'm not talking about Yreka. It's in the truce agreement."

I lick my lips. "Okay, then I want to change the truce agreement."

Those red lights are flashing in her face, and they wash her eyes a darker blue. Little flyaways curl and frizz all over her braids. "Penny."

"We both get to amend it."

"Penny." It's not a sigh this time. Maybe it's a warning. Maybe it's a plea.

I'm not heeding either. Our timing is never right. So I'm going to make it right. Because we're running out of time.

"I want to talk about Yreka."

Her breath sucks in, so sharp it's gotta hurt. "You're the one who put it in our truce agreement."

"I've changed my mind."

It sparks in her face: annoyance. And it makes her snap, just like I knew it would: "Why?"

Three words. If I say them, they'll change everything. I don't know if I'm ready. But God, I am willing to find out.

"I heard you."

"What—"

"In the motel. In Yreka. I wasn't asleep."

The ripple between us is like air shimmering on a hot day. It changes your perception.

"You . . ."

"I heard you."

Her hands clench. I want them in mine. To soothe her. How can she not know it's okay?

Because it's never been okay.

We've bickered. She's waited and I've run. I've lied and she's been in the dark. We've made mistakes and been mistaken and not talked about the right things. We've dodged and darted like tadpoles around each other.

We've lost too much. We've gained good things that can't make up for those too-much losses.

We're here. Once again, we're *here*. Her and me, breathing in each other, pulled together by so many things I don't know if I could list them all now.

I don't think I believe in fate.

But I do believe in this.

In her.

In the thing that is *us*.

She stares at me. The hazards click on and off.

"Say something. Please, Tate."

And it's all she needs to spring to life.

"You are infuriating," she says, but she's stepping toward me instead of away. "You make the simplest things *so* complicated." Her eyes spark in the red haze. Three more steps. Another three and she'll be right in front of me. The thought makes my entire body flush. "Being around you is like being dropped in a labyrinth with no guide, no string, and absolutely no sense of direction."

"I could say the same thing about you!" I shoot back.

"I am a straightforward person," Tate insists. "I am not a labyrinth."

"Are you kidding me? You have so much shit going on under the surface you could wreck the *Titanic*."

"So now I'm cold like an iceberg?"

"No, you're deep and immovable like an iceberg. Big difference. You're the one bringing up Greek mythology! Who does that? Am I

366

upposed to be King Minos, sacrificing people to the Minotaur in the abyrinth metaphor?"

"More like whoever created the labyrinth no one could solve," ate shoots back.

"That would be Daedalus."

"Oh my God, of course you know the dude who made the maze," he mutters to the sky. "See, this is exactly what I mean: I try to make a metaphor and now we're talking about mythology. Simple"—she hrows her left hand to one side—"Complicated." The right hand gets hrown to the other, and her arms are wide.

Beckoning.

So I go.

One step.

Two.

And then I don't have to move anymore.

Because she's closing the space between us. A leap of a movement, heart-jolting and hopeful. When she looks down, I know. I just *know*.

Timing's finally right.

"You piss me off so much," she says again, but there's less heat behind it now that I'm so close. Her hand finds mine, and my fingers find a new home, curled safe in the palm of her hand.

"You love me," I say, and the smile that spreads across my face is a full-tilt dare. Fearless in the face of the truth.

She stares down at me, her thumb rubbing over my knuckles, the fight all over her face.

"It's okay," I tell her. I lean forward, my lips brushing against her hand, holding mine. I think about the porch and her lips on my bandages, two years ago. About the barn and the reckless *pick me* feeling she'd stirred in me. I think about sitting in that waiting room with her, the clock ticking. Of early mornings and that silly water bottle of hers and way too much oatmeal. "I loved you before I understood it, too. And once I did, I didn't think I deserved it. And I *knew* you deserved more than me."

"Hey," she protests, ever my defender, even when it's against myself.

"Hey," I say back, soft, and I tilt up, because I have to go on my toes for this to work if she doesn't bend—

But then she does.

I tilt and she bends and her hand slips around my waist and my fingers hook in her belt loop and it's like all the times before, that shuddery moment of leaning in before it all goes to hell.

But no one interrupts this time.

This time I don't hesitate.

This time, neither does she.

This time her lips find mine, and she tastes like peanut M&M's, and I probably do, too. Her hand lifts from my waist to cup my face, and she kisses me like we've been separated by a war. One of our own making. I can't breathe. I can't think, in the best way. I'm about to die and be reborn right there, especially when her fingers press this spot under my jaw that I didn't even know was a spot.

Which, of course, is when the truck lets out a mighty screech against the combined affront of the broken axle and Berry the Bear's extra weight and tilts farther to the right. Which would be fine, except the movement causes the final tie keeping Berry upright to *snap*!

"Shit." Tate grabs me out of the way just as Berry careens head-first into the side of the mountain, eager to be one with the earth

368

again. The enormous blackberry de-cleaves from Berry's shoulder at the impact and rolls lopsidedly past us.

"Oh my God," I say in the stunned silence as we stare after it. Then I just start laughing. "This. Fucking. Day."

She looks over at me, and the smile that crinkles her eyes is like the perfect freefall. "That bad, huh?"

"There were some major bright points," I say, and I hook my fingers in her belt loops again, tugging her forward, into me.

"Yeah?"

This time, I kiss her.

This time, it's a very long time before I can answer "Yeah" back.

64

TATE

AUGUST 11

SO YES.

I'm the one who breaks first. Later, I will make the argument that she goaded me into it. But I make the first move. I kiss Penelope Conner in front of a six-foot bear statue that then tries to smash us dead in the forest after we bicker about Greek mythology and the *Titanic*.

The stuff of fairy tales. And I'm not being sarcastic.

Kissing her is like waking up after a hundred years. It makes everything new.

(I feel new everywhere she touches.)

Loving her isn't new. It's a permanent state I've grown used to.

But being loved *by* her?

It's like touching water for the first time.

I just knew.

(I was home.)

PENNY AND TATE'S TRUCE AGREEMENT
(Est. June 22.
Amended August 11)

- We don't tell the moms our real anniversary date.
  Easier than explaining the whole thing.
- I will have your back.
- You'll have mine.
- I'll love you.
- You'll love me.
- It might be hard sometimes.
- But we'll be happy most times.

ACKNOWLEDGMENTS

I tried to come up with a cute way to number this in six parts, but I'm a writer for a reason. Numbers have never been my thing.

A book is a team effort on so many levels, and I have some incredible and talented people to thank who were involved in the creation of this one.

Huge thanks to my editor, Lisa Yoskowitz, who ushered me and my debut into the publishing world all those years ago and nearly a decade later really got my little ode to fanfic structures and slow-burn sapphic tension. Life threw me so many roadblocks when writing this book, and you responded to them with such grace and guidance and ease, and I'm so grateful.

Thanks also to my fantastic UK editor, Rachel Boden, for her wonderful insight and notes that encouraged me to dig deeper.

Thanks to my agent, Jim McCarthy, who after many books full of murder from me did not blink when I said, "So, I wrote this book about almost kissing and rural medical access. . . ." I appreciate you and your taste in cat cardigans so much.

Thanks to Lily Choi, whose structural eye was a tremendous boon to this project. And thanks to Caitlyn Averett for all her assistance.

Thanks to Kathleen Cook, whose keen eye for detail and timelines was greatly appreciated—and needed because my timeline was off by a few days!

Thanks to the incredible design team at Little, Brown Books for Young Readers, who created the most amazing cover. Special thanks to Kim Ekdahl, who brought Penny and Tate to life with her beautiful drawings, and Jenny Kimura, who gave us such a gorgeous and thoughtful book design, inside and out.

Thanks to Cheryl Lew, Emilie Polster, Andie Divelbiss, Savannah Kennelly, and Christie Michel for all their efforts promoting and marketing this book.

Thanks to my wonderful friends who had to listen to me moan about how hard this one was to properly structure: Elizabeth May, Charlee Hoffman, Dahlia Adler, Jess Capelle, Sharon Morse, R.C. Lewis, Romily Bernard, and everyone in the Trifecta.

And thanks to K, who had to drive through yet another forest fire while I wrote this one. One day, love, I promise, I will not be on deadline when we have to evacuate.

ABOUT THE AUTHOR

Born in a mountain cabin to a punk-rocker mother, **TESS SHARPE** grew up in rural California. She lives deep in the backwoods with a pack of dogs and a growing colony of slightly feral cats. She invites you to find her on Twitter @sharpegirl.

HAVE YOU READ THE BESTSELLING
THE GIRLS I'VE BEEN?